Potter
Princeton
1979

THE STONE AND THE VIOLETS

THE
STONE AND
THE VIOLETS

Milovan Djilas

Translated by Lovett F. Edwards

HARCOURT BRACE JOVANOVICH, INC.

NEW YORK

"The Girl with the Gold Tooth" originally appeared in *Harper's Magazine*. "The Ambush" was first published in *The Times Saturday Review*, London.

ISBN 0-15-185100-X
Library of Congress Catalog Card Number: 76-174507
Printed in the United States of America

B C D E F

CONTENTS

The Stone and the Violets
3

The Brothers and the Girl
17

The Girl with the Gold Tooth
63

Under the Yoke
78

An Eye for an Eye
86

The Doctor and the Eagle
108

Two Wolves
112

The Ambush
116

Birds of a Feather
135

The Old Man and the Song
178

vii

Contents

A Montenegrin Jest
187

Tsar Dukljan
208

About Marko Miljanov
212

THE STONE AND THE VIOLETS

THE STONE
AND THE VIOLETS

Beneath a leaden spring sky the procession wound through the rocky defiles. The stony hilltops merged with the sky. The procession, moving silently in clothes of dull, winter colors, became one with the rock walls and the sparse tufts of undergrowth. In the harsh grayness, only the weapons, which were scattered here and there throughout the procession, mainly at its head and tail, clinked and shone.

A group of about twenty men dressed in various styles—some in uniform, some in national costume, some in town clothes— walked about a hundred feet in front of the procession. They moved steadily onward, paying no heed to the procession behind. But the interval between them and the procession did not vary; it seemed as if the procession were making sure that it remain unaltered, so as not to disturb the sullen, solemn ritual in which they moved over the uneven stony land.

The three men who led the group were the only ones unaffected by the unbroken silence and the slow measured progress of the procession. They walked, now alongside each another, now in Indian file, as the narrowness of the path and the stones dictated. Among them, a huge, swarthy, mustachioed man, the commander of the partisan detachment, stood out. His heavy boots, fur-lined jacket, and otterskin hat made him look massive, even ogreish. The other two were the pale, bony commissar of the detachment

3

and the heavy-jowled, ugly-featured secretary of the regional revolutionary organization. There was a fourth man with them—the lean, dark, youthful-looking middle brother of two of the men condemned to death. He took no part in the conversation of the commander, the commissar, and the secretary, but kept a little aside and a little behind them.

After these four came five other men, walking one behind the other, bound with wire and surrounded by guards. They were the tallish, red-faced commander of the insurgent battalion; his younger brother, a stocky, broad-shouldered peasant youth; two counterrevolutionary officers—one dark, small, and bony, the other of medium height, with reddish hair and beard—and, at the end, a tall, upright old man in ceremonial national peasant costume. All of them, the condemned men and the guards alike, marched as if in a daze, but also so carefully that not a sigh, not a displaced pebble could be heard. Had the guards been without arms and the prisoners unbound, there would have been nothing to distinguish one from the other.

The conversation of the commander, the commissar, and the secretary, though carried out in low tones, dealt only with everyday affairs; there was no mention of the decision they had taken that morning, or of what now, in the early afternoon, was happening and must soon be brought to a conclusion.

Nonetheless, through that casual and indefinite conversation there broke out from time to time discordant and violent dissensions, which had been latent in their morning discussion. These were not about the fate of the prisoners—the previous night, before they had gone to sleep one beside the other on the floor, they had agreed that the prisoners, except for the middle brother of the battalion commander, deserved the death penalty—but about the manner in which the execution should be carried out.

In fact, the prisoners differed both in their offenses and in their ideological convictions, so when the commander had proposed that morning that they all be shot together and without delay, the commissar had protested. "Comrades," he said, "I would not like

4

you to think that my disapproval is in any way connected with the fact that the battalion commander and his brothers are of my kin. But till yesterday they were our comrades and brothers in arms, and it is neither just nor proper that they should be executed together with counterrevolutionaries and lie with them in the same grave. And this, too, is important: we must not shoot the officers in public. Up to the present we have not done so with reactionaries, and now we have even less reason to let their kin, on the pretext of love for them, make a shrine of their graves. It is a different matter with the battalion commander and his brother. We must shoot them publicly and explain their crimes. For even if they have wavered and trodden underfoot the laws of the revolution, they did not cross to the enemy side, and we should not prevent their kin from burying them and mourning them as men. They lived different lives and had different viewpoints; let them die in a different way and rot separately."

By unwritten, but customary, law the secretary had the final word. But as he had not yet expressed any opinion, the commander once more said: "That is of no importance. Must we kill them? We must! That is the important thing. Everything else is by the way. The enemy may break through at any moment! We are throwing sick and wounded men into the front line, yet here we are, keeping a whole battalion inactive for fear that we stir up unrest over a few criminals! I, too, do not think that the battalion commander and his brother are on the same footing as the officers, but we dare not waste time, especially on a public execution for which we must summon the people together and withdraw units from the front. I can explain the difference in the crimes of the battalion commander and the officers to the people and the soldiers later on, though I do not see any great need to do so. For whatever must be—must be! Shooting is shooting, and a grave is a grave."

The secretary still remained wisely silent, so the commissar began again: "The trouble is that there are shootings and shootings. The battalion commander is probably—not probably, but incontestably—more guilty than the officers. For the officers have done nothing; they, like most of their class, are our enemies. They have kept quiet so that they could choose a favorable moment to join the counterrevolutionaries, whereas the battalion commander, though he was never our enemy, refused to burn his village, which we, in principle opposed to burnings, could not in any other way prevent becoming a lair of infection and a fortified outpost for the forces of reaction in the nearby town. Tomorrow, perhaps, the officers would reinforce the enemy army, but the battalion commander by his action has today confused our own army and caused it to waver, when the very existence of the revolution and the future of our people are at stake. Nonetheless, the battalion commander should not be placed in the same grave as the officers. Let him die as he lived—a revolutionary who, for personal and sentimental reasons, wavered in a moment of weakness and transgressed the rules and regulations of his own movement. The fighters and the people will understand and approve and for that very reason will forget him the sooner. By shooting him we strengthen order and discipline in our own ranks; and the people will be satisfied and the fighters encouraged if the battalion commander and his brother are shot publicly."

The commander did not reply, a sign that, as was usual with him, he had begun to defer to the commissar's political reasoning and was thinking of some new and different decision. Then, just at the right moment, the secretary spoke: "The guilty men not only are our fellow countrymen but also come from our own district and are known to us. What's more, all three of us have kinsmen among them. One of the officers, Comrade Commander, is a cousin of yours, and the second one is also some sort of kin to him. The battalion commander is a blood relation of the comrade commissar, and the old man is my uncle who, since I was an orphan, took me in and brought me up. Therefore this is a test case, not only for the revolution but also for ourselves. For we are not men like other men. We exist only by a continual denial of the past and a rousing of the future within us. That is our fate

6

and our vocation, and whoever has not realized this within himself is not true to his ideals or to the revolution. Therefore I cannot agree either with the commissar's observations, though they are right and just, or with the military and undoubtedly justified reasons of the commander. Till now, the revolution has thundered in our social relations, but now it has penetrated into the very souls of the revolutionaries. The weakling will succumb and the strong man will become even stronger! We cannot win if we do not master these weaknesses and recognize them as the monstrous heritage of reaction. If we do not expel the weaklings from our ranks we shall burn together with all the dung of counterrevolution. Doubts and uncertainties will arise among the people, and the enemy will take root among them as long as we revolutionaries show consideration and mercy toward ourselves, toward the weaklings among us. The people can be educated and liberated only by example, by our ruthlessness, and by our blood! That means, today, here and now, an identical solution for all opponents of, and renegades from, the revolution. For, as we all know, example is the best teacher and the highest standard. My uncle has bayed only too loudly against us, encouraged by the thought that no one dare even look askance at him so long as he has me, the secretary, as his nephew. When we silence him with lead, my conscience will be as clear as that of a newborn child. For our ideal and for our revolution it does not matter who is what or what sort of person he is; what matters is that he be subordinated to its aims, and he must, if he can, to some degree, put them into practice. Aims are more important than persons. Our aim is history, not ethics! Do not misunderstand me. That does not mean that we must torture no matter whom, whoever he be, but—when it is inescapable—wear him down to the limits of human endurance and in the manner most appropriate. Therefore, in this case, it is both more practical and ideologically more just to shoot them publicly all together, and so make it impossible that their common grave become a center of reaction or of reactionary lamentations."

The commander had no serious reason not to accept the secretary's view; one public shooting would not prolong the holding of army units needed at the front. The commissar, encouraged by the secretary's words, which had both enlightened and inspired him, proposed that the best soldiers be summoned from their units to attend the execution and that he personally prepare a speech for the occasion. His proposals, as also those of the commander and the secretary, were based on experience and confidence in victory. They were accepted and amplified with common fervor and conviction. But the insoluble problem remained: how to shoot the guilty men publicly and at the same time avoid lamentations over their grave.

Finally, the secretary remarked with a smile: "Don't be afraid that their tomb may become a shrine. The supporters of the revolution will not meet there because the officers will be there, too, whereas the opponents of the revolution will not do so because the battalion commander and his brother will be there. The problem is only that they be killed and hidden in some secret place that will not be exposed all the time to the eyes of the people and thereby remind them of their fate and our ruthlessness, even though that be necessary and justified."

The commissar broke in as if inspired: "Let's throw them into a bottomless pit, as the people in days long past used to do with mortal sinners. I remember that I myself, when I was a shepherd lad, came across such pits in the stony hillsides around here. I will look for one of them, in a hidden place, while you do everything else that may be necessary."

But the secretary would not agree that there was no more to be said until they had had a talk with the middle brother of the battalion commander, whom it had been necessary to pardon because of his sincere repentance. This had been confirmed by his statement revealing the crimes of his kinsmen and the information he had laid against his brothers. "Naturally," said the secretary, "he can no longer be secretary of the village revolutionary organization, but he must be given the chance as an ordinary fighter to wipe out his sins against the movement and the revolution. However, in his case, I am not sure if I was too lenient or too harsh, so that it would be a good thing for you two to weigh the matter."

The guards had brought the middle brother.

From the secretary's impression of the night before and his conversation with the brother, he expected to be faced with a man contrite, reasonable, and intimidated. Yet now before him stood a man of open, even carefree, attitude, who, as soon as the secretary called on him to confess his misdemeanors to the comrades before him and to explain his present attitude, burst out eagerly and unrestrainedly: "I have already told you all the facts, but they cannot even approximately lighten the terrible, shameful darkness of my soul and thoughts! Comrades, I have many times desired your deaths, but that thought and the baying of my younger brother to throw a bomb at your command and your committee I have plucked out of my mind and the marrow of my bones. Even last night, I, comrades, while confessing my sins before the comrade secretary, was continually thinking how to deceive him and how to save my selfish and worthless life, the life of a dog. That abject vileness has drawn from me even greater sincerity, and I have cast the burden upon my own brothers; yet they are less guilty, for they are less perfidious than I. I have cast my burdens upon them as a trick, in order to deceive the movement and the revolution. Even now, comrades, do not believe me. Always be suspicious of anyone who even in his thoughts and dreams wavers in our ideal and in our holy struggle. For such men, in fact, deceive first themselves, their own conscience, and their own being. And I am one of the blackest of them, for I have sinned without reason, without excuse, because of my own depravity. My blood and the blood of my brothers cannot purify me! I deserve to be burned alive. Let no trace remain of my body or of my filthy soul! One thing I would wish, comrades: that before my shameful death you lead me from village to village through all my homeland, to show me to the people. Let them make me a target for their

9

curses and let the young, new men gain knowledge from my shame and from my fall!"

Not one the them, the secretary least of all, was able to guess the end of his outpourings, still less suspect what he would vomit from his innards, and the secretary took advantage of the first pause to cut him short before some fresh tide of confession and supplication began: "I have already informed these comrades of the sincerity of your repentance. And insofar as they have no comments to make on your statement today, I can inform you of our conclusion. We are relieving you of all responsible duties and are transferring you to a unit as an ordinary fighter. We are giving you this chance to confirm your repentance and to prove it by your actions. You will go with us to this execution and, if the need arises, you will expose their treason and attest your loyalty."

"Is not that too great, too noble, a reward for a traitor?" the middle brother asked in bewilderment.

"Our aim is not to destroy men, but to remold them," replied the secretary firmly.

With that, the morning session had closed. The other prisoners were not interrogated. Their crimes were known, and the sentences were passed, though they were not revealed to anyone. In any case, each of the three leaders was too busy and each hastened to his task: the commander to give orders to the army units, the secretary to inform the revolutionary organizations and, through them, to summon the people, and the commissar to find a pit and make preparations for the actual execution.

Each one had carried out his task, and now they were marching at the head of the procession, stumbling along one after the other because of the roughness of the path.

"How will the people get here?" said the commander in alarm, halting. "And where does this path go?"

"It wasn't an easy place to find," retorted the commissar. "Without the help of the shepherd boys, members of the youth organization, I would never have found it. But, as you will see, the place is well chosen."

The commander marched on without hesitation, and the secretary, coming up beside him, explained: "Don't worry about the people. They will follow us, and they're used to scrambling among the crags."

They could no longer walk without stumbling and were silent, not being used to broadcasting their conversations, even though they were of no importance and could be overheard only by men who within half an hour would be dead and thrown into a bottomless pit. Soon they, as well as the prisoners stumbling on the rocks, found themselves isolated from the procession by the crags and outcrops on the sharp bends of the rough path.

They went on in this way for about ten minutes. Then a stone gully, surrounded by steep walls, in which every footstep or blow of a stick, every cough or sigh, was clearly distinguishable, opened before them, and the condemned old man, the secretary's uncle, shouted unexpectedly and violently, as if there had been a rock-fall: "Would you turn your own seed to stone? Has my bread become leprous to you, nephew? Why don't you kill us and bury us like men?"

"Shut him up!" stormed the commander.

The commissar halted, probably to explain to the guards how to carry out their leader's command, but the secretary waved his hand: "Let him be! It's not important. It is all that is left to him!"

They had already emerged into the oval gully, not more than fifty yards wide. It was, in fact, a somewhat wider, level karst valley, to whose bottom melting snow and rain had brought a little earth from the surrounding bare stone crags. The old man fell silent, and the commissar hastened inexorably across the gully and stopped about ten paces from its edge, waiting for his companions and holding a largish stone in his hand.

"There you are!" he said, pointing to a small ring of stones, about knee-high, in the rough soil.

Only then did the commander and the secretary notice the

black crevasse in the rock. The commissar threw his stone into the pit. They listened carefully to the dull, heavy thud of the stone against its sides and remained standing tensely even after the sound had been swallowed in the tremendous abyss.

The commander was the first to make a move. Looking around him, he said: "A wonderful choice!"

The secretary, too, announced: "Really wonderful! What is more important, there is plenty of room for the people to find places all around it."

The commissar smiled with satisfaction. "I had that in mind. It's like a theater."

Only then did they notice the prisoners and the guards, there behind them, pale and apathetic, and the people who flowed into the gully like a turbid stream. But they had already decided on their duties: the commander to line up the prisoners and arrange the firing squad, the commissar to explain to the army delegations the crimes of the condemned men and the reason for the execution, and the secretary to assist the members of the organization to place and control the people.

Everything happened more quickly and in a more orderly manner than had been forseen. The people obeyed the soft-spoken orders smoothly and rapidly. The condemned men also lined up obediently and remained sullenly silent, motionless and ill at ease between the pit and the craggy walls around them. After the people had taken their places and squatted down in a semicircle on the rocks, the silence was such that the twittering of the wagtails on the hillside and the gurgle of the waters in the depths could be heard. That stony dumbness, with only the voices of the birds and the sound of the waters, seemed to startle the commissar, who was busy with the soldiers. With long, hurried paces he made his way to the rocks around the pit and clambered on top of the highest of them.

But as soon as he began his speech, the condemned battalion commander began to shout, his veins standing out as if about to break his bonds: "Long live the revolution! Long live the revolutionary movement! Long live national freedom!" Incited and given heart by his shouts, the other condemned men also began to shout, each about what lay close to his heart and for what he wanted to be remembered. The brother of the condemned battalion commander, licking away his tears, shouted that he was guilty of nothing, only that monstrous and unseemly words had escaped him when he was angry. The red-haired officer also wept and shouted that he was guilty only because he was an officer; while the dark officer, stifled by fury and by his bonds, hissed unintelligible words aimed both at his killers and at his pusillanimous colleague. The old man, the secretary's uncle, knelt down and, beating a stone on the rock in front of him, began to pour out curses as from time immemorial the people have done when they wish their words to come true. The members of the revolutionary organization also protested and grumbled, as well as many of the younger men, the fathers and mothers of fallen revolutionaries, the wives and sisters of revolutionary fighters, and the poverty-stricken, maltreated, and embittered peasants. Some even began to throw stones at the condemned men.

The commissar shrugged his shoulders helplessly, looking around him for the secretary, who was lost to sight. He scrambled down from the stone as if the furious wave of tumult had washed him away. The secretary emerged from among the rocks and the people and signaled to the commander with his hand, as if waving a sword, to get on with the execution. The commander shouted an order. Though it was not too loud or even very clear except to the soldiers, it cut through the tumult and agitation, though not through the outcries of the condemned men. A deafening volley drowned his second order. The condemned men fell, all except the old man, who only swayed, gripping in his hand the stone with which he had forged his curses. He ceased shouting to utter his last curse, but instead of words a stream of blood flowed from his lips, dyeing his white mustaches. Then he, too, toppled over. The dark officer and the youngest brother of the battalion commander unexpectedly raised themselves, the former on his right elbow, the latter supporting himself on his two arms.

"Filthy swine!" shouted the officer, baring his teeth.

"Forgive me, brothers!" sobbed the young man. "Perhaps I can still live. Let me redeem myself as a fighter!"

But a fresh volley silenced them and beat them down.

The commander carefully inspected the corpses, his pistol at the ready, and fired a shot into the heads of two who seemed to him to be still alive. The army delegates, instructed by the commissar, seized first the battalion commander and threw him into the pit, and then the others. But no one was listening for, or heard, the thud of their bodies on the rocks in the depths; the people responded with savage, spontaneous yells to the words the secretary shouted from that same stone from which the commissar had tried to speak.

As soon as the secretary had got down from the stone, the middle brother of the battalion commander approached him. "You told me," he said, "that I might have to give details of their treason and perhaps confirm my loyalty. But, you see, I have had no chance! What do you think—would it be suitable if I were to start a kolo?"

"That you must judge for yourself," the secretary replied, joining the commander and the commissar, who had moved away from the pit toward the path.

"People! A kolo, a kolo! Let us dance and sing over the corpses of the traitors!"

The kolo quickly got under way, and in its flowing, singing variations the petty vindication of the middle brother was lost.

Watching the kolo, the commander remarked: "It's growing clearer."

"Do you mean—symbolically?" the commissar said, smiling.

"Take it any way you like," broke in the secretary, and added: "It's a nasty business—but it had to be."

They started back, but were halted by wailing from somewhere among the rocks. Two women, almost at the same time but from different directions, pushed through the circle of the kolo and made their way to the pit. One of them, dark and bony, was recognized by the three leaders as the sister of the executed brothers, and the plump blonde as the wife of the red-haired officer.

"Hell!" shouted the secretary. "Didn't we agree to put a guard on the path? Didn't we stress that we must prevent precisely these two disturbing and working up the people with their mourning and keening?"

"The guards were posted," the commander retorted curtly. "They must have found their way here without using the path."

"Someone must have told them," the commissar said, "or else they followed the procession and bypassed the guards."

But the women were no longer mourning or wailing. The sister, the first to arrive, sat down on a stone and leaned her head on her hands; then she spread out a black kerchief, as mourners do before they begin their keening. But noticing the officer's wife with a posy of violets, she quietly stood up, tied the kerchief under her chin, and hissed: "Were you thinking, you sow, that I would keen over your traitors also?"

The officer's wife looked at her for a few moments in astonishment and placed the posy on the stone. Then, flushing, she snapped at her opponent: "Did you think, you common dirt, that I would bring flowers for your bandits?"

The kolo stopped in dumb silence. But when the two women went on shouting insults at each other and at the executed men, several of the peasants began to laugh and urge them on with jeers. The commander, too, laughed loudly, while the commissar watched with vague curiosity and the secretary looked at the scene pensively and enigmatically.

Amid the furious hisses of the women and the gay mockery of the crowd, from somewhere or other a bearded and bent old man, leaning on a knotted stick, reached the edge of the pit. Someone shouted: "Quiet, quiet!" And, in fact, a murmur, becoming more and more subdued, accompanied the movements of the old man. He walked slowly, paying no heed to anyone. Obviously he was not frightened, or perhaps, being so old, he was already indifferent to his life. As soon as he reached the pit he slowly took off his brightly colored sheepskin hat, crossed himself, and, sighing out "May God give rest to their souls!," took the posy of violets from the stone and slowly threw it into the pit.

"Who is he?" asked the secretary.

"Some crazed old fool from the caves," the commander replied.

The commissar added: "He is an old man."

And the old man, with clumsy haste, put his hat back on his sunburned, almost bald skull, and, leaning on his staff, started off in the opposite direction to that from which they, the prisoners, and the people had reached the pit.

His gray, tattered peasant clothes merged with the stone, and in another moment he disappeared.

Belgrade
January 4–12, 1968

THE BROTHERS
AND THE GIRL

To the memory of my brother, Milivoj Djilas

Shrewd and hard-working, my father lived to experience an old age such as he least of all expected. From the wars against Turkey and Austria-Hungary and the struggle for the unification of the southern Slavs he emerged with a heightened reputation and the rank of a senior officer, which enabled him to acquire a fine property in the Sanjak, where the Moslems, after the Turkish collapse and the Montenegrin invasion, sold their lands for a song. Still upstanding, but unsuited for service in the new and more modern army, he was, like the majority of Montenegrins of his generation, granted a pension on which he was able to live comfortably on his property, though he was not rich. But just when he hoped to go on living peacefully, his way of life and thought was completely disorganized, for his children had become not only adherents but also promoters and leaders of the revolutionary movement in that district. Unfortunately for my father, I was sentenced to a heavy term of imprisonment just after my elder brother had been dismissed from government service and my younger brother arrested and expelled from Belgrade, where he was studying, and sent home. The authorities also resorted to an irritating supervision over the house and family as the most effective measure of pressure and intimidation. As always when there is oppression, it revived banked-down hatreds and encouraged toadies and flatterers to inform against our family. Relatives and friends deserted us; they rarely, ever more rarely, came to our *slava*—our family feast—which my father continued to celebrate in defiance, the more assiduously and formally since he considered that bearers of ill tidings, even were they of the same faith, should never be trusted.

It would be long and tedious to describe the whole troublous path that my father had to tread from rejecting his children's beliefs to accepting them and, in the end, supporting their ideas and their activities. My mother, however, seemed to be quite unaware of this transformation. She was a mother; she thought and lived in the destiny of her children. Illiterate, she was by tradition a protector of the persecuted, as in Turkish times. Although at that time it was comprehensible even though it appeared unnatural, that path was trodden by the majority of the families of the revolutionaries, especially those from patriarchal homes. Hope for the future, honor, and courage were more important than what was real and possible, than property or comfort. Fathers, just because they themselves had been fighters against oppression and inspired by myths, became, in this new struggle and with new myths, the children of their own children.

Therefore, as my father grew older and his destiny became more and more identified with that of his children, he lost all interest in his property, although until then he had loved it and cared for it as something living and born to him. Furthermore, he—and his children with him—felt that in a more cultured, more developed milieu the pressure of the authorities would be less effective, less insolent, and the possibilities for employment greater; he therefore consoled himself for the loss of his property, sold it at a low price, and moved to a little town on the Sava, a fertile but cheap district, since our family would now have to live exclusively on his pension. And our family was numerous. Other than the two grown-up and unemployed sons there were five other children, and I was the only one who did not have to live at my father's expense, since I was already completely devoted to revolutionary activities in the capital and living mainly on the generosity of those who held similar political opinions or by whatever jobs I was able to pick up.

In his new surroundings the supervision and pressure of the authorities were less noticeable, though Father and the family did not find peace and security. Though already remarkable and attractive, because of its special customs and way of life, our family would soon have made a reputation such as inevitably accompanies those who are in conflict with the injustice of the existing world. It was soon noised abroad that we had, in fact, fled from our own district because not only the children but the father as well were dangerous subversives, and our new home became a headquarters about which began to collect all those who protested and who dreamed of justice and human good fortune, the more inevitably as in the little town itself there was not yet any illegal revolutionary organization.

Despite the hope that we would find peace and quiet, our family from the very first day of its arrival became transformed into a center of discontent, drawing upon it the more and more vigilant supervision of the authorities. For a man carries his own world inside himself—a man is his own world, unable to dissociate himself from what he is, from what he must become. All those in the little town and its surroundings who were longing for something new, for their own world, considered it an act of courage and also a duty and a necessity to visit our family and associate with my brothers.

2

I don't know how and when the girl got to know my brothers and became friendly with them. It must have happened soon after the arrival of our family. In her final year at the teachers' training college, she cut short her schooling, either because of lack of money or because she had been expelled for her political activities, but in any case, she was filled with revolutionary fervor. That was sufficient reason for her to get in touch with my brothers as soon as she heard of their arrival in town and who they were and what sort of men they were, and she soon became a daily visitor to the family. She used to stay with my family almost as much as with her own, which was in a nearby village. Such an association among persecuted fellow thinkers was quite natural, and my parents themselves were already quite accustomed to it.

She was much younger than my brothers, only just in her eighteenth year, and certainly also much less experienced, or— as it used to be said—still ideologically and politically undeveloped. With a fervor that was also coldly calculating and controlled, she soaked up every new item of knowledge, whether from books or from conversation, and resolved it in her own mind quietly and unobtrusively. When I visited the family in the spring, I noticed that she was an eager listener, but one who concealed her own inquisitiveness. She easily understood even the most complicated theories, but never revealed how much of their teachings she absorbed and what conclusions she drew. By that I do not mean that she was not an intelligent and devoted activist. She soon formed in her village and in the vicinity a series of youth groups, and later displayed courage and resolution in prison and under interrogation. It was, in fact, a different manner of accepting revolutionary teaching and methods of work.

It was through her that I for the first time realized the make-up of the new revolutionary generation. I don't know if it was better or worse, but it was certainly different—no less brave and self-sacrificing, but a generation to which revolutionary action was something normal and everyday, something to which a person submitted deliberately and consciously, without any accentuated renunciations. It seemed to me that this girl would be able to endure all sorts of torture and even death itself, not merely because of idealism and self-sacrifice, but also from some inner, personal calculation; the word "calculation" is not a good one, for it carries the idea of material benefit, but I am unable to find a better one in view of her careful consideration in everything. In accord with that judgment, it seemed to me that she might equally well become a traitor—not a coward, of whom there were many, and who, in the strict sense of the word, could not be called traitors, but one who could change sides and become transformed into an embittered adversary. But in her case, that could happen only if there were some inner contradiction between her personality and the ideas and practices of the organization which she might understand in some unacceptable way and so come to some conclusion of her own. I was bound to put before my brothers my impressions of this girl—naturally, in the simplified and dogmatic terms which we then used and which, to us, most suitably and completely explained the world we longed to establish. Broadly speaking, I said: "She is very quick, intelligent, and energetic, but it seems to me there is still in her much that is individualistic, not to say provincial; she does not surrender all her personality to the idea. But she is young and can be developed, and certainly she can already be made good use of, especially for work among young people."

I could not say that my brothers agreed with me, though they knew her more intimately and more closely. But they saw in her much that was different and that I, knowing her only a short time, had had no chance to notice. Today I see that they, each in his own manner, introduced into their opinion their personal feelings and all that had already been created between her and each one of them separately.

3

My elder brother had noticed, especially in her ambitions, that she still had something provincial about her, but considered that that was unimportant. But first of all, I must explain what my brother, what all of us at that time, meant by provincial feelings, by a small-town person.

Provincial people are, as everyone knows, petty business people, artisans, small merchants, and lower officials, and provincial feelings are their habits, morals, and desire for obtaining advancement by favor and for a secure life in their own little houses for their own families. But for us revolutionaries such ideas also embodied all forms of conformity and adaptation to established, inherited, and inevitable circumstances. In an unindustrialized country, revolutionaries, even when they originated in the working and intellectual classes, were by inherited emotions and by the influence of their surroundings weighed down and cramped by the desires and habits of such provincial persons. And though these provincials were in no way active political opponents, they were, by their very way of life and viewpoint, an obstacle—mental and psychical, rather than social—to conversion into a revolutionary and thereby to revolution. Revolutionary action and personal involvement in revolution, though apparently beginning with clashes with the provincial milieu and separation from it, of necessity extended to and even beyond an ascetic renunciation and disdain of realities, to a personal enthusiasm in which one regarded oneself as the germ of the new man of the future. It was essential that each one must kill within himself all that had until then existed, so that he could influence others and change human relationships. My elder brother's comment about the girl meant that she had not yet freed herself—that was the expression we used—from the sediment of provincial ideas and the desires of her family and those about her, and that she had not identified herself personally with the struggles and visions of the new world.

When I look back today, I can see that I and my brother were, in fact, mistaken; not even then was she in any way essentially provincial, but there was something of that in her daring and new, but also cautious, behavior. She had cleansed herself of everything traditional and everyday, as if she had been born without that burden, and insofar as she had retained some trace of those forms of life and thought, it was only for the strengthening of the revolutionary movement and, indeed, of herself also, in her role as a revolutionary. She was prepared to struggle with her whole being, just as every other tempered and developed revolutionary, and it was just in this way that that highest and most longed-for quality was expressed.

In fact, it was all a misunderstanding. In my brothers' and my own accepted and considered scheme it was only possible to include her partially and reservedly. For us, the revolution and the new ideas had a higher, final sense, and we devoted ourselves to them with that passion and enthusiasm of which only those are capable who are convinced that they have found the truth that will in the end lead to brotherhood and peace among men. Therefore we lived and struggled in a continual wavering between faith and desire to submit our personalities, to identify ourselves with the universal, and the impossiblity of any full and final realization of anything of the sort. Whenever we succeeded, by dream and ecstacy, by endurance and exploit, in freeing ourselves from our own inner conflicts, we were glad that we had confirmed the rightness of our ideas, that is to say, the sense and possibility of our own happiness. But she accepted the revolutionary viewpoint and revolutionary activities as something self-evident and therefore profited also by other forms—those provincial forms—if they favored the spread of ideas and the consolidation of the movement.

In connection with that I remember one detail. When we offered her some small sum from the party funds—for she was so much taken up with her political work that she had no time to earn any money for herself—she accepted it as something quite natural and comprehensible. Whereas I and my brothers, like most of the other revolutionaries of our stamp and of our generation, if we had to take party money for our own most necessary and most essential needs, always did so with the pangs of conscience of a believer who steals from a shrine, every time in the hope that it would be the last occasion.

But that did not mean that she was any more venal or desirous of comforts than we were. She was a different kind of personality, and I would say that that was so because of conditions we did not fully understand, though they were in part the result of her own revolutionary activities. For us, the revolution was a dream and an end; for her, it had become life and inevitability.

4

Today the judgment of my younger brother seems to me more accurate, though at the time I did not consider it reliable, because he had fallen in love with her. He thought that she had unusual and brilliant qualities in every way and disagreed with my elder brother's judgment, and also with my own, which had been based on his views and my own first impressions. He claimed that the individualism and provincialism we saw in her were, in fact, neither one nor the other, but, rather, her own perspicacity and inventiveness in the execution of her revolutionary tasks and her own personal life. He could come to this conclusion, even if it was prejudiced, because he was more intimate with her than we were and also because he was younger than we were—seven years younger than my elder brother and three years younger than I—and was, therefore, if not a member of the new revolutionary generation, at least its herald.

But even he did not quite penetrate into her personality—if such a thing was possible—mainly, so it seems to me today, it was because his ideas of morality and behavior were markedly different; I would say old-fashioned, if not antediluvian. All three of us were overburdened with moral scruples, each of us in his own way. But in him this was so conspicuous and intransigent that it seemed that his whole character was linked to moral issues, as if all his actions and desires were conditioned by morality. He was one of those honorable men whose misfortunes must sometimes be confirmed by the dishonor of others, in the very existence of dishonor on earth. That did not mean that he was naïve, or that she was immoral and that he was aware of it. No, it was simply that she was something quite novel to us—and, I now see, to others also—so that we were not fully able to understand her.

The Brothers and the Girl

Thinking back for a moment about her personality, still so enigmatic after so many years, I am forced to the conclusion that she would have become friendly with my brothers even if she had not been a fellow thinker. It obviously attracted her that they were Montenegrins and mountaineers, quite different from the Serb plainsmen along the Sava valley. That was, I believe, decisive for her, a new experience; she did not suspect that concealed in just that link with them was her first definite political ascent. Even today I cannot erase the impression that she insufficiently desired the confirmation, the stressing, of her personality, though it cannot be denied that she was prepared at any moment to sacrifice everything, even life, for any revolutionary task, though inessential and wearisome—if there are any such in revolutionary organization or in revolution. Yes, she was just such a personality, unrestrained and heedless in her advance, blazing the trail for revolution, identified in her with her personal success and with her destiny. As such, she was irreplaceable and incomparable in revolutionary work; she went everywhere, unyielding and inventive, ready for anything.

Not even my younger brother could really know her; he least of all, so overburdened was he with ethics and already in love with her. He realized that she was not an individualist, in the sense in which the term was then understood, and still less a provincial. Like his elder brother, he noted her quickness, her political gift, and her practical ability. But these were only some of the many strands of her personality.

This, too: My younger brother considered that she was a very pretty girl. Even my elder brother said that she was handsome, a word that with him meant not only beautiful but also attractive, though not exceptional. It seemed to me, when I saw her for the first time, that she could not be called a beauty. But in that, too, my judgment turned out to be superficial, inaccurate, when I was compelled by later events to delve more deeply into her personality and to assess her physical appearance.

She was slim, but not thin, of medium height and pale complexion, and with black hair. Such girls may often be found in the small towns of Serbia. But in contrast to the majority of such girls, she had a fine, slightly curved but delicate nose and thin nostrils. Still more striking were her eyes, variable in color, more tawny than dark, quite in harmony with her face, which was flecked with fine freckles that became flushed in moments of excitement.

Later, I got to know her appearance, and remembered it down to the smallest detail. But at that time, though she was in love with my younger brother, I did not pay any special attention to it. She was, for me, only one of many comrades from the movement, rather prettier than some, not so pretty as others. In truth, it must be said that pretty girls were a rarity in the revolutionary movement. Someone commented: "Ugly women find compensation for their ugliness in revolutionary self-sacrifice." Perhaps that was not quite true, but power and wealth attract beauty, and we revolutionaries did not promise either one or the other.

More than eighteen months were to pass before that girl impressed herself upon me by her personality and her appearance as a separate and distinct individual, and twelve years have since passed and I am still, as you can see, trying to understand her.

5

Both my elder brother and I were pleased that our younger brother had at last found a girl, though we knew that in fact it was she who had found him. For though my younger brother was by nature very reserved, there was at that time among the revolutionaries a current of opinion that the true revolutionary must be self-controlled even in matters of love and must be continent even to asceticism. Like many other things among the revolutionaries, that, too, had the authority of a mystical rite, though there were not many who held to it or carried it out to the letter.

My younger brother was just one of those who did. He was already in his twenty-fifth year, well-built and handsome, though with too big a nose and a little stooped, as is often the case with tall men of great strength. Nonetheless, he behaved as if he had never known a woman. Perhaps he had had some love affairs in his early youth, but he never spoke of them, nor did anyone know of them, and it is more than probable that he had passed through some unhappy and painful experience. We could scarcely suspect him of any relations with women. He did not go to women of easy virtue, and whenever the talk turned to love affairs there was a sort of modesty and even melancholy in his smile and his silence. The rich and ebullient love life of his elder brother astounded and even repelled him. Such emotions were bound to be deeper in him, insofar as he was, in any case, taciturn and reserved, and his development into a young man and a revolutionary coincided with the strict limitations and rules of conduct of the revolutionary movement.

The intimate life of us three, indeed, was not only an expression of three different, though akin and intimate, personalities, but also of three layers of the same generation, of the same revolutionary movement.

My elder brother, though he became a revolutionary at the same time as I did, if not a little later, matured at a time when there were no sexual prohibitions in the revolutionary movement. Indeed, they were regarded at the time as provincial prejudices. Passionate in everything, especially in matters of love, he was impetuous and self-willed. Easygoing, even libertine, in his relations with women, he was driven in his youth to many quick love affairs, after he became angry and embittered by the refusal of his girl to follow him on his risky and rebellious path. Above all, he was fine in a typically masculine way: he had big eyebrows, a striking bone structure in a pale, uneasy face, with firm lips and strong teeth, and was in everything strong and a trifle rough— direct and even brutal. He did not know how to, could not, hide his love affairs, and I was astounded, especially when I was still a boy, at the number and unexpectedness of his conquests; it seemed to me that there was no woman who could resist him or who was able to remain true to him. Since the revolutionary movement re-quired a platonic and comradely relation with its adherents, after he entered it he behaved in this way toward them, without, how-ever, changing his attitude toward other women, though he was convinced that in malleability revolutionary women did not differ in any way from any others. He did not want to have a woman comrade, some woman from the revolutionary movement, to whom he must be exclusively bound. Perhaps with him that was more a longing for unrestricted freedom than an irresistible need to change his women. It seemed—and, indeed, it was so—that he was a rebel who had penetrated into modern times from some primeval, mythical national past. Struggle, insurrection, war were for him as much, if not more, a realization of his most essential everyday needs as an eagerly and patiently awaited moment.

In contrast to his, my love life began late and remained un-fulfilled. At the time when I could enjoy my youth I was in prison, and after that I was caught up in the puritan and dogmatic phase of the revolutionary movement. I linked myself firmly with my future wife, so that to associate myself with the victory of the new current in the movement—I was one of its supporters, though not one of its initiators—was no hardship for me. But today there is no reason not to confess it: though I remained faithful to my wife and to the newly established code—conceived as the ultimate truth and the most exalted ethic, since it arose from the need for an inner consolidation of the movement and for distinguishing us revolutionaries as above and outside ordinary men—other women countless times took my eye and countless times I desired them. One might conclude that what with my elder brother was fact was, with me, desire. That was in accord with the difference in our characters. If I see myself correctly, I am easily inflamed but also deliberate. Entry into the revolutionary movement was for me a true and moral obligation, as much as a realization and a duty.

For my younger brother, it seemed, there were no such inner nuances and conflicts. Revolutionary work was for him a way of life and a viewpoint on life, and when the work of the movement drew him closer to the woman he loved, he ceased to lust after other women. Certainly, not even in his case did everything happen simply and easily. Yet such were the results.

In telling this story I have intentionally simplified everything so that I can show as clearly as possible, as comprehensively as possible, both the drama and the actors. It does not seem to me important in what order or how the events occurred. I have attempted to show men as they actually were, how they behaved and what happened.

6

My elder brother and I, and also the rest of the family, would scarcely have known that my younger brother and the girl had become intimate comrades, as the expression then was, had she herself not openly avowed it. She understood easily and at once all the harshness with which relations between men and women were treated in the revolutionary movement; but also the good will and support, almost romantic, that the functionaries showed to such lovers or married pairs—they did not distinguish between them—if their relations were in accord with the current viewpoint and the needs of the movement. For such relationships forecast the future new society and eliminated from the movement intrigues and jealousies. The influence on sympathizers and ordinary citizens was considerable. The revolutionaries became models of moral purity, and the members of the movement themselves were transformed by their moral catharsis and devoted themselves without afterthoughts to revolutionary tasks. The love life, the most intimate life, of the revolutionaries became a means—far more important than was believed—of external uplift, of spiritual fusion of the movement. Therefore the girl accepted and nurtured her relationship with my younger brother in revolutionary purity and constancy.

From that summer, ever since the relationship became public, she began to behave as if she were a member of our family. Our parents accepted her as such, since they were already accustomed to the relationship between my comrade and me. They looked upon such relationships almost as marriages, and regarded them as natural for the new times and the new people. Thus the bond between those two appeared to my parents as a real love match, and to the revolutionaries, and also to me, as one more confirmation of new relationships between men and women. My elder brother, from his point of view, was the most satisfied of all; his younger brother had broken away from his senseless and unnatural asceticism, without clashing with the aims of the movement.

My younger brother was as if transformed. Not only did he become more gay and talkative, but also wiser and more assiduous. I remember noticing suddenly that his thoughts were clearer and more discriminating, that he sharply observed realities and faultlessly carried out important undertakings. His blue eyes lost their hidden inner fury, and his face and whole bearing no longer expressed suffering renunciation. He began, of a sudden, to drag himself away from the house and from books. He passed the heat of the day on the Sava, in the early evening went to conspiratorial meetings, and returned late at night. I did not know how they consummated their love, nor was I interested, but I heard from my sisters that they often, neck and neck, swam across the river and disappeared into the reedbeds, spending the day on sandy islands they alone knew. In the evening he saw her back to her village. They met on the paths, in the meadows, and on the hillocks. It happened, too, that he would sometimes pass the evenings with her people, and then she would accompany him home and spend the night with him in his room.

That meant love for him and, I believe, for her also, love coordinated with their tasks and with the aims of the movement to which they belonged. He could not, did not know how to, love in any other way. She, too, loved, undoubtedly in her own way, taking care that the needs of her youth did not clash, at least noticeably, with the demands of the revolutionary movement.

Such a dilemma could not exist for my brother; if he did not have a comrade, he quite simply renounced all love life. She, however, considerea—or if she did not consider, she gave way to it—that revolutionary morals were something inevitable, like political attitudes and actions, and so every member must submit to them at every moment when it was necessary for the movement. For she had her own personal needs, inclinations, and wishes, while my younger brother seemed as if he had no other existence outside the movement; his personality was fused to the greatest possible degree with revolutionary ideas and activities, which, for him, were linked, if they were not identical, with primal justice, which he regarded as ultimate justice.

By pointing out these differences between those two, I do not mean to underrate her or show her as a person of less value, unworthy of my brother's love, although I—I openly admit it—later often hated and despised her, because I, too, though to a lesser degree, was weighed down by ethical ideas similiar to those of my younger brother. Today, when I think it over coldly, I can see that she in many ways surpassed my brother; she was more resolute, more capable, sharper and with a keener mind, and, furthermore, she was in no way an intriguer or an opportunist.

I knew nothing of her past in matters of love, if, young as she was, she had such a thing. She realized that she must take a comrade from the revolutionary movement if she wanted both a lover and to remain in the movement. This did not mean that she did not love my brother, but that she loved him in a manner only possible according to the ideas, emotions, and conditions by which she had to live. She did not exist only for the revolutionary movement, but it existed because of her, because of the way of life it inculcated and which was hers.

7

Sometime in the late autumn or early winter of 1939, there was a wave of arrests in the little town where my family lived and also in the girl's village. Among those arrested were my brothers and the girl. The local police, probably hoping to uncover a wide-spread organization and thus win promotion and recognition, arrested everyone who was friendly with my brothers and seized as material proof left-wing books, which were openly sold in the bookshops. Every trace of the organization, which was then just in its beginnings, was lost in the confusion the police themselves created.

Finding themselves in a stew which had been brought to the boil too soon, the police were forced gradually to set free those they had arrested. After two or three months, my elder brother and the girl were released, and sometime at the beginning of spring, my younger brother also. The term of his expulsion from the university had by now expired, and in the spring of 1940 he came to Belgrade.

I would have found it hard to notice in him, always so taciturn and reserved, any special mood, had it not been for his vivacity during the summer months. Perhaps what I came to know later made me imagine that I noticed changes in him at our first meeting—a sort of discouragement, an exaggerated and suffering seriousness. I remember clearly that I asked him about the girl and what would happen to their relationship and how long they would be separated. He avoided a direct answer, saying something of this nature: "Conditions have changed, and now all that is no longer of importance." If I went on trying—I do not remember if I did or not—to get him to explain that change and the present unimportance of their relationship, he did not refer to it or, if he did, did so only vaguely. I was left with the impression of something uncertain, unclarified, though I thought: He hasn't changed; he is still reserved and withdrawn. In any case, he must stay in Belgrade for his studies, and those two for the time being cannot be together.

Rarely, even by chance, did we see each other. War was tearing Europe apart, and a mortal fear oozed from every pore of the ruling classes. The revolutionary movement, confident in its vision and its analyses, burst out on all sides. I was overloaded with work. In addition, like almost all the known revolutionaries, I had to live illegally, with false papers and in other people's apartments. That made it impossible for me to enter more intimately and surely into the misfortunes of my younger brother.

The intimacy between us was of a special nature. We were only brothers, whereas he and my elder brother were also something more. As all children of more or less the same age, we two had quarreled and fought. My elder brother had always protected him, among other things because he wanted to establish over me that same ascendancy that I had over my younger brother. When we became young men these quarrels ceased, but I continued to feel shame and reproach that I had been unjust to my younger brother, and he remained reserved with me—a reserve that continually increased—as if he were still afraid that I would not want to understand him and that I would laugh at him. Furthermore, we had lived our youth apart, I at my studies and he at his secondary school, I in prison and he at his studies. My elder and younger brothers had in the meantime drawn closer; they had had to live together with our parents for a longer time. But that former protective, almost parental, attitude of my elder brother remained, arousing in response a feeling of respect and consideration.

Between my elder brother and myself, however, there was an intimacy from the time of his youth and my boyhood; he continued to confide all his passions and love affairs to me, and I told him all my dreams and hopes. It so happened that we did not see each other for long periods, a year or two perhaps, but nonetheless there would be established between us, from the first moment when we met again, a cordiality as if we had never parted. Our love was inexhaustible, as if we only existed when we were together, one and inseparable.

If I wanted to know something more, something more intimate, about my younger brother, I felt that I could find it out more easily through my elder brother than through him himself. And that is what happened—not because of my insistence, or because of the frankness of my younger brother, but because of the irresistible impulse of the elder one.

8

In the autumn of 1940 my elder brother finally succeeded, through personal influence, in obtaining a post somewhere in the Voivodina. Before leaving for his new job he came to Belgrade, in order to get the most recent political directives and orders and to make the necessary arrangements for his appointment, and also to see me again. This last was, at that time, more an imperative necessity than a pleasant need.

It was October, and the afternoon sun picked out in a golden haze the steep and shady streets of Kotež Neimar. We spent the whole day walking, until the sun set in the bloodstained west over the limitless plain of Srem. Then I had to go to a meeting and he to his train.

My elder brother told me what had happened, I might even say made his confession to me.

Immediately after their release from prison he and the girl had met—they had had to meet because of the political activities interrupted by the arrests—and they had become intimate. I did not want to find out how and in what circumstances it had happened; it was ugly and painful to ask questions about anything of that sort, but from his account and from my knowledge of his passionate nature, and even more from the manner in which he described it—he flared out at himself with the most violent and unbridled expressions—it seems to have happened as much by chance and his careless and casual manner as by her deliberate and considered intention.

"I began it all as a game," my brother told me, "simply not believing that that was just what she wanted. It seemed to me then that all I had to do was to hold myself in check, but now I doubt it, as if some devilish, irresistible curiosity led me on to get to know my younger brother's girl as he knew her, to identify myself with him through her. One thing is sure: it was not so much that I desired her, but that something drove me on to see to what degree she would resist. As soon as we were alone together, I was astounded by her behavior and expression, which was more suffering then seductive. It was as if she were rigid inside. She did not say a word, she was deathly pale, and her lips quivered.

"As soon as I touched her, she pressed herself against me and drew me to her, but as if she did not really want to and regretted what she was doing. She did everything as if against her will, but drew closer to me and surrendered in advance to my every movement. And I, though taking the initiative, as a man does, also did everything unwillingly, movement following movement inevitably. Kisses were transformed into embraces and love bites as soon as her body wound about mine and the whiteness of her breasts, perhaps unintentionally, shone before my eyes."

As soon as it was over, his conscience reproached him. He said to her: "This must never happen again. We are not strangers, but are bound, both of us, to him, to my brother." She agreed with him: "Really, that this should happen between us makes no sense. First and foremost we are comrades, revolutionaries." Only then did the ideological rules and prohibitions enter my brother's head. "He is my brother," he said, "and that seems to me the most important." But he did not get the impression that that was in any way a moral problem for her, as it was for him, but more an inconvenience, because of possible and superfluous complications and repercussions. She went on: "You know, I long for him so much that the fact that you are brothers draws me to you irresistibly." "But that is shameful, both in our eyes and before the movement!" my brother shouted. She retorted uncertainly: "I agree that there is no sense in it. That is important." Then she added, worried and passionate: "But what can one do, if a man draws one irresistibly, when that is everything in the world except our common struggle?" Only then did my brother remember that she, during their union, had whispered with anguish: "How sweet you are, my dear, my darling!" He knew, incon-

35

testably yet inexplicably, that when she cried out she was thinking both of him and of his brother, and what seemed even
stranger to him, in those moments it had not worried him at all.

Later, in conversation with me, he recalled the folk stories
about the frequent sinning between best man and bride, and
even between bride and father-in-law, and came to the conclusion that there perhaps existed some special kinship and affinity
that drew them together. But lust and thoughts of her had never
tormented him, for nothing had drawn him to her, and he had
the impression that she, too, had been indifferent to him until
they were alone together. Then everything had begun, as it were,
of its own accord, from a glance or a chance contact, and they
could neither resist nor avoid the act of love itself.

The day after their first union, he found a false consolation
for himself. His younger brother was not married to her, and he
should not marry a woman of this sort; too much importance
should not be given to the whole episode, though in the future
they must avoid anything of the kind.

"That's how it is," he exclaimed, stopping and clenching his
fists. "When a man wants to be a beast, he can always find a justification for his beastliness and becomes even more beastlike."

The house in which our family lived was one of those one-story
houses whose rooms are arranged one beside the other facing onto
a courtyard, each one separate from the next. My elder brother
had his own room at the end of the courtyard. The following evening she came to him. Everyone in the household except he
went to bed early. She had indeed brought some work with her,
but all the time it seemed to my brother that the work was only
a pretext. "For perhaps, in my filthiness," he confessed, "I unconsciously laid all the blame on her." They discussed everything
that was necessary, and then once more came that moment when
she became rigid inside and began to grow pale and to tremble.
"Perhap I, too, looked at her in just the same way," my brother
said harshly and angrily. "We did not say a word. As if by chance,
I moved away against the wall. She interpreted that as if I were

making room for her, and perhaps I really was, and without a word she quickly took off her shoes and slipped out of her dress. Lying to both her and myself, I said: 'It's really late. You can't go alone to the village now, and I don't feel like getting up and seeing you home. Let's lie beside one another like brother and sister.' And she added coldly and almost sarcastically: 'Yes, like brother and sister—like comrades.'

"I really wanted it to be like that and that nothing should happen between us," my brother cried. "But I secretly suspected, even knew, that it would not be so as soon as she lay down beside me. I did not want, and yet I wanted, it to happen! She went to turn out the light, and when she came back to the bed she was completely naked and she whispered casually: 'You know, I agree with you. We ought to be like brother and sister, like comrades, but I am used to sleeping naked.'

"That night I gave myself up entirely to enjoyment with her," my elder brother went on bitterly. "It was an orgy, if such a thing as an orgy really exists. I did with her what I have never done with any other woman! In a way it was deliberate, intentionally perverse, and carefully thought-out enjoyment. She not only silently and freely submitted to all that I did, but led me on with feverish shudderings. What she was searching for the devil alone knows! But I sought also the enjoyment that my brother must have had. I wanted to try everything he might have been able to imagine and experience, and her acquiescence roused me to still greater fury and led me on to untried, mad follies. What was more, my self-reproaches because of my brother, and that terrible acquiescence and the ever-harsher realization that I was a filthy beast and a traitor to all that I was and am, not only did not restrain me, but excited me again and again to transports unknown but suspected, to the depths of enjoyment of her womanly essence or, the devil alone knows, to the depths of my own filthiness."

From my brother's narrative it appeared that she took part in these enjoyments freely and untiringly, though probably she did not have his gnawing pangs of conscience and humiliation. For in the morning she tidied herself calmly and discussed the daily political activities with him as if nothing had happened. What is more, she was not at all embarrassed when the inmates of the house, who had risen early, found them together, despite my brother's precautions, and even went to our sisters and had a cordial conversation with them till it was time for them to go to school.

In the family, however, there was a gloomy, uneasy atmosphere; no one reproached my brother, and they behaved toward her as they had always done, though more stiffly and coldly. To the people of the household it was as if someone near to them had committed some serious crime about which they had to keep silent, and my elder brother felt as if he were the criminal.

While she was chatting with his sisters that morning, he came to a fateful decision. He made up his mind that there would never again be any sort of intimacy between them and that he would tell his younger brother all that had happened.

9

According to my brother's account, it was not the attitude of the family, and still less the satiety after that night, that made any renewal of their relationship impossible. Of course the mood of the family affected him and caused him—not to decide, for he had nothing to decide, since everything had happened of its own accord—to realize the senselessness, the madness, of their intimacy and that he would come to hate her with a hatred more frantic and unreasonable than was his passion for her. In his consciousness, in his memory, there lasted indelibly—this was noticeable even while he was speaking to me—the inexhaustible suppleness of her body, transformed into a naked and madly sweet shuddering which was transferred to him and permeated him as if it were his own. From that he knew that these enjoyments could never be repeated and that he would be horrified by the memory of them. That occurred to him while he was dressing and again

at breakfast—they sat opposite each other like distant acquaintances—and even when he saw her home and informed her of the
finality of his decision.

She, however, understood his decision as a momentary stifling
of his conscience, similar to that after their first union in love.
Later she again tried to get into close contact with him, always as
if by chance, as in a simple game. But he did not let himself be
seduced and ensnared. Hatred and repentance were more powerful in him than the delights that arose unforgettably in his memory, ever more persistent and ever more beautiful.

Till then, he had not attributed any special significance to his
relationships with women. If they wanted to lie with him, he im-
portuned them; if they didn't, he called them silly geese who put
on airs. But he never classed them as either chaste or dissolute—
they were what they were, born and conditioned to live sexually.

For the first time, there arose in his mind the thought, or the
suspicion—for it could not be called a realization—that in the
act of love between a man and a woman there was something
much deeper than mere enjoyment or a need, more fateful than
the founding of a family and the renewal of life, some kind of
personal confirmation of the eternal existence of the human race,
some kind of union of personality with eternity, the cosmos, and
incomprehensible law. He expressed this much more simply
and more emotionally: "I coupled with her as a beast with a
beast and felt, somehow, as if I had turned the whole world upside down!" But he did not stress, nor could I measure, how much
this feeling was conscience, because of his transgression against
his younger brother, and how much delight with the girl herself.

For the first time, he was forced to consider the problem of the
spoiled woman—or, to put it more exactly, the dissolute woman
who simply has had no time or opportunity to become dissolute.
"There is no reason to blame her," he concluded. "It is in her
blood and in her mind; not with all men, but only with those she
is close to ideologically. Lust and ambition with her are one and
the same thing."

But his judgments of her were unsure. Though he could not deny that she was passionate and unrestrained, and—most significant—in a manner attractive to both brothers, she also devoted herself with no less impulsiveness and energy to other activities, especially political.

It was obvious that the relationship with my elder brother did not have the same significance for her as it had for him, particularly from the moral standpoint. First, she did not have the feeling of kinship which, bred in brotherhood, afflicted my brother in relationships such as they had created. For her, these feelings were quite separate from one another. She even argued with my elder brother that by her union with him she had revived and intensified her love for his younger brother. Perhaps it was for that reason that she was quite unable to understand why he attributed such significance to the fact that the man he had deceived was his own brother. She said, indeed, that for her what had taken place between them made it impossible for her to marry the younger brother but only because—so it seemed to my elder brother—my younger brother and the family would never become reconciled to such a marriage. She recognized, and even condemed, their breach of the revolutionary norm and considered that they had proved themselves weak and inconsequent. The main thing was to remain scrupulously devoted to revolutionary activities. Moreover, having come to know the relationships within our family, and especially among the brothers, she could without apprehension reckon that her love affair with these two would never become public and notorious in the movement and so make political work impossible. Just because of that she could still less understand why my brother felt himself bound to tell his younger brother. Was it really necessary to make his brother unhappy? Why spoil for them all something that had been beautiful, the fruit of sincere love and passion? Why expose the intimate side of her life, even if it had not been without blame?

It seemed to me that my elder brother had come to his conclusions too casually, too easily, about her inborn dissoluteness, or perhaps he was trying to delude himself in a useless search for consolation because of what had happened. Perhaps she restrained herself, but neither then nor later did she ever show herself to be a woman who changed her men or who surrendered easily. Her private life was regular; she was in so prominent a position that any irregularity could not long remain unnoticed. The explanation of my elder brother that she, by making love to both brothers. was aiming at dominating the organization and its activities was even less credible. She was, undoubtedly, ambitious, loved power and authority, but always along the line of consolidating the movement, identifying her destiny with its destiny, and never in a manner either sly or secretive. He himself stressed that in later political work with her, despite the intolerance that had developed between them, he did not encounter any difficulties from her.

10

I still remember his tormented appearance at that time. He was, as always, pale. But now he had a sort of bitter and sarcastic intolerance—he seemed thin, with something weak in voice and manner, if not in thought. I believe that even on my deathbed I will remember his eyes, which, temporarily lit by the sun, sought for, begged for, peace and consolation from me.

Naturally, he had told everything to our younger brother—on the first evening after his release from prison. But even while he was telling him, it was clear to him that it would have been better, had he been able, to have said nothing.

"But what could I do?" he exclaimed, afraid to look me in the eyes. "Could I remain forever a traitor to him? Could I dare to allow him once again to take up an intimacy with her who had been unfaithful to him or whom his own brother had seduced? No, I had not the strength to remain a beast to the end and to keep silent—and that was just what I should have done!" By this confession to his younger brother, the whole depth and complication of unhappiness and suffering into which they had fallen was revealed to him.

My younger brother had understood his love for the girl as the final realization both of his own desires and of a love connection compatible with all that the most idealistic of revolutionaries then believed. For him, that relationship was not only the realization of the joys and needs of love but also the final conception of life and ideals—their ideals. The evil was not only that he must fall back once more into a long-lasting asceticism, but also that just that pure and idealized relationship between comrades which he had sought, and in which he had trusted in vain, was shattered. He knew—and that became obvious to his elder brother—that he would never again desire, much less create, a full, unconstrained, and unhypocritical love relationship. Not even his relationship with the girl had been quite that, but he had understood it as such, just as he now imagined it, and just that dream, that ideal world which for him was the most complete and the only acceptable reality, had been demolished. For years he had waited and longed for just such a relationship, had prepared himself for it, and now it had gone forever in the most painful, ugly, and unexpected manner.

It had seemed to me that he, so devoted and integral in his honor and idealism, would sooner or later be disillusioned, and not only in love. But what affected him most was that the disillusionment should come from his elder brother, who had been like a father to him, and in whose love and devotion he had until then believed unwaveringly, and from her, so young and modest, whom he had first taught love and idealism.

He did not in any way blame his elder brother, and that was perhaps the hardest thing of all to bear. After he had listened to him in silence, his expression changing every moment, he withdrew into his room and threw himself on his bed. Several times that night our elder brother had stolen up and peered through the window; his brother continued lying there, fully dressed, gazing at the ceiling. In the morning he complained to his elder brother that he was in pain, that his teeth hurt him, but at once repented of it and added: "It is nothing; it will pass." That evening the girl came. It was at once evident to her from his appearance and from the icy restraint with which he greeted her that he knew everything. She sat down, pale and subdued, and then went out into the night without asking him to escort her.

The next day my younger brother arrived in Belgrade. My elder brother remained with the family and went on seeing the girl. But she no longer tried to draw closer to him. Only once, she said to him: "It might all have ended without so much—so much unhappiness."

But my elder brother, though he had expected his younger brother to suffer, had not been able to keep from telling him everything. "Something drove me on," he told me, "even though I suspected how it would hurt him. I could not refrain, as I could not refrain from my relationship with her. I said to myself: He is your brother. You must tell him everything! And I knew that I was not talking to him because he was my brother, but because I could no longer hide all that shame from him, a shame so much greater because it was I who had done it."

Both then and now I thought it would have been better if he had said nothing to my younger brother, though I did not approve of his continuing his love affair with the girl. But to my elder brother it was not essential that he confess, though he put it forward as a reason. As in everything else he did, there was something unrestrained, passionate, and self-revealing in his telling the truth.

I did not, however, tell him what he should or should not have done; everything had already been done. I went on calming him and trying to restore him to good humor, even using the argument that he was treating all this from a religious viewpoint—broken faith to a brother, the prohibition of incest. That was the only thing that made any impression on him; it struck him in his revolutionary conscience, revealed that he was not a logical materialist and atheist. But it did not reconcile him. He said: "Yes, perhaps you are right. There are still within me remnants of religion and clan atavism, but the main thing is that it is dishonest and repugnant, a betrayal. For the realization of sin and the pangs of conscience a man need not have a God."

11

I was impressed so strongly and painfully by his confession that only after several days did it enter my mind that it was my duty to put the whole matter before a political forum, so that my elder brother and the girl should get a well-deserved castigation and the movement should not remain in ignorance of their weakness. That was my duty, the more so because such procedures were already the practice of the movement. I myself had been one of those who had introduced them, and I had taken part in the investigation of several such cases.

But I did not do so. Even now I cannot really decide why I did not carry out my revolutionary duty. It was a question of my own brother, and that considerably hampered me. And I was convinced, and still am, that any discussion would have done more harm than good, though it might have strengthened the self-criticism and discipline of the membership, it might also have driven away and scandalized some of those who had just joined the movement and were overburdened with every kind of weakness. What was more, I knew my elder brother as well as any man can know another, and it was clear to me that all that had happened had no connection whatever with his devotion to the revolution. Dragging the whole affair to the notice of the movement could only make him smart internally, deepen the humiliation of our younger brother, and isolate the girl, who was still young, from revolutionary activities. So I quickly reconciled my revolutionary conscience, though today I wonder if that was really a transgression of the rules of the movement or perhaps a dull, secret longing for the girl.

Also, the whole episode was for me so unpleasant and emotional that I simply stifled my scruples and did not do my duty. Moreover, I did not even remember to point out to my elder brother that just this case, his own example, confirmed how right the movement was when it preached the free choice of partners but also monogamy. But that was how it was; the painful human side led me to act as I did.

I considered it my first duty to help my younger brother. But there was nothing I could do. As I have said, I was in hiding and he, too, did not have a permanent apartment, so that several days passed before we met. And that was a good thing—if there was anything good in all this. For I was so moved by my elder brother's account that, had we met the following day, I would have begun to speak openly of it. However, calming down and reconsidering in the course of those few days what I should do, I came to the conclusion that it would be better if I could induce him to tell me what was depressing him and that in any event I should have to be careful and considerate.

But my younger brother remained silent, parrying all my devious attacks. He was so obstinate and set in his attitude that it was soon clear to me that any interrogation or reminder of what had happened to the three of them would tear open his wounds, which he had with great spiritual effort succeeded in covering.

He looked worse from every point of view. Even before, he had not been well-dressed and had been poorly fed; our father had had to take care of the other children. But now the wretchedness of his appearance was striking. I managed to collect, from friends and my own small reserves, some clothing and shoes and a little money. He took them mechanically, scarcely noticing and not differentiating the nature of things. And that, too, was how he ate. He took food as if it had neither taste nor smell.

Perhaps my impressions were exaggerated. I had expected in advance that he would be listless and indifferent. I never saw a man who was to such a degree, not exactly unhappy, but enclosed in some world of his own, and at the same time so devoted, so wrapped up to his last thought in the revolutionary movement.

45

It seemed to me that he found in his surrender to the revolution some special personal passion, as if he were escaping from this world, the world around him.

His friends had scarcely noticed the changes in him. He had always been devoted to the movement and alien to any form of amusement. He was once more that youth of earlier times, serious, taciturn, with a melancholy smile, but I noticed in him even bodily changes: that stoop was now more noticeable, now no longer only an expression of strength, but also of some hunched withdrawal into himself. His melancholy smile lasted longer than there was any reason for it to do so, and remained rigid and petrified on his face until he wiped it away by some internal tremor. His eyes seemed expressionless, without the nuances of their youthful, keen blue. They were not warm, but pure and sad.

I believe that he suspected I knew everything and was grateful to me that we never spoke of it. We mentioned our elder brother casually, and he spoke about him with his earlier respect but, I would say, also with greater and almost compassionate love. He loved me, too—I felt that incontestably—more solicitously than before. He was afraid that I would be arrested and he worried about my lungs, which had got worse. I am convinced that he would have forgiven both his elder brother and her, and probably would have accepted everything as a misfortune, like death, though not resigning himself or finding any final, comprehensible explanation.

But there was not time for him to forget all that happened—if he ever could forget. Nor was that new love between him and me able to flower. I was left with the sorrowful realization that I had not helped him as much as I would have liked, that he had not overcome his unhappiness. The invasion of our country in April, 1941, cut short his recovery, as also the course of so many personal destinies, but it could not, either for him or for my elder brother or for her, sweep away their feelings toward one another or toward all that had happened to them.

12

In the fever of preparation that led to the insurrection, my younger brother went to our parents, and my elder one to Montenegro. The latter began the armed struggle in our native district, first by an ambush and then by an attack on an enemy garrison. His moment had come.

The last time I was with him was on the eve of the outbreak of the struggle. Frenzied, he had rejoiced childishly when I informed him that the time had come to begin armed attacks on the occupying forces and the local authorities. He had no talent for detail and long discussions, and still less for political finesse. He became his real self only in open fighting. Recalling him as he was in those days, I often think that there are men who are as if created for particular situations and circumstances, and that it is just in them that they display the gifts and the power of which until then they have not been fully conscious. They become overnight the leaders of the masses who instinctively submit to their thoughts and orders, recognizing spontaneously their inherent ability. Such men spring up especially in moments of struggle and insurrection, when all authority, customs, and ideas are called in question. My elder brother was not at the head of the revolutionary forum, but he emerged as the head of the insurrection, not merely because it was he who began it, but, rather, that he, though it appeared that he had no sense of organization, found means that answered to his ends, to the times and the circumstances.

My younger brother I did not see. He was busy with political agitation and organizing militant groups in the villages. About the girl I heard only that she was leading a youth organization, that organization whence came the greatest number of fighters. From reports, my impression of her was confirmed: persevering, disciplined, but pondering every new attitude and directive with such intensity that it seemed visible how she thought, how her thoughts were transformed into clear and concrete forms of action. She was able to comprehend realities and snatch at every possibility. But it did not seem that she, like my brothers, was carried away by enthusiasm for the war and the insurrection. For her, they were realities more or less like any others; man must take up arms if he wants to live and to survive with his ideals, desires, and plans. On such as she forums, staffs, and officials can always rely. They may be sure that such members will not rush ahead or withdraw too early.

We met once in Belgrade, where she had come for illegal literature, on the eve of the insurrection. Naturally, I did not speak with her about her former relationship with my brothers; she never came to know that I knew all about them. Neither then nor later was there any need for such talk, and it seemed to me that if I had mentioned what had happened I would have placed her in an uncomfortable and humiliating position, not so much because she would be ashamed, as that she would always be afraid that by bringing all that to light her reputation and also her role in the struggle would be smirched, even if she did not end up before some party commission of investigation.

Especially on the eve of, but also in the course of, the insurrection I did not make any reference to my elder brother about what had taken place among the three of them. How could I darken the rejoicing he felt at what he had expected and awaited for years, through persecution, humiliation, and imprisonment. But I came to know, and myself noticed, that even though the insurrection was for him just that way of struggle, if not of life, in which he found his real self, he brought to every skirmish, every clash, too much foolhardy courage, as though he were passionately playing with danger. When he led the attack on the garrison, he personally went right up to the building itself, threw a bomb and, after it, his own shirt, soaked with petrol and blazing, thus exposing himself to unnecessary danger. His heroism made a deep impression on those taking part, and rumors of his exploits spread among the people, but—and in that many agreed

—he could have achieved all this with less exposure of himself and others. He would wait, standing in the middle of the road, for a lorry filled with military police, so that they, had they been bolder and more capable, could easily have killed him. Such men usually do not last long in war; born for it, they also die in it. My elder brother also died. But too soon and certainly not inevitably.

On that night it was necessary to seize and mine a bridge of the greatest importance to the enemy. The bridge was guarded by local militiamen, stiffened by a small squad of gendarmes in a fortified post on a hillock nearby. It was a moonlit night, and, meeting gunfire and still unaccustomed to night fighting and attacks on fortified posts, the insurgents scattered and withdrew in panic, though they did not take to flight. My brother went up to the fortification, feeling, by some sense that only born fighters possess in the course of an engagement, that the center of resistance was there. Two or three of the bolder men followed him. Mad luck served him. The fortification was silenced, deafened by the roar of his bombs, and the enemy soldiers were defeated and dispersed. My brother did not stop at that, but ran along the road, catching up with and killing the flying and demoralized gendarmes. In war it usually happens that a defeated enemy, whether as a group or as individuals, loses every wish to resist and surrenders to certain death. So it was then. But my brother did not know when to stop and went on farther—into an unknown and unreconnoitered area.

He came upon one of the village guard units that the occupiers had begun to form, especially along lines of communication. The insurgents, with good reason, despised them, seeing that they were for the most part made up of desperate peasants mobilized by force. That guard, too, would probably have fled without a fight, but, as ill-luck would have it, someone called my elder brother by name just as he turned into a crossroads where an ambush had been set. His name was widely known; he had often visited that village and had worked as a teacher there. Among the guards were some who were only waiting to acquire some bloodstained glory. My brother fell with a groan, hit by the first shots. There was an exchange of fire over his body, but in the confusion and panic the insurgents did not succeed in dragging him away. Next day his body was hanged on the concrete pillar of the burned bridge as a warning, and later exhibited in the little town nearby, as had been the bodies of notorious haiduks in days gone by.

Not even I thought that my brother had gone to his death intentionally. But his recklessness in battle and the fury with which he fought and settled his accounts with his enemies and, above all, his indifference to his own life told me, and especially tell me today, that some inner discord drove him on, some gnawing of conscience because of his sin with the girl. Probably he would have been killed anyway, but not so soon, and not in so reckless a manner. I recall that he had the bearing and the way of thinking of a man dedicated to death; not only did he never dream of life in times of peace, but he also behaved as if there could be no life for him outside war and insurrection. In that there was something great, but also something despairing, as if he had found there not only the reason for his existence but his escape from it as well.

I used to think that that was my impression only. But a few years later, at the commemoration of the insurrection in the little town in which we had settled, it was the girl herself who, when my elder brother was mentioned, remarked, as if by chance: "He should not have been killed; at least not then and in that way."

13

In the death of my younger brother, however, there was not any kind of unconscious intention. It was. if I may so put it, a logical continuation of his troubled and suffering existence.

At the end of 1941 his detachment—he was its commissar—

was smashed. The commander fled to liberated territory, and my brother remained to muster the fighters, who were mostly demoralized. But soon even those who had remained with him were either killed or captured. Wounded, he was betrayed and was taken prisoner in some village. They took him to Belgrade, to the camp at Banjica, where they collected the peasants from the insurgent districts and sorted them out. Here they separated the organizers and party members from the ordinary peasants.

My younger brother was in peasant costume; at that time many of the organizers of the insurrection stressed their ties with the people in this way. At first he was among the mass of peasants, but then someone recognized him and betrayed him to the camp commandant.

Prisoners were interrogated in the building of the special police and not in the camp, but the camp commandant had been for twenty years an interrogator of revolutionaries at the Belgrade police headquarters and was well known for his ruthlessness and experience. On the eve of war, regarded as unsuitable for the new conditions and probably also because of political rivalries, he was relieved of his post. He was appointed exclusively as executioner and camp commandant, a post eminently suitable for him. But he considered this as unjust and in the camp tried to expose revolutionaries and revolutionary organizations and to carry out interrogations. Since that sort of task was infrequent there and was not, strictly speaking, within his authority, he was able to carry it out methodically and unhurriedly, the more so as his personal career and prestige were involved. The administration of the camp and the life in it were under day-to-day control of the Gestapo, so that my brother found himself face to face with a bloodthirsty Balkan tyrant and with the investigators of the German secret police, who worked with refinement and scientific skill.

The camp commandant at once began with some of the harshest and most long-lasting tortures. Though I was not able to find out everything about this unequal contest between my brother

—they put him into solitary confinement at once—and the united forces of the two police authorities, I quivered with horror at the details I did learn about what he had had to endure. This was revealed in the accounts of the surviving inmates of the camp—and they could not have known or seen much—and from the not very explicit but nonetheless eloquent documentation.

The interrogation of my brother lasted a full three months. From the documents it could be seen that at the very beginning the camp commandant in the course of his official duties advised the special police whom he had found, whose brother he was, and that his interrogation had begun. In that short report he said that the prisoner remained obstinately silent and only stated that he wished to die honorably and that he would not speak. The commandant, not without irony, said that he would make every effort to soften him—he used just that expression. My brother's statement under interrogation was attached—just one sentence: "I want to die as an honorable man and I will not speak." That was just as the commandant had reported, but here it sounded quite different, not theatrical, not disdainful, not even revolutionary, but merely a reduction of everything to moral, I would say human, values. No other document remained except a circled number alongside my brother's name in the roll of the prisoners, meaning sentenced to execution by shooting at Jajince.

From the accounts of the camp inmates, I learned that all that had remained of my brother at the end of his three-month torture was a bloody and toothless skeleton with huge undimmed blue eyes. He was disordered in mind—for everything except keeping silent—and his limbs were dislocated and broken. He could not walk by himself, but had to be carried to his interrogations on a blanket. And that was all—so little and so much.

I cannot link the death of my younger brother with what took place between him and the girl, and between her and my elder brother. That my younger brother fell into the clutches of his torturers had nothing to do with all that. Nor can it be linked with his heroism; that word does not seem to me exact, for it was something above heroism—a conscious, fanatical, impulsive, but deliberate act. It was a question of honor as a condition of my brother's existence, as a noble death, as the culmination of his life.

My younger brother died honorably for the revolution. He would have died thus had there been no revolution. Life itself would have forced upon him the choice between betrayal, honor, and life. But the fact was that he, as also my elder brother, died poisoned by the bitterness of life. He had told me that the girl was present in his misfortune. I saw in his death, in the manner in which he understood his death, not only the inevitable and logical continuation of his personality, but also his love for the girl and his disillusion at the behavior of my elder brother and that he had decided upon it without too much anger, even without reproach, but with suffering resignation.

Therefore I have often thought that the lives of my brothers might have taken quite another course if it had not been for their relationships with the girl. Perhaps their revolutionary tasks would have been apportioned differently—for both tried to be as far away as possible from her—and perhaps their inclination toward self-sacrifice would have been less, and not so intense. Yes, everything might have been different—at least so I would have liked to imagine, and would have thought, if what had happened had not happened.

The girl was in no way to blame for their deaths. She went on with her revolutionary work in the most difficult conditions, living in hiding and building up disbanded organizations anew. The movement throughout the whole district was based on her, and she held firm. Whenever we met by chance after the war, she avoided mentioning my younger brother, from which I concluded that she had in her own way loved him; his tortures greatly afflicted her. When I unintentionally showed her the account of his interrogation she said: "Only he could have made such a statement and died in such a way."

That is the story of my brothers and the girl.

14

Yet she is not the most important reason that has compelled me to relate all this. It was, instead, what happened later, or, rather, what did not happen, between me and the girl, by then prominent and a married woman.

After the war I did not meet her very often and never intentionally. I did not try too much. Though I did not blame her for the deaths of my brothers, I still felt that she should never have allowed any intimacy with my elder brother. The reason for my coldness I hid as best I could. Nonetheless, I felt that she was trying to break down the barrier between us and to create a warmer, friendlier atmosphere. I never noticed anything incorrect in her efforts, and I did not think of anything amorous. In any case, at the end of the war she got married and later had two children. Her marriage seemed a happy one. They lived quietly and contentedly, as far as their public duties permitted.

So passed the first six years after the war, and so, too, would have passed all the others had we not met at the celebrations for the tenth anniversary of the outbreak of the insurrection in her district. I avoid celebrations, probably because of their pompousness and insincerity; on these occasions, in fact, men speak about themselves and the present day. But I felt forced to attend this celebration because the insurrection in that district was closely linked with the work of my brothers. I knew that she would be there, too—I had already spoken about it to her on the phone—but I did not attribute to that any great or special significance. It was, as I remember, a little unpleasant for me to meet her there, for I knew that the meeting would revive the memories of all that had happened between her and my brothers, the unexplained and inexplicable aspect of their deaths known only to me, and, doubtless, also to her.

I noticed her on the dais, and we exchanged a few words. But as long as the official part of the celebration lasted—and, as usual, there were too many speakers and they all spoke for too long, even though it was a hot summer day—it was as if I had not noticed, nor was there that unpleasant feeling that I had expected. My thoughts wandered as they always do whenever I am faced with such more or less similar laudatory speakers and speeches. Still, I thought unceasingly and intensely about my brothers. The mention of their names and of the place where they had been active, and the presence of men who had known them, no doubt had an influence on these feelings. But the recollections were dark and vague, and I experienced a strong feeling of their existence, the continuance of their life in me. Most frequently the thought occurred to me: All this, these men would not be here and this celebration would not be taking place if my brothers had not died. I was filled with sorrow and emptiness and, even more, with a sense of absurdity, an evident discord between their deaths and what we were doing there, and that, too, intensified the feeling of their continuance in me, to such an extent that for a moment it seemed to me that they truly existed bodily and lived within me.

The last speech was almost at an end when I felt as if someone behind me were watching me intently. It was not in any way different and separate from that feeling of my brothers within me, but was somehow linked with it, as if my brothers themselves were watching me and enjoyed watching me. Though I do not believe in mysterious thought transference, I was aware at that moment that someone behind me knew exactly what I was feeling and thinking, and that that person especially knew very well that continuance of my brothers within me. The orator was still shouting something, and I realized that it was she who was watching me. It was unpleasant, and I turned to look. She was in fact standing behind me, but a little to the left, and not looking at me but somewhere indeterminate, over the crowd, at the distant mist-covered green hills. I remembered that I, too, had been looking at those hills in just that way, scarcely aware of the speaker's words and not distinguishing individual faces. How strange she looked! Pale and rigid, despite a slight perspiration, her features illuminated by some vivid inner picture, by some clear and moving memory. Her lips were parted a little, her teeth white between the dark-red lips; I thought to myself that her teeth must be very sharp. I don't know what I looked like myself, but I thought that not only did I look just like her, but also that I was unable to look any different. It was clear to me that she was thinking of my brothers. In that, however, there was nothing strange; all that was strange was that correspondence with me in the manner of our thinking, in the identity of feeling for my brothers. I was, of course, astonished and confused by that, and firmly convinced that she would turn around and notice that look and that feeling in me, or that I saw that look and that feeling in her. But that did not happen. She stood as before. The intensity of the same experience showed more and more strongly in her expression, and I noticed that she clenched her white plastic handbag so tightly that her knuckles and the tips of her nails were white. I was afraid lest she turn around and see the identical expression on my features, yet at the same time I longed for that to happen, probably because memory and emotion had gripped me so completely that I felt isolated, eager and impatient to be with someone near to me, with someone who understood me. I thought: What has been has been! Now she and I feel the same grief and we can share it together.

I was convinced that that momentary link with her arose exclusively from a mutual and contemporaneous feeling for my brothers, and that in her there was nothing else but a common grief that brought us together and swept away my concealed intolerance and her embarrassment and humiliation before me. But that was a commonplace and obvious conclusion.

15

As I said, she did not turn around, and I was so saddened by that that I could hardly wait until the end of the speech to approach her, just to remind her of my presence. But there is no doubt that she was unconsciously aware of it. The speaker ended by shouting some slogans, and she gave a start and looked at me.

I don't remember who made the first move. I believe that we both responded at the same moment. She smiled, sadly and with understanding; in that I recognized a shade of complicity, an unrestrained but banked-down continuation of that mutual emotion she felt for my brothers. I wanted to say to her: "What can we do? It had to be so, and you and I understand each other." But I managed to warn myself: No, she does not know. She must not know that you know everything that happened between her and your brothers. I was at the same time longing to seize her hand, even to kiss her! There was nothing especially erotic in that, or so I tried to convince myself, and nothing that might have been unwelcome to her.

I concealed my words and desires. She approached me and, with caressing sorrow, whispered: "We two are still alive. We mourn and we rejoice for those two." There was no doubt that she understood my feelings. And from that moment all barriers began to fall between us, moral and social, emotional and physical, with a speed that, even had I wished, I was unable to follow or recall.

We walked beside each other, I in shirt sleeves and she in a short-sleeved blouse, and our elbows touched, and I said to myself, almost aloud: This is a woman whom I could now, at once, marry.

When I say that, it must be borne in mind that my relations at that time with my chosen comrade were frank and harmonious and that I, by my actions and thoughts, belonged to the movement and regarded every involvement in love affairs as illogical and insincere and a destruction of my whole personality. I do not say that women never came into my mind. I would be lying if I did not admit that such thoughts often occurred to me, most often when I was lying wakeful at night beside my comrade. But those were only fancies—not facts! It is action that is important; I do not consider myself a waverer just because I do not translate thought into action and because I know that I should refrain from action. Even in those imaginings the objects of my desires were not my comrades with whom I worked in the movement. If anything of the sort arose in my mind, I would immediately expel it and replace it by the image of women who were not members of the movement or who had joined it after the revolution and either did not know or did not greatly care what the relationship between comrades should be.

But in those moments when we two were going down from the dais I wanted her, regardless of everything else, despite the fact that she was the wife of one of my comrades. That desire was indeed so immediate, so heedless, so definite, that I realized and accepted it almost as if it were the act of love itself, in no way shameful, in the presence of my comrades and the people.

The touching of our elbows did not fall among those chance contacts of hair, breasts, hips that arouse desires of which we have until then not been conscious. No, this was not the desire, awakened yet ecstatic, furious and irresistible, for union in love that is not fulfilled because momentarily the conditions are not suitable. I was quite certain that she wished for the same thing, and that she knew what I wanted and longed for. How else could I interpret the intentional persistent pressure of her arm and the words, her words, spoken mournfully and passionately, after we were in the crowd: "We see each other so seldom, as if we were not linked by those whom we have loved most of all." Indeed, all that we did later was a tacit but deliberate search for conditions for the realization, the completion, of the act of love.

I had previously regarded her as pretty, though not a beauty. But now her body acquired for me a quite different appearance and significance. Suddenly it became for me very familiar; every little bit of it lived for me as if it had been my own. Even her clothes I felt as my own, and her every movement was seductive and as if intentionally made to draw me to her, to her body. That body, which was so frankly and unrestrainedly offered, I saw and accepted as incomparably beautiful—not beautiful, perhaps, but formed and adapted to offer me alone a great, new, and absolute enjoyment.

She had changed considerably since the time I had known her as a girl. But I saw her, recognized her, as she had been then, though she was now both more beautiful and more striking. It was almost as if I had been trying to revive her appearance as a girl, which I had forgotten and which I now considered had been of no significance for me anyway. Her freckles had almost entirely disappeared, but I could still perceive them through the pale brilliance of her skin. Her curly hair was even thicker and was combed in a different way, but it retained the freshness that I had forgotten. Only now did I remember that it was her eyes, so varicolored, with greenish and tawny lights, which had been so in harmony with her then freckled face and had given her features that roguish yet sensitive expression. She was fuller in the figure but had kept her girlish suppleness, her soft hips, and the provocative firmness of her small breasts. I had never thought of her fingers, but now suddenly I began to recognize unremembered details—they were thin, with shining knuckles. So, too, I could say for her lips, the upper one a little upturned and the downy golden lower one sharply retracted, both thin, dark, and red. All of her suddenly became so familiar that I suspected, even saw, the moles on the most invisible, most concealed parts of her body. I felt that I enjoyed her naked and submissive to my hands. Then, too, I knew her way of thinking—devious and realistic— her psyche, all its secret nuances, and especially her manner of giving herself—fiery and intense. She was all mine, even though nothing took place between us. I was sure that she knew me just as well, if not better—knew me and claimed me.

16

Though it was not so long ago, I could not say how that afternoon passed. It seemed to me that even without concrete details my impression of it was both more real and more intact.

The guests had to be continuously in the company of their host and fall in with his plans. But we two were at the same time conscious only of ourselves, as if separated from the others. It all happened spontaneously and was due in great part to the fact that although she, too, was a guest, she was to some extent the hostess as well, because of her youth and because she had been a good friend of my brothers and the family. Thus, through continual reminders of our common memories and visits to well-known places, we created a sort of public intimacy, which served, before others and perhaps even more before ourselves, to conceal our mutual desire. So it happened that one or the other of us, but more frequently she, proposed something regardless of our host. Below all that was taking place openly flowed our secret understanding and familiarity, like an underground river that knows nothing but itself.

At lunch we were seated fairly far from each other on the same side of the table. But we found a way, by leaning forward and toward our neighbor, to look at one another. It especially excited me to see the way she drank the wine; as she did so, she looked at me, but not in the way one sees in the films, with a glance of half-closed eyes, as if proposing a toast, but with feverishness, her eyes glued to mine as if to drink her own or my blood. The glass in her hand I felt as a prolongation of herself. So indeed I felt about all the things she touched. It seemed to me that her lips absorbed mine and not the wine; she really drank as if she were kissing. If I did not have the same expression, I certainly did something or looked in some way so that she had the same impression of me. For when lunch ended and we were once more running after each other, she said: "They gave us seats far apart!" To which I added: "But just the same, we were near."

She proposed that everyone take a rest after lunch. The host agreed, and I did so, too, secretly rejoicing that there might be a chance of being alone with her, hoping that either she would come to my room or I would go to hers, though the little hotel was wide open to the glances of the staff. Because of the shortage of accommodations, I had been put with a colonel, an elderly and distinguished invalid from the district, who, portly and slow, was only too willing to lie down. I lay down fully clothed, and though I have the habit of sleeping after lunch I was not able to close my eyes. I got up as soon as the colonel began to snore and went quietly down the corridor, with the deliberate intention of meeting her, without yet knowing how to manage it, but sure that she, too, wanted it. I listened. Which was her room? I made up my mind. I decided to open the doors of all the rooms, pretending to have made a mistake, until I came to hers, or to ask someone. But it did not come to that. She appeared in the corridor. She, too, was not alone in her room, nor could she sleep. We went toward each other. But not even for those few moments were we alone; servants and guests were continually passing along the corridor. We looked at each other, ashamed, as if caught *flagrante delicto,* and then hurried down the stairs. In the restaurant we met those who had not gone to rest, and I suggested that we go for a walk instead.

At last we found ourselves on the banks of the Sava. The greenish river seemed unmoving in the heat. There was something passionate about it, as if it were offering itself with tepid, outspread languor. The opposite bank breathed with willows like a foaming wave. Suddenly she approached me, touching my arm with trembling, hot, excited fingers. "Why don't we swim across?" she asked me in an equally hot and excited whisper. "I could get a swimsuit. It would freshen us. It would be really wonderful."

I remembered that my younger brother had swum over there with her on just such hot, clear days, perhaps among those very willows and from this very place. And although some inexhaustible desire drew me to her and the river with sullen force, I was filled with such terrible shame, for myself, for my dead brothers, for my comrades present there, that I almost inaudibly muttered: "Yes, it would be wonderful, but it would be silly to leave the others."

Though I was appalled at my lust and hers, I could not shake myself free of it—or from the thought of my brothers, though they were now far away in my memories. I could not free myself. With the dying day my longing for her became a dark and sullen misery, and the memory of my brothers farther and farther away and more importunate. I was afraid of the night, afraid of her—and of them—of ecstasy with her and of betrayal of them.

The shadows fell on shame and memory, and passions and realities flamed up and spread. I went away before dusk, unexpectedly for her and for the others, in fear of what I might do in the darkness. But it seems to me that on that afternoon I understood more intimately, more finally, both my brothers and the girl.

In prison, at Sremska Mitrovica
April 6–22, 1959

THE GIRL
WITH THE
GOLD TOOTH

The armies came and went, and the authorities in the little town were constantly changing, and all found joy and solace with her, regardless of their creed or the flags they waved and that led them through the massacres. But the war could not go on forever, and one army finally won. It had occupied the little town before, but then it could not call itself victorious.

Now that army, even though war was still raging furiously somewhere far away, entered as undisputed victor; the defeated armies had finally withdrawn, leaving behind their piles of ashes, mounds of men shot hurriedly, and all the savagery of hate and bitterness. The victorious army was bound to be, also, the aveng- ing army, and because it had fought in the name of the idea and the promise of a new life, it had to confirm this by purges, in its own ranks and in the life around it, of what it considered old and hostile, the elimination of everything that hampered its author- ity or sullied the purity of its faith.

Thus she, too, the girl with the gold tooth, was brought before a military court—since there were still no real courts, the army commanders passed sentence—even though she was not guilty of anything except that she liked to amuse herself with everyone and took pleasure in dancing and singing, good dinners and love.

She was the prettiest girl in the town; everyone who dared to say so admitted it. Good husbands did not dare to admit it to their wives lest they reveal their hidden desires, and the young men did not dare to say so before their girl friends lest they refuse to join them on the evening walk. When they did not gossip about her, they preferred to keep silent. But the children—for they know everything and dare everything—sang tauntingly about her beauty, and the old women—they forget all that they ever knew and are envious of everything—spoke evilly of the hussy who led their grandchildren astray and disturbed the happy marriages of their sons.

She was no whore; nor had she any need to be. She came from a middle-class family, was the daughter of a respected father and the sister of a well-known fighter for the new life. She was born in the hill country, whence her family had come to settle on the outskirts of the little town in a house with a garden that stretched down to a little stream and the river. Her father had also bought a market garden nearer the town, an orchard and a vegetable plot on the far side of the river, right on the steep bank, but one which could not be seen from the house because it was screened by other orchards and meadows. That, together with her father's little pension, was enough to enable them to live peacefully and comfortably.

But she did not want to live like other girls; she was different. Breaking away from the mountain-peasant way of life before she was fully grown, she had in her early girlhood decided to enjoy everything the little town offered: sweetmeats, young men, silk dresses, parties, comforts, and love—in fact, what every girl wants if she can get it. She explained: "I am neither one thing nor the other. I want to be a town girl and would never have been able to remain a peasant. So, by chance, everything in me is mixed up."

But those with whom she was intimate knew that that was not the truth, at least not the whole truth. She was, indeed, a town girl, but not like the others. She had kept something of the freshness and robustness of the mountaineer; the town girls were for the most part thin and pale. Her body was firm and compact, full, plump, and eager for enjoyment. Strong in the hips and breasts, she had a soft throat and full, unmuscular haunches. Her hands were large and strong, but with delicate and cushioned fingers. Her head seemed a trifle bent under the weight of her thick, black tresses. She laughed frankly, blushing coyly like a peasant girl, but she also liked the direct and impudent town manners and sallies. Her skin was dark, but she looked after it carefully, and her greenish eyes flashed mildly from under thick brows. She loved ornaments, heavy silver bracelets and huge gypsy necklaces, but her dresses were simple, in pastel shades. In the village she would have been a young woman with hordes of children, game for anything and skillful at deceiving her husband under his very nose and putting horns on him. In the town there was no hurry for her to get married, and she could deceive her lovers to her heart's content. She could not stand any excess and least of all scandal, but she liked to hear how the women decried her from envy and jealousy. This was not hatred—she hated nobody. It was her only compensation for the bad repute and gossip she had to endure. She was not mercenary, though she gladly accepted presents and still more gladly gave them.

She had a gold tooth, the right canine, or eyetooth, which, when she laughed or spoke, flashed from the ripe redness of her lips. It used to be said that the gold cap had not been necessary, that she had had it put in to add to her attractions and had had it done by a dentist, who had stayed for a while in the town, for the love she gave him. That gold tooth was like a symbol, by which she was known and remembered. It put the seal on her beauty, was a sort of invitation, and revealed her tastes. Those who knew her usually added to her name the words "with the gold tooth," and she was known to those who did not know her personally, and did not care what her name was, as "the girl with the gold tooth." The tooth stressed and outlined her personality.

She had not wanted to get married when she was younger, and later, when she had the reputation of a light woman, there was no opportunity, despite her father's pride and the burgeoning of her beauty. She used to say: "It is never too late to get married.

I am still in flower. When I'm an old bag I will find a way." Her father used to beat her when she was in her teens for hanging about kissing in the gateways and bushes and, more often, in the orchards above the river. She went there by preference, even in winter, for on the steep banks behind the willow and alder clumps were hidden dens and little level patches from which all she had to do to keep watch was to raise her head a little, and to keep her head down to remain invisible. Later her father kept his hands off her to avoid scandal and because, despite everything, he loved his only daughter as she him. She fussed over both him and her younger brother, regardless of whether they considered her guilty or innocent.

She might have been about twenty-five years old when the war and the insurrection broke out and foreign armies overflowed the land and intruded into her godforsaken little town and carefree life. Yet, though like others she was horrified by these events, she was neither frightened nor bewildered. The foreign army officers were only interested in her beauty and her way of life, and the locals—students who knew everything and rigid officials, frightened petty merchants and apprentices—all in one way or another burned their fingers at her flame. They secretly desired her, or she bewitched them with her smile and her songs if they had not already experienced her unforgettable embraces and incomparable limbs. She said, half-seriously: "They have learned love from me and, you see, now they are ready to tear each other's eyes out!"

Therefore she behaved as if the war had changed nothing essential, as if nothing essential in her life could change. There were shortages of materials and of new clothes, but she always had plenty of dresses and, being skillful at sewing, she was always able to appear in something new. The garden and the orchard still bore fruit, the cow gave milk as it had always done, and laborers were cheaper than ever, so that serious shortages and heavy tasks did not exist. Though women became more open and casual, she was pretty enough and young enough and skillful enough to be able to go on choosing her men. Changes and difficulties were mainly due to the fact that she was now alone. Her brother had gone to the forests, to the insurgents, where there was a place for him; and her father, after interrogation and preventive custody, had been interned in a foreign land.

Vital and independent, she rapidly found a way out of her loneliness. She made friends among the girls and the women left forsaken as she was, and though she became more selective, she went on amusing herself freely with men, seeking refuge in flirtations and pleasures to stifle her grief for her brother and father.

The most handsome, most witty, and most impetuous men were the officers of the occupying army. But she did not consort with them willingly, because of her brother and father, because of the hostility in the town, and also because they were foreigners, who could bring her no joy except coarse bodily satisfaction. If anything took place between her and one of them, it was by chance and momentary, in a furtive manner. As luck would have it, the occupation army did not remain long in the isolated one-horse town, only entering it during temporary offensives against the insurgents.

Thus the girl with the gold tooth went on living and enjoying herself as before. She looked on love as uncommitted, and accepted both one side and the other—revolutionaries and counterrevolutionaries.

The little town was taken and retaken several times, and it happened that those who took the place of those who had been there before threatened her and called her a bandit's whore. But she, familiar with armies and accustomed to insults, paid scarcely any attention. After a few days she would choose a new lover from among the newcomers, if, indeed, he were not one of her earlier lovers, sometimes from times of peace, for she changed less often than was said of her, preferring to stick to well-tried lovers, as all who are skilled in enjoyment prefer.

Though the war flared up with more and more merciless devastation, only the merest chance, so she thought, could disturb or menace her life. Yet everything was overthrown and destroyed, even her loves; they took her hastily and without tenderness on the eve of withdrawal and after shootings had been carried out. And she gave herself more frequently, from habit and impatient desire for the return of her former carefree existence, rather than from any carefully considered passion or enjoyment. All that remained was the ghost of her former pleasure. But she was satisfied even with that, as if assured that, as soon as the war ended, her real life would be restored, either as it had been before or in some other way.

It turned out quite differently, though for the little town the horrors of war diminished as soon as the enemy and the counter-revolutionary armies finally withdrew. She, too, could have withdrawn, had she suspected any danger, if she had not dreamed of peace and did not have to preserve her own home. They arrested her the second morning after the entry of the victorious liberation army, though she had had a love affair with its commissar before the war and had had frequent love trysts with the information officer during the war. There were many arrested, and therefore, even before the setting up of some sort of courts, they had to hurry with the sentences. The first shootings were carried out on the same day as the town was liberated, and they brought her for interrogation on the evening of the day she was arrested.

From earlier occupations and liberations of the little town it was known that interrogations before the military command were of little importance, merely a part of established and almost ritual order, since the sentences had for the most part been decided upon before the arrests were made. But this time it was the final liberation. The leading persons of the command were her good acquaintances, and she did not feel guilty. Therefore she stood before the investigators calmly and even joyfully, though she understood that in war ideas of guilt and justice often changed and human lives depended on mood and inclination as much as upon laws and regulations.

She looked at the commissar with recognition and smiled at him, awakening memories and the knowledge of delights known only to him and to her. But he responded with a complete lack of understanding, probably simulated, and coldly said to her: "For such as you there is no place in our new society. You have entertained the enemies of our homeland with song and have amused yourself with bandit officers."

She replied with a ringing and involuntary laugh, though chill with apprehension. "I do not ask who has what politics; I took pleasure with and entertained only men who pleased me. You at least should know that."

The commissar retorted indifferently, with a harsh smile: "For you, it seems, there is no difference between giving pleasure and amusement to enemies of the people and to fighters for national liberation! And what do you mean by 'you at least should know that'?"

Before she could make up her mind what to reply he shouted, seeming paler than she had ever seen him: "I know very well what you meant!" Looking at her with eyes that did not want to, perhaps were no longer able to, meet hers, he continued: "You wanted to remind me of our former intimacy and, certainly, to influence me, perhaps to blackmail me. But that was at another time; the land was not yet occupied and betrayed, and I, too, am today another, a new, man. Look, here are my comrades!" He pointed around, and only then did she notice the information officer, with his pencil poised over his notebook, and a motionless and attentive civilian, whom someone had previously pointed out to her as more important than the military commander, though she did not know, and until then had not cared, what his duties might be. The commissar went on: "You see, here are my comrades, and I am glad to be able to tell them openly: 'We were lovers.' But at that time I was not politically aware, and today I am ready to pay for my fault by repentance before my comrades and objectivity toward you."

He went on speaking, but she no longer understood him, though she still heard him; she realized that she was lost. She could no longer recognize him, with his tight belt and made-to-measure uniform, though he was still the man of former times, slim and blond. Her tears streamed. She heard the reserved and mysterious civilian say: "Everyone is free in his personal life, but also responsible before the people and society," and noticed that the information officer, going down a list with the red point of his pencil, no doubt a list of those arrested, had put a circle around one of the numbers, certainly the one opposite her name.

She remembered her brother and father. But her father was far away in a camp, if he had not already died or been killed, and her brother—her brother was on their side. Yet she pulled herself together and snapped at the commissar: "Have I not got an equal right to be one of these new men?"

"Everyone has that right," said the commissar, sitting down and continuing as if he were talking to someone else. "But he must win it—by struggle and by loyalty. We would be betraying ourselves if we had mercy on such people." The important stranger added: "What would the people who have suffered so much and have paid with their blood think of us?" And the information officer concluded mockingly: "We would have to resurrect everyone if we looked aside and let such persons go."

Quite collectedly, she remarked: "You forget that I have a brother in a very high position among you! What will you say to him? He will never forgive the murder of his sister." But the unknown man readily retorted, as if he were waiting for just this reminder: "We have kept that in mind. In truth, it touches us closely that you are the sister of such a comrade. We can tell you that he is so incensed at such a sister that he has behaved as such a comrade should behave; he has left it to us to decide, convinced of our revolutionary conscience."

She sobbed hopelessly. Someone grabbed her firmly by the arm and dragged her away. That must have been the information officer, for his voice near her ear shouted to someone, most likely the sentry, to wait at the head of the stairs. The hard unyielding hand, which did not let go of her arm, led her down a long and mildewed corridor and took her into soft and sweet-smelling

70

light, laid her down on a soft, yielding couch, and began to stroke her hair and face with velvety palms; a voice spoke to her in warm whispers. She pulled herself together as the information officer reassured her, holding her hands in his.

"We do not spare ourselves in the struggle for a new life. We want to save and to resurrect, not to suppress and to destroy. But we are all uncompromisingly against the evils and lies of the old order and of all who serve it, and we seek all those who belong to it, so that we may root them out. Naturally, we, too, are men. We differ from one another, and our duties, too, are different. All eyes are fixed on the commissar; even if he does not burn with the idea and his duty, he must remain pure and upright. And the secretary of the committee, that other one, who spoke little but wisely, he could be a saint among saints if we believed that there are such things as saints. I, however, am different, and my duties are different. I admit that I am weak about women and that I am forced, in my work, to take advantage of all sorts of people and all sorts of means, for the enemies of freedom and of our people are not subdued by defeat and have no fear of anything. My work, I admit, is dirty and horrible, if it were not undertaken in the name of the highest ideals and for such men as the commissar and the secretary. But without such men as I am and work such as mine is, they would not hold out forty-eight hours, and selfish and evil men would quickly tread underfoot today's freedom and our dreams of the future. I work in darkness and torment, and can do things that would not become them to do. We two could once more be together, be near each other. You are pretty and attractive, and you have something, some sort of frankness and candor in giving that I have not found in any other woman; nor will I ever find it. Even more, all sorts of men come to you, and you live in circles and milieux that are alien and inaccessible to us. I could convince those two that this is so and that you would be able to go by new paths, and I could induce them to show mercy and understanding. Everything, now, depends on you."

"What have I done wrong, what can I do now, that everything

depends on me?" she asked, drying her tears, listening to him and realizing, though she scarcely recognized him, in his tight-belted new uniform, as the swarthy and dark-browed man she had known.

Instead of replying, he embraced her. But she pushed him away and stood up. He darted a glance of malicious wonder at her and then shook himself, grinning softly and obscenely. "Surely you know what you ought to do. You are irresistible and experienced."

"How wrong you are!" she shouted. "I have never given myself to anyone against my will. I cannot, will not, do anything like that! It is not in my nature. I am not a whore. Even were it not for my father and my brother and the citizens, I could not for my own self-respect do anything of that sort. How can you, you especially, even propose such a thing, you who have been, who want to be, intimate with me?"

He stood up, looked out the window, and remarked: "No one is forcing you; nor can anyone force you. But think it over. Human nature is changeable. There is no whoring in that! If your brother or father were to hear anything, we would explain everything to them and convince them that service of this kind serves higher ends, which are just as important as any other. What is important is that you would not be doing it for personal profit— though, naturally, there would be some personal profit—but for society and the idea. As for my relationship with you, I am not the commissar or anyone like him, who must confess and repent. I think that, even if we were not old sweethearts, it would not be unpleasant to have a little fun together. As a man in a responsible position and a man who used to be dear to you, I state: In my eyes you would be neither dishonest nor unchaste, since the work I offer you would in fact be your sacrifice for the new, shining, noble life."

"I would like that, I ought to do that!" she exclaimed, gazing around her and trying to find something firm to grasp. "But I cannot understand! I cannot, I cannot!" His hand, once again firm and unyielding, led her out again. Somewhere in the dark corridor his voice went on mumbling in her ear: "As a man in a responsible position and a man once dear to you, I must tell you: I have already ringed your number and it is up to you tonight, for tomorrow may be too late, to do or not to do what you should do, for yourself, for your brother and father, for society."

Before she could recover herself and think what she should reply, a hand, even harder and stronger, seized her at the top of the stairs, and she stumbled down them, sobbing. They took her to a cell. Brushing away her tears, she informed the two prisoners already there, a peasant woman suspected of betraying hidden insurgents and the wife of an officer who had fled: "They will kill all of us. Me, too, me, too—and I don't understand. I am not guilty of anything."

They interrogated the two women the same evening—a little longer, a little shorter. Then everything was silent; they had gone to supper. But throughout the night, until dawn, they took away men from the other cells, men who did not return—and the three of them, in the morning, hoped that they would be spared one day longer, if they had not already been forgotten. For they knew that shootings take place at night. Till then, all the armies had acted thus. Night has no witnesses, and by night there is less trouble and inconvenience for those who have to do it.

Daybreak brought not only encouragement but also hope, and lulled them with the details of everyday life—washing, breakfasting, cleaning and putting in order the cell and themselves. The women forgot, or did not recall, that this was a victorious army, which did not always find it necessary to conceal what it did. Men came for them about noon, when they were least expecting it and still less could conceive, on that bright, warm autumn day, that there was really to be a shooting, despite the fact that the commissar informed them of that curtly and icily in the prison courtyard.

They were escorted by a couple of soldiers in partial peasant costume and by the information officer; he was there, so he explained, in case the soldiers have pity on weak women or try to take advantage of them. The three women, unbound, walked through the little town, weeping but consoling and encouraging each other. The peasant woman wailed that she had not been allowed to go to confession, though the soldiers tried to convince her of her foolishness and grumbled at her. The officer's wife was weeping softly and sadly for her little son, to whom they had not permitted her to say good-by. The girl with the gold tooth walked silently, pale, lethargic, and pensive, wondering if this was really happening to her. It occurred to her to turn to the information officer and accept his offer and to recall his recent flirtation with her. But she did nothing, lost and disillusioned, perhaps ashamed of such weakness in front of her fellow sufferers and the people of the little town, which, deaf and empty, peered at them from behind drawn blinds.

The three women knew where they had to go; there, in front of the fortress where other armies had carried out their shootings. They went neither hurriedly nor slowly, in step with the soldiers, in the terror and silence of the indifferent, unknown, alien town, by the street that led past the house of the girl with the gold tooth, across the little bridge and into the orchard, into the area of her love trysts.

They knew that they would be shot and not hanged; the revolutionaries shot women, too, whereas the counterrevolutionaries hanged them, because they considered that only a man was worthy of a bullet. They went by a well-known road and to a death they knew. But death itself they did not know—that no man knows—and they marched on, legs leaden and glances vague.

The girl halted before her house, gazing at the windows through which she had been awakened in the morning and behind which she had gone to sleep at night, and from which she had seduced the young men and affronted the conventions of the little town. But the windows remained closed and the small, dark, limping soldier shouted at her, pushing his rifle barrel into her back, "Come on, come on, we have more important things to do!"

and his companion, tall and dark, remarked unrelentingly: "If there is anything of yours there, then it is no longer yours!" The girl moved on without a word, stumbled on the cobbles, and took hold of the peasant woman, just as the officer's wife was holding on to her.

They crossed the little bridge. In walking, the girl kept to the right, whence, from the darkened gardens, could be seen the black shingles of her home. The garden fence, through which she had sometimes brought her lovers, was breached and falling down. It had been like that yesterday, a month ago, and even a year ago. But the garden, which the girl had constantly tended, was bright with color from the still-unwithered autumn flowers. Once again it drew her eyes, but the guards were in a hurry, and she stumbled and once more caught hold of the peasant woman.

They wanted to continue along the road. But the guards turned to the right, along the little path by the edge of the orchard above the steep riverbank; that way was shorter to the willow thicket in which they carried out their shootings. Now they walked in Indian file, along the path by which the girl used to go to meet her lovers, by those hidden hollows in which, between the river and the skies, she had passed many ecstatic moments, oblivious of life and death, evil and good. She must have remembered loves linked with that path and recalled childhood memories linked with the little meadow, to the left of the slope, now turning yellow, on which she had pastured the cow and where she used to play with children of her own age. She went on, attentively and silently, to impress every detail on her memory. The information officer, too, must have remembered the past and those hiding places; he stamped harshly with his booted heels and looked straight in front of him, sullen and frowning.

No one said anything. The women, hurried on by the soldiers, were now themselves hurrying. It was almost a mile to the willow thicket, there behind the hillock, which sloped down to the water's edge, cutting off the waving course of the meadows and gardens. The guards, too, hurried. They were now in the open, and the women, seeing that they no longer had to walk along the path in single file, once more took each other by the hand—the officer's wife, the girl, and the peasant woman.

They had walked thus for about a hundred paces when a dulled shot—it was, in fact, two shots—struck down the girl's companions. Perhaps the information officer had told the guards to kill her first and without warning, to shorten her suffering on the long road to death and save her from the horror of gazing into the rifle barrel, and the guards had made a mistake, or had attached no importance to the order in which women who were very shortly to die in any case were to be shot. Perhaps the information officer had only given a sign and the guards had fired at those on the outside, since they were the easiest marks.

Be that as it may, the girl remained standing with empty hands, ready to cry out, to beseech, to implore—there was no one she could cling to. She turned, ready to cry out, to whimper, to remind, or to ask. But the guards were quick, and before she could utter a sound both fired at the same moment into her breast. She again spun around and fell face down, between the women with whom until a short while ago she had been holding hands, and whose hands were warm from her touch, as were hers from theirs.

The information officer motioned to the soldiers, who slung their rifles, telling them to roll the women down the steep bank into the river. But they did not understand, and he explained: "The river is high—throw them in! We haven't time to bury them. Let the waters carry them away." They obeyed him, first taking hold of the arms and legs of the peasant woman. They swung the corpse, as bathers do when fooling around with another bather, and heaved it into the water. Then they did the same with the officer's wife.

But when the thin soldier took the girl by the legs, the limping one said, taking a knife out of his boot: "Hold on a bit! This one's got a gold tooth. Pity to let it go to waste." As if he had heard what was said and realized what the soldier intended to do, the information officer, saying nothing, hurried back to the town.

In prison, at Sremska Mitrovica
June 20–21, 1959

UNDER THE YOKE

We could not get away from the Morava. It kept appearing now on one side, now on the other. It was turbid and swollen, like a widow's eyes that have not had their fill of weeping, slow and heavy like a cow in calf. It was somehow enigmatic; one simply did not know where it was flowing. Had the train not been moving and had we not known that there is an end to all things, it would have seemed that nothing would keep us away from the Morava until the end of time—the Morava, which is the greatest of the Serbian rivers and is Serbian from its source to its mouth.

The train, dirty and smoke-laden and crammed with people, was continually halting and hesitating—as always in wartime. The people had collected from everywhere and were of all sorts: black-marketeers and refugees, vagabonds and laborers, Vlachs and Šopci, but for the most part Serb peasants. No one was silent, and yet everyone seemed to be silent. For no one spoke of what hung over us and what everyone knew: the train for Skoplje had not left that morning, and from the laborers whom the Bulgarians had collected from the villages along the Morava to repair the track and dig trenches, and from those who had returned from the south by our train, the rumor spread that the guns were already roaring around Kumanovo. The French and the exiled Serbian army had broken through the Bulgarian-Austrian front, and their advance had been as inevitable as the coming of the seasons, as human hopes.

For in the autumn of 1918, heaven and earth, conquered and conquerors, were sated with war. As the rumor spread, the mood of the people suddenly changed. They sensed that the Bulgarian soldiers guarding the stations were without leaders and that the collapse of the Bulgarian regime was imminent, as leaves must fall, as plague and flood must pass.

The good news was swifter than the train. Fresh passengers entered, silent yet joyful, as if that merciful, beneficent, and seductive autumn sunlight had been born within me. Already we began to feel sorry for the Bulgarian soldiers. They were not so much to blame. It was war, and some blind force had driven them to evil. But it was not fated that we should wallow in joy and forgetfulness, even on that one morning.

Even had I not been a stranger there, a Montenegrin, I would not have been able to remember at which station the three Bulgarian soldiers got on and still less exactly what took place, but I shall never forget all that I now have to tell you. For it was so sudden, so pregnant with crime and evil, that I, a Serb, and the other passengers, even those who were not Serbs, were so fettered by impotence and horror that we ceased to be men.

It happened somewhere on the line along the Morava, and I remember only the main event and the main persons involved. The greenish Morava, as if it, too, were a person and a participant, flowed unmoved and immortal, indifferently, between banks weighed down by orchards and fields of maize under the mute, untroubled sky.

Who was I to remember and to understand? A destitute, unlettered wretch, fleeing from Montenegrin ignorance and penury, who went from house to house seeking shelter with relatives at Toplica but found there only ashes and desolation worse than in Montenegro, and then went on his way, living on a crust of bread, to see if he could find some compassionate householder who would grant him a bare existence and shelter from cold and misfortune. What had I to remember and to understand?

There remained only shame, bitter and inconsolable—to the grave. Yet it was not shame, for we were neither Serbs nor men.

Or perhaps all of us were so drained of feeling that we had become the sort of man who could bear anything, the sort of Serb able to forget anything.

As I have said, three Bulgarian soldiers entered, somewhere or other on the right or the left of the Morava. It seemed to me that they must have entered the carriage behind us, for I had not seen them at any of the little stations, though they may have jumped on the train when it was scarcely moving. But however it happened, they came with rifles and fixed bayonets, and we who were unarmed were instinctively aware of them and on our guard, though we pretended not to see them. They had not come in like other men, and were peering about them like thieves but with harsher, more inconsiderate, military bearing.

The first to enter was a swarthy sergeant, a rough-looking lout with bushy eyebrows and twisted mustaches. As soon as he came in, pushing the passengers aside to right and left as if forcing his way through cattle or weeds, it could be seen that he had something evil in mind. He kept glancing from side to side with glinting eyes, unblinking and expressionless like a snake's. I could see that those eyes rejoiced that they were without human mercy.

Behind the swarthy sergeant danced a puffy blond soldier with pale mustaches, merry eyes, and red lips. He seemed the precise opposite of the sergeant. He winked at everyone roguishly, sputtering gay, teasing jests. He brought with him a sense of human gaiety; or perhaps the world is so arranged that one man radiates terror and another hope, so that a human heart is bathed now in dismay, now in salvation.

The third soldier—the third soldier was neither terrible nor mild, neither dark nor fair, neither one nor the other, but in some way both one and the other. As far as I remember, he was of average height and average in everything else, mousy, moderate, and as if nothing interested him in the least. I don't know how or why, but in that universal dismay and confusion I was most chilled by that soldier. Such men seem to know nothing of inhumanity, but obediently carry out whatever their superiors command, in order, so they believe, best to insinuate themselves into their good graces.

Even had I known any of the passengers, I would now have forgotten what they looked like. What had I to remember them by? We all showed ourselves to be one and the same—without reason and without personality. But, as I have said, I remember those the Bulgarian soldiers halted beside and on whom they exercised their authority, since as long as I am conscious of myself, I cannot forget them. I remember their names and their faces, their eyes and their hands, and every detail of the horror that overtook them.

They were Dmitar, a bony yet still strong old man, his wife, Stojana, toothless and soft and gray as a sack of flour, and their daughter-in-law, Milojka, a black-eyed young woman, firm and robust in her thin skirt and embroidered blouse. They were sitting in a corner with their bags and baskets, and though there were other women in the carriage, the soldiers went to her, to the young wife, Milojka. Just as we had been aware as soon as the soldiers entered that we would not be spared force and violence, now we knew as soon as the swarthy sergeant set eyes on Milojka that she would be the victim. There was no other woman so young and so attractive. Except for Milojka there was no woman so clearly Serbian in dress and appearance, with her pale face and raven hair, modest looks and folded hands.

I do not know Bulgarian. But I understood and still remember every word the soldiers said in their language.

The swarthy sergeant asked old Dmitar who he was and where he came from and whether the young woman was of his kin. Dmitar, hand on breast, bowed deeply, as they used to bow in Turkish times, and said that he came from some village near Niš and that the girl was his daughter-in-law and he was taking her home; times were troublous and uncertain, as they could only be in wartime, and he had thought it wiser if he got his daughter-in-law away from the main roads and the open country.

"And where is her husband?" the Bulgarian asked.

"Killed. Missing in the war," the old man replied.

"You're lying! She would be wearing black if he had been killed, and you would not be taking her home. She's waiting for him to come back to her from the Salonika front."

"I have heard nothing of him since Serbia was occupied," the old man excused himself, as if he were to blame for not knowing for certain whether his son had been killed.

The old woman, Stojana, fell on her knees. "May I be struck blind if I know whether he is dead or alive."

The swarthy sergeant, as if in jest, said: "If he has been killed, then a wife is no use to him, and if he hasn't—then let her pay for him."

The fair soldier tried to make everything a joke and a bit of fun: "Certainly she must have been longing for her husband. Wouldn't it be nice in these hard times if some young men had a bit of fun with her?"

But no one smiled. The old man began to tremble, clenching his horny hands on his stick, and the old woman began to implore the soldiers: "Be merciful, good sirs. You, too, must have a wife, or a sister. . . ."

The young wife, Milojka, sat motionless, still more rigid, her eyes downcast. I was reminded of a girl at communion or a lamb before slaughter. But the sergeant paid no attention either to her or to the old woman's entreaties, only ordered the mousy soldier: "Make some room there, Asen."

So we—did it matter?—learned that the third soldier was called Asen.

Asen quickly shooed the passengers away from a corner at the opposite end of the car. I don't know why they chose to free just that corner, for they could equally well have chosen the corner where old Dmitar was. But they chose that corner as if they were ashamed to move the father- and mother-in-law, and wanted to be as far away from them as possible. Perhaps they especially wanted to lead Milojka through the whole carriage in sight of us all, as the best man leads the bride on the first night in the presence of all the wedding guests.

"Come along," the sergeant summoned Milojka, and since she did not move he ordered the fair soldier: "Bring her!"

Opening his wide lips in a gay and malicious sneer, the fair soldier took the young woman under the arms and, I might even say almost gently, pulled her along. "Come along, dear. Don't be afraid and don't be stupid. We won't hurt you. We only want to play with you a little."

The old woman knelt and clasped the sergeant's boots, sobbing and imploring, while the old man muttered something; he was reciting a prayer or a curse, and his hands showed white on his staff.

"Bring her, Asen!" the sergeant shouted angrily, kicking the old woman away as if ridding himself of something superfluous and unpleasant.

The fair soldier nodded and waved his hand, as if to excuse himself. "She'll come, all right."

Asen went up to Milojka on horseman's bandy legs, tore off her kerchief, and with astonishing skill loosed her hair and wound it around his fist.

"Go, daughter," the old man groaned, and added, as if to himself: "Soldiers, force . . . God and man will forgive her."

The old woman keened as if someone of her household were being lowered into the grave, but the sergeant angrily kicked her in the ribs. "You're mourning for Serbia! Mourn then, mourn! You won't have to mourn much longer."

As if that was just what she had been expecting, the old woman sobbed and whimpered. And the young woman, till then stony and resistant, went calmly and obediently.

Then Asen took off his bedroll, unfolded his blanket, gave one corner to the fair soldier, and tucked the other under a trunk near the window. So the young woman and the sergeant disappeared behind a curtain of blanket, and Asen, rifle at the ready, turned to face us.

The fair soldier took a peep over the blanket, turned toward us, and crudely winked and grinned, while Asen stood cold and motionless, as if nothing was happening or would happen behind the blanket.

We did not dare look at each other. Whenever any one of us looked at another, it was as if he weren't seeing him. It was shameful to be a Serb, unbearable to be a man.

It did not last as long as one might think, yet long, terribly long, too long to be endured. Nonetheless we endured it—to the end. When the sergeant came out from behind the curtain, doing up his trousers, grinning embarrassedly, he snapped at us: "That's the way it is. You are the losers!" and the fair soldier disappeared behind the blanket. Then, finally, Asen did, too, expressionless and severe, as if he were reporting for some fatigue duty or other. Had we attacked, we could have overcome the soldiers, especially when they were busy with their shameful task. But that did not occur to any of us. We knew, too, that the Bulgarian command did not approve of such behavior, but they would certainly believe their own soldiers and not us. A sort of weakness paralyzed our minds and energies, as when lightning strikes or there is an earthquake—each of us was thankful that misfortune had not fallen upon him.

When the soldiers had tidied themselves, shouldered their rifles, and leaped from the moving train, Milojka, hands rigid on her gaily colored apron and looking straight in front of her, slowly went back to her seat. Nobody dared to look her in the face, until the old woman took her hands and covered them with tears and kisses. The old man wept silently, bent over his staff. Milojka did not let a single tear fall. She only pushed back her hair, which had fallen over her face. She sat motionless and rigid, looking somewhere out the window, I don't know whether at the left or the right bank. . . .

And I who am writing this, forty or more years after I heard it, have not remembered either the teller or where he told it. Did it really happen like that? Shall I always remember the soldiers,

the carriage full of passengers, and the unhappy young wife behind the blanket, somewhere on the Morava in the land of Serbia?

In prison, at Sremska Mitrovica
March 23–25, 1964

AN EYE
FOR AN EYE

I was no different in any way from the other peasants in my village. I was a man and a Serb, like other men and Serbs.

I had no schooling except four grades of elementary school which I had finished at Toplica before my father moved to the Bačka, where he had been granted some land as a veteran of the Salonika front. My grandfather, like many of the men of Toplica, had settled there from Montenegro, but when his sons divided his property each got so small a parcel of land that they had to hire themselves out as day laborers. Had it not been for the war and the collapse of Austria-Hungary, I, also, would have been nothing more than a day laborer, unless I could have managed to pick up the rudiments of some craft.

We lived well in the Bačka. I was twelve years old when we settled there in 1920, and I quickly adapted myself to the new conditions. By the time I became a young man I differed in no way from the Serbs of the Bačka—perhaps a little in accent, and my father still kept up some of the old habits and customs. In the Bačka the land is more fertile than anywhere else on earth; it demands hard work but it returns a good yield. I will not say that I was among the most industrious. That, no! But I was not lazy. I loved to go to the tavern on Sundays, as did the others, but more because of the dancing and the talk than the drink. I was no drunkard. Nor was I a womanizer—there were plenty of those—

though I won't say that I did not enjoy myself now and then. And cards and dice never interested me. I was quiet and moderate and never long at odds with anyone; nor did I fly into a rage unless someone tried to kick me in the face. I was pious. I never blasphemed God and his saints. Even now I keep my *slava* and celebrate Christmas and all our other Serb Orthodox feasts.

I had no luck in marriage. My father arranged a marriage for me in our native district, but my bride fell ill with consumption as soon as she came to the Bačka—different water and different climate—and soon died. She had had no children, for which the poor girl had tormented herself and me. After her death I did not marry again. The local girls did not willingly marry colonists, and I could find women enough. So I grew to a man's years and awaited the war, always postponing marriage from one day to the next.

The war turned everything upside down. Nothing was left of our life before it, or of my plans for the future. The war, so to speak, turned me upside down too. It did not change me, nor did it change others, but it forced me to live on the other side of the coin. It was as if I had never known myself until then. Or others, either. It seemed as if the war had come so that everyone would cease to know himself or others; or, to put it another way, the snow falls so that beasts will reveal their tracks.

Ours was a mixed village—old Serb settlers, Hungarians, and us Serb colonists. So we were always divided in everything, except that we colonists always sided with the local Serbs against the Hungarians whenever there was anything political in question. There were no great antipathies. It was more like neighbors who quarrel and yet love each other. We were guests of the Hungarians and they of us; we were friendly and helped each other. And though all of us held firmly to our own faiths, it happened occasionally that a Serb would marry a Magyar girl or a Hungarian a Serb girl. But that, too, was as it should be between neighbors. Sometimes it even seemed comic to me when my father said: "Don't trust the Magyars. Just let them catch fire once and you will see what they will do." Later, I often remembered his words, for so it turned out: men can be seen as they are only when they have the chance to do to others whatever they have a mind to.

I might have expected every sort of evil from the war, but that our Hungarian neighbors, with whom we had eaten and drunk, made merry and shared our sorrows, should so turn against us—that I did not expect.

They and their occupation authorities first of all, and most violently, vented their fury upon us colonists. Because of the land and God only knows what else! They held that the lands of the nobles which our state had parceled out after the First World War should have been theirs, for until then it had been Hungarian peasants who had worked the land—and that would have been fair enough if their state had not lost the war. Now they were only waiting to snatch the land from us. For my father, the loss of his house and property was not too hard to bear; war had given them to him, and war had taken them away again. But for me it was. I could not reconcile myself. It was as if I had lost my life as well, and as if all my life had been spent in vain. If only our Magyar neighbors had been content with taking our property from us! But with what hatred and enjoyment they took it, while doing all they could to humiliate and oppress us! Some of them at once joined the Magyar gendarmerie and thus had power over us. They were the worst. There was no authority above them, nothing to restrain them.

Our next-door neighbor Janos seized our house and property, though we had always been on friendly terms. He had his own house and land, but they were not enough for him, and he installed one of his sons and himself in ours. My father was in no hurry to leave his home, so Janos kicked him out with his jackboots and stood, short and dark, in front of the open door, snarling: "It's been yours long enough; now our turn has come!" I said to him, my mouth dry and the words sticking in my throat: "Good, brother Janos. Your turn has come, but why beat my father?" And he: "He ought to be beaten and killed. Until we wipe out all you Serbs, there is no existence for us Magyars." And I again to him: "But we neither beat nor killed you Magyars." And he: "You couldn't. You didn't dare to because of the Great Powers. But we can. The Great Powers will help us do it." My father said nothing. He was no less angry and embittered than I. But it all seemed comprehensible to him, and I could have sworn that he was thinking to himself: Magyar Janos is right. It so happens that he can do as he likes, but in our case we cannot do as we like.

Most of the colonists, without land and in fear for their lives, fled to Serbia. My father, too, wanted to go, but I would not let him. I would not leave the land even though it was no longer ours. It is hard to leave something on which a man has spent his life and strength. We remained, therefore, in a local Serbian household. I worked as a day laborer to feed myself and my father. But in wartime everything turns out differently from what a man dreams and plans.

In August, 1941, the Hungarians began to collect the Serbs to send them to camps, now from one village, now from another, until our turn came. They made a selection from the local Serbs, usually the most prominent among them, and took us colonists to a man. This evil took us somewhat by surprise, although we had been expecting it; not even those who had said that our village would be overlooked had really believed it. Early in the morning of August 17 they drove us, whenever and however they found us, into the courtyard of the municipal building—women, children, and old people as well. There they sorted us out, as they would have cattle—the young from the old, the children from the adults—and put us in various groups.

They separated me from my father—we were never to meet again—and I heard later that the old man had never reached the camp at all. He fell by the way and was beaten to death.

As for me, still strong and able to work, I was put with the younger ones in the courtyard of some village worthy's house. His family, too, had been collected for the camp. There were about fifty of us, some men, some women, but mainly men. They lined us men up against the courtyard wall—we thought they were going to kill us—and the women, all the young girls and married women, they lined up against the house wall so that we could look at them, but we were forbidden to speak to them. It was, I remember, a very hot, stifling day, yet they would not give us water, although there was a well in the courtyard. But we forgot our thirst and our misfortunes, even forgot that we expected to be killed, when we saw the shame that took place before our eyes.

At the end of the courtyard there was an extensive stable with a door wide enough to admit a hay cart; such stables were common all over the Danube plain. There, in that stable, they began to rape our women, the Serb girls and the young married women.

They did not shut the stable doors, but left them wide open. Intentionally! When one of the soldiers wanted to shut them, an N.C.O. shouted at him: "Don't shut them, clot! Let these Serb brigands see how we improve their stock!"

Even though we realized what was happening, we did not want to believe it. First they threw down hay from the hayloft and spread it out on the floor of the stable so that it would be soft and they would not dirty their knees. This and everything else they did conscientiously and without haste, as if preparing some especially important task, like some—may God forgive me!—rite in which every detail must be exact and properly carried out. They even brought a basin and a jug of water to wash themselves afterward, so that their uniforms would not be stained and everything would seem as much as possible like a real act of love, for which married couples or older lovers prepare every comfort and remove every obstacle beforehand, aware of the enjoyment that awaits them.

First of all they set aside two girls, the youngest and prettiest— one was the daughter of the master of the house and the other the sister of my good friend Mitar—and took them into the house for the officers. Right up to that moment we had been of two minds about what would happen; until then they had behaved severely toward us, but without brutality and oppression. We might even have believed that they were taking the two girls in for some sort of interrogation had not one of the officers, young, dark, and short, greeted the householder's daughter at the doorway with a crooked, silly smirk. The girls, too, had not realized or were unable to believe. They went in without resistance, though pale and embarrassed. Soon the sound of a struggle, blows, and commotion could be heard from one of the rooms; the householder's daughter was defending herself. Probably she could not conceive that they would do such a thing in her own house—and she was by nature untamed. From Mitar's sister in the other room there was not a sound; probably she was numb with fear and horror.

Yes, each one of us knew what was happening in the house, right there in front of us, even had the windows not been open. But we kept silent, pretending to ourselves that we did not know what it was all about, and, in truth, we would not have been able to look each other in the eye. I glanced at Mitar, but he did not wish, did not dare, to look at me. He behaved as if it were not his sister there inside, and as if he did not suspect what was being done to her. The householder's daughter was finally overpowered. A soldier went in to help the officer, and we could hear panting and struggling, like someone choking, and not long afterward a submissive sobbing.

The Hungarians behaved as if they knew we were glad that we could not see what was happening. The sergeant, red-faced and with upturned mustaches, ordered two of the gendarmes to bring Mara, the wife of Jakov, a colonist from my district. From then on that sergeant took charge of everything, and everything that took place later was at his command. I could not understand how men could carry out such orders. One of the gendarmes, a youth with fair, almost white, hair, refused, and the sergeant sneered: "What! Not up to it yet?" and ordered another man to come.

But Mara protested: "I will never allow anyone except my

man, while I am alive!" The gendarme struck her on the breast with his rifle butt. She fell winded to the ground, and he dragged her by the arms across the courtyard. Jakov could not control himself; perhaps shame drove him—and we were not yet accustomed to what was happening. He rushed to the aid of his wife. But he did not reach her; the sergeant fired a shot into his back. Jakov gasped, turned and looked at his murderer with disbelief, then put his hands to his breast. Blood spurted from between his fingers and he fell. The sergeant went up to him, swearing as only Magyars know how to swear, and, since Jakov was still rolling his eyes, fired a shot into his chest, probably into his heart. When Jakov still did not die, he fired yet another shot, into his head, till the skull split open and the brains poured out on the flagstones.

I remember those first details with unusual clarity. What happened later I have forgotten, and in fact there was not much to remember. Everything was a repetition of what happened to Jakov's Mara, only not all of the women protested and not one of their brothers or husbands dared to go to their aid. Not because we were afraid—I don't think any of us feared death—but because resistance was pointless, and we would have died vainly and absurdly.

The gendarmes relieved each other by command. When all those in the courtyard had had their turn, others came in from the street; although different in appearance, they all acted in the same manner and afterward looked the same, as if gloating and yet ashamed. They always went to the stable in pairs, and if any woman resisted, one of them would sit on her head and hold her arms stretched out on the ground, his back turned, and look down so as not to hinder the other in his shameful task. They did everything skillfully and methodically, not sparing blows, looking at those in front of them—and perhaps not even looking at them—as if they were under orders. If it so happened—and it did happen —that one of the women, realizing the uselessness of resistance, gave way to her fate, the other gendarme would wait, watching with enjoyment what his mate was doing and urging him on with shameful jests.

So it went on—I have no idea how long—until everyone had been satisfied, and all the women had been raped. But the truth must be told: there were some who, like the fair-haired boy, did not want to, or could not, take part. The married women, I would say, bore it the more easily, and even among the girls there was not so much shame as impotent grief. Weeping and entreaties only excited the gendarmes, and I noticed that they fell most willingly upon the girls, but I would not say that this was because they were afforded any greater enjoyment, but because it confirmed their power and authority more definitely. The sergeant, after he had satisfied himself with one of the girls, delivered a little speech to mark the occasion: "We have taken your land and dismembered your state, and now we have conquered your women, too!"

When it was over, there was a silence more agonizing than all that had gone before. The gendarmes began to eat—the house was full of food—and they allowed us to sit and mingle with the women.

They threw the householder's daughter out of the house, and she, bloody and disheveled, began to scream and curse them. They belabored her with their rifle butts and threw horseshoes at her as long as she made any sound. I heard that she died later from her contusions.

Mitar's sister also came out of the house, crumpled and disordered, bruised and dazed. After her came Janos' son, Imre, he who with his father had settled in my house, a still-unmarried and powerful youth, like his father in appearance. He had just enlisted in the gendarmerie and did not even have a complete uniform, only shirt and cap. He was buttoning his shirt as he came out, and, as if on duty, he turned to Mitar: "As a woman, your sister has no defects. But I prefer more experienced women, so that I don't have to teach them their job." Mitar looked at him calmly, as if they were talking of everyday matters, but his face twitched. I was unable to believe that a neighbor could do such a thing to a neighbor, to a girl with whom he had danced the kolo and who had grown up with him. But so it was, both with our lands and with our women.

Now we looked at each other without shame and even talked to each other—about everything except what had just happened. We wanted to believe, to deceive ourselves, that it had never happened, and still less that the Magyars had done it; we could not recognize them. None of us so much as mentioned what had just taken place. We moved Jakov's corpse aside like some object, and even the sergeant, pouring wine from a flask over slices of sausage, calmed down. Only occasionally a woman whimpered and then quickly became mute under the reproaches of her comrades who were resigned to their shame, and under the feral glances of the conquerors.

Midday passed, and a good part of the afternoon, though I could not say how, or what we did. I remember only that I tried to console Mitar's sister, but she acted as if she were offended and looked angrily at me. I withdrew, thankful that my wife was dead, that my two sisters had died in childhood, that I had no daughters, and that my father had not been there to see the horror and the Serbian shame.

The stifling heat had already lessened when the rumbling of a truck could be heard. Then the gendarmes began to push us into it, not separating the men from the women. They took us to a camp in Hungary, a fair and rich land but an enemy land. Men and women were separated there, though we were able to get in touch with each other and exchange messages—Mitar was regularly in touch with his sister. For the most part they used us for agricultural work on the estates of the nobles. We were deep in their land, near Lake Balaton, and they considered that we had nowhere to escape to and so put few guards over us—about one to every ten, and those mostly old men or invalids. We were not hungry; they fed us so that we could work. But I never reconciled myself to slavery in Hungary.

I could not forget how we Serbs had suffered for hundreds of years, and that the blackest days of all were now, just when we had hoped we would be able to live as men should. How long had Montenegro—or so my grandfather had told me—endured evil! There where there were no songs except laments, and every second hearth had been extinguished. And how Serbia had suffered in the times of Karageorge. And Bosnia, and the Voivodina. We Serbs were fated, I thought, to struggle for bare existence alongside other peoples. As my grandfather had, and his grandfather, and my own father, so, too, must I struggle with my enemy as long as I had breath in me. All this weighed upon me like some talisman, some holy testament, handed down from the distant past, from the unhappy Serbian past. I would have gone to war to fight as best I could, but our rulers had betrayed us, had grown rotten and corrupt in power and lordship and revenge. Even in the camp I thought about how I could fight and struggle, but could not think of any way to do so.

It was soon noised abroad—and written about even in the Hungarian newspapers—that the people in our unhappy land had risen in rebellion and that many of the insurgents had fled into the forests and were attacking from ambushes. The newspapers said that the Communists had started it all, and indeed they had, as I see now. But I was not interested in who the leaders were, only that the time had come for the Serbs to rise. We in the camp began to talk about it, and I made up my mind to escape and to fight against the Hungarians the best I could.

Several of us, including Mitar, agreed to run away. We did not dare confide in the others—there were informers among us, as there always are when a plot is being hatched and wherever force holds men down. And our exploit was made still more difficult because it was autumn, and Mitar wanted, at all costs, to get his sister out, too. So we waited until the spring of 1942. I must admit that we were encouraged—the Germans had not taken Moscow or conquered England, and the newspapers for the hundredth time had liquidated the last insurgent bands in Montenegro and Bosnia.

The Magyars in no way respected our holy days and drove us out to work on Orthodox Easter as if our Saviour had never been crucified and risen again from the dead for us Serbs. I had managed to get hold of a long file, and that morning I had it hidden under my coat—that was the day agreed on for our flight.

About that time, as luck would have it, who should have come to our camp but Imre, the son of my neighbor Janos, who had raped Mitar's sister after the officer finished with her. The Hungarians from Hungary had not cosseted our Hungarians as they had expected. Imre and others had been sent to the eastern front, and he, after being wounded, had been posted to our camp as a guard. Mitar and I planned our flight for a time when it would be Imre's turn to stand guard over us.

He accompanied us on that Easter, and, by agreement, as soon as we entered the forest I thrust the file into his stomach. One of our men was killed, but we were able to seize two rifles. I wanted to beat Imre to death, but Mitar would not let me. He pulled the file out of Imre's guts and with it scooped out his eyes, really scooped them out, not just pierced them, saying: "That is for the pleasure you got from my sister, my good and lovely neighbor!"

All my life, even now, I have never been able to stand the sight of blood or any sort of torture. It was a torment to me to kill a chicken. But what Mitar was doing—he had to hurry before the other guards caught us—filled me with a sort of enjoyment, as if I were intoxicated, and I saw everything clearly. I was only sorry that we could not torture Imre at our ease, taking pleasure in his entreaties and his bloody tears until his soul left his body. For a chicken is an innocent thing, but a man, a Magyar—well, he is guilty of human suffering and Serb misfortune, and it is not right for him to die easily and unaware.

But Mitar held back, or perhaps was horrified at his own deed, so I was forced to cut short Imre's life with my own hands. I just had to, had to experience that also, since there was no other way. I drew the knife I had taken from Imre, seized him by the jaw, and turned him over like a sheep. He no longer seemed to know what was happening—he did not lift a hand in his defense. I called out: "Imre, this is me, your neighbor Stojan, whom you threw out of his home. Now I will cut your throat!" "Slaughter me," he said, "but don't torture me. Have pity on a man's sufferings!" "I would have no more mercy than you had," I said to him, "but we must hurry." Then I pierced him with the knife, but not too deep, so that his life would flow out with his blood and not suffocate in gasps. So I slaughtered him at my ease, and there was nothing terrible in it for me. I even felt pleasure in Imre's warm blood on my hands, before my eyes, and on my soul.

When I think back, I see that we worked unskillfully and hurriedly; later we became more skillful, for killing men becomes a craft like any other. We got too bloodied, and we were surprised that he had not died at once, as soon as I drove the file into his guts. We were afraid that he might still be alive, and though there was no sound from him, and the blood continued to spurt out, I remember that I hacked and hacked with the knife until I had hacked off his head, and even then it seemed to me that the body was still living and the head still conscious. Yes, one must know, one must learn; there is nothing easier than to kill a man if you know the right place to strike, and if he twitches it is of no importance—his arteries are still working and his blood flows—for he is full of blood, and it cannot all flow out in a moment.

We knew where Mitar's sister was working, and that same day we took her away and killed two guards. Counting her, we were now a band of six. I was chosen as leader.

Even had we been able to get there, there was no place for us in the Bačka; there is too much water there. And the local Hungarians would have risen against us to a man, and because of us would have exterminated the Serbs. So we stayed hidden among the forests and creeks, trying to approach the Danube, since we had heard that on the other side, in Slavonia, there were insurgents. The posses were not especially active, but every Magyar,

97

even the children and women, would have told the authorities about us at once, and we would not have had any food had we not taken it by force. Thus began a most terrible life. All men, all Magyars, were against us, not because the authorities and the police made them so but of their own free will. They could not bear us to be living there alongside them.

We hated the Magyars. But not one of us ever said that we had to kill them all—children, women, old people. That came somehow of itself, from the conditions in which we lived and fought, and also from our memories of the Serb misfortunes. There was no life for a Serb as long as the Magyars were the stronger. First we killed a little girl—so that she could not betray us when we left. Then we cut the throats of a forester's whole family; they had caught sight of us when we came on their house unexpectedly, and we had to save ammunition. The child in the cradle we wanted to forget, but the only one of us who had until then been aghast at the killings reminded us: "How can we leave it, without father or mother? And this is that sort of struggle—to the last man, either ours or theirs." So we cut the child's throat, and it, too, was, as we put it, weaned.

We found countless good reasons for slaughtering the Magyars to a man. Most frequently we stressed: The fewer Magyars, the more Serbs. And quickly we revealed this unspoken reason: There is no real enjoyment in killing the enemy until you can feel his life ebbing away under your hand, and you can achieve that in the simplest and easiest manner—by cutting his throat. We enjoyed the terror we spread around us, the horror with which we were recognized, and the curses that accompanied us. But man quickly becomes satiated with every enjoyment, even killing, and so we thought of new ways. We wanted to become the devil in the eyes of the Magyars, and we were only too happy to do so, believing that God himself had directed us to avenge the Serbs and at the same time to pleasure our own hearts.

It came to rape almost by chance, without any real reason. In the forest we came across a shepherd girl scarcely fifteen years old.

We intended to cut her throat, nothing more. I noticed lust in the eyes of my companions, but they did not say anything; either they were ashamed or their desire was not very strong. Mitar's sister urged us on: "What sort of men are you! Have you forgotten what they did to us?" The shepherd girl did not understand Serbian and looked at us in terror; we had already made it known who we were. She thought that we meant to kill her and began to implore us to spare her life. She did not guess what we intended to do, and none of us had yet made up his mind to be the first. Then one said: "Give her to me. I'll have a go." Realizing at last what we had been talking about, the shepherd girl seemed to forget that her life was at stake and began to resist. But Mitar struck her with a rifle butt and knocked the wind out of her. We pulled her down and sat on her head, stretching her arms out on the ground, just as the Magyars had done with our own women. We took her in turn, but without any enjoyment. Mitar's sister kept guard. We felt awkward in front of her, but I believe that she secretly watched and even enjoyed it all. It excited and pleased us that we could do whatever we liked to the Magyar girls, even what a man and a woman do together only with good will. It excited us that we no longer had to be like men with a Magyar girl, but could be like beasts who pay no heed to the powerless female's wishes.

There was one of us who did not want to, or could not, though he was young and strong. And the helpless shepherd girl would have remained lying there, uncovered and bloody, had not Mitar said: "She will betray us in any case. We must kill her." But it was unpleasant for us to do so, after the pleasure we had had from her. Then Mitar's sister said: "Surely you won't let her conceive a Serb child?" So I waved my knife, and the girl screamed as I thrust it into her entrails. We fled, leaving her to die.

We went on like that, slaughtering all we met, raping, burning —men, women, cattle, and property. The posses became more frequent, giving us not a moment's breathing space. If in our flight we had not come across a Serb village near Baja where we found shelter, we would soon have been destroyed. That, too, happened by chance. We were uneducated and did not know that there were, that there could be, Serbs in Hungary. We usually passed the night where we were least expected, concealed in some forest, resting and reconnoitering. Selecting an isolated house, we would kill the inmates, take whatever we needed, and then disappear as quickly and as far away as we could. So when on one occasion, on the outskirts of a village, we came upon a house with our Orthodox icons and a *kandilo* burning before Sveti Nikola, we looked and wondered. Speaking in Magyar, as we always did except among ourselves, in order to hide our tracks more easily, we asked: "Where did you get those icons?" The householder replied, also in Hungarian: "We are Serbs, Orthodox." "Serbs? How can there be Serbs in Hungary?" But so it turned out. We began to speak in Serbian, and they spoke good Serbian. Then we asked them about Kosovo and our Serb rulers and our Serb saints. They knew about them, and they knew all the *slava* customs. They were true Serbs, no question of that.

Having found a base, we were able to make better preparations for our attacks, and we carried them out as far away as possible from the Serb settlements. But we soon noticed uneasiness and hesitation among the local Serbs, who began to ask if we were not some of those who killed every Magyar they met and inflicted every sort of shame upon them. We had to hide our exploits from the Serbs. Then there began to be waverings among us. Why were we killing all the Magyars when, as we could see, they had not killed all the Serbs in Hungary? As soon as we started asking ourselves such questions, we stopped raping and killing indiscriminately and liquidated only the most notorious oppressors. The Serbs grew proud of us and regarded us as their avengers.

But we could not go on without losses. Even before our flight to Baja, the young man who had not wanted to take part in the raping died. A householder pierced his stomach with a pitchfork, and he himself begged us to finish him off so that he would not fall into the hands of the gendarmes. Others, too, were killed; we did not allow anyone who was wounded to be captured. At Baja our little band from time to time increased in size. Now and again some peasant would join us, either for profit or for revenge, and when the attack was over would return to his everyday tasks. But of those who had set out together only three remained by the summer of 1944—myself, Mitar, and his sister.

In the middle of the summer, when we least expected it, Mitar's sister was wounded. We had fallen into an ambush at night. We carried her, but the posse caught up to us in the morning; we could clearly hear the dogs and the shouts of the men. She implored Mitar: "Kill me, Brother. I would die sweetly by your hand!" I saw that the posse would catch us if we did not leave her—and we did not dare leave her alive for them to rape and mutilate. I could not say a word for sorrow, and my tears flowed; I had become as accustomed to her as to my own sister. Mitar, too, wept, but she did not shed a tear, only went on imploring. At last Mitar turned his rifle on her, and she caught hold of the barrel and put it to her heart. "There, there, Brother!" Mitar pulled the trigger, and she cried out and jerked away from the barrel. Our poor comrade had found peace. So was she killed, and we never ceased mourning for her.

Shortly afterward Mitar, too, was wounded. There were about fifteen of us in the band when someone betrayed us and we came upon the gendarmes in the midst of the forest. But the forest saved us; we slipped away and dispersed among the trees and in the marshes. Wounded, Mitar wanted to kill himself, but I would not let him. I carried him on my back. I cared for him and healed him. I was afraid his wound would become infected, but I saw with my own eyes that marsh mud cleanses a wound.

That autumn the Soviet army broke into Hungary, and by winter had totally conquered it. I began to hope that I would enjoy to the full the misfortune of the Magyars.

We knew that in our country everything was topsy-turvy, that the Communists had raised an insurrection, created an army, and introduced their sort of order. We had even come into contact with their partisans. But we did not want to join the Communists, for they were unbelievers, and, what was worse, they did not kill all Magyars, only the policemen and the fascists, whereas to a Serb all Magyars are the same, and he will be happiest when not one of them is left. We were used to our own way of fighting and to associating with soldiers of our own faith, and we had set up a network of supporters.

It did seem to us that we ought to be able to get along with the Russian army, even though it, too, was Communist. The men were Slavs and loved us Serbs; so it was and so it will remain, with Communism or without it. We would never have been crossing ourselves with three fingers, nor would our state and our name have been preserved, had it not been for the Russians. Not all are like this—they, too, have their politicians, their Communists, and their commissars—but the true Russian, he who for ages past has not changed, nor will ever be able to change, he is a Slav. He knows that he cannot exist if he does not suppress other tribes, and he is ready, when necessary, to exterminate them.

In their army, as in every other army, there were all sorts of men. No wonder! All those who do not begrudge their lives are welcome in war; and so their army had convicts and every kind of riffraff who liked to plunder, rape, and kill. Of them I do not speak; there are such in all armies, and everywhere they are an evil against which all men must fight. Nor do I speak of those whom the horrors of war had turned into beasts. It is no joke to cross thousands of miles of blood and fire and desolation in one's own innocent land, and be mild and understanding when one reaches the land and the homes of those who did it. But such men, embittered and crazy, are quickly satiated with doing evil to their enemy. They kill or rape one or two, and then something happens inside them, and later they grieve and are sorry.

I speak for those others, such as I was myself—those who exterminate their enemies not for profit or from bitterness, nor those who are of criminal or perverse disposition, but those who, like me, would not tread on an ant, much less consider doing evil to a man. I do not know how to express it accurately, but I am thinking of those who do such things because they know— or not so much know as believe with their whole soul and every artery of their body that they cannot do otherwise—that this is the way they must act if they themselves are to survive, not so much themselves as individuals, but their people.

At first the Russian command behaved as if the reins had slipped through their fingers, and they allowed the bloodstained soldiers to wreak their will. But soon they restored discipline and began to punish oppression and looting; they shot those who disobeyed, regardless of rank or service, as only men can who receive orders and carry them out unquestioningly. Yet who can supervise, day and night, every soldier in so great an army, who can know every ear and every grain on every ear? Men of similar type, men of similar inclinations, find each other out, just as dogs smell each other out. So we rapidly and easily found Serbs and Russians who agreed that the Magyars should be exterminated.

None of us, not even I, knew any Russian. Nonetheless we served as interpreters for those Russians. We knew Hungarian, and Serbs and Russians, although their languages are not much alike, understand each other; a lot of words are the same, while others are similar and some are quite different, but even the latter can be understood when a man has the will to understand. So we led such Russians to do as we had been doing in Baja. The Russians did everything well, except that they did not kill willingly. This we Serbs carried out. For the Magyars were on our own doorsteps and in our homes, while Russia was far away. Nonetheless, the Russians wanted to display their power over the Magyars and drive them into the black earth, so that it would not enter the minds of even their grandchildren's grandchildren to lead Hungarian armies onto Russian lands.

I realized that it was important even for these Russians to find some justification, some pretext, for their command and for their own conscience. We tried to persuade them to go on killing and raping, but they hesitated: "It's not right. The Magyars, too, are people." And we: "Yes, the Magyars are people, but we are calling on you to eliminate fascists." "Oh, well, fascists—that's different," and they at once agreed.

Such pretexts were not needed for me and my band. Why? Fascist or Communist—to me the important thing was that they were Magyars. There was no sort of command over me and nothing weighed on my conscience, which told me: "Exterminate the Magyars, so that they do not exterminate you and all the Serbs."

Unfortunately, this period did not last long. The Russian command shortened the reins, the war ended, and we then had to carry out our task secretly and finally to disband and run away, we to our own land and our Russian friends to theirs.

But I, too, felt some qualms, after listening to those Russians trying always to find some pretext or excuse for what they were planning against the Magyars. I, too, began to turn things over in my mind and look for pretexts, though rather different ones. More and more often I forced myself to recall the evil and oppression that the Magyars had wrought on us Serbs—in my own village. I recalled the smallest details—and those the most gruesome—and gladly listened to and remembered every crime and oppression that they had wrought in other villages. I began to speak to myself and to my comrades: "Since they could, and since they began first, then so can we, and they had better look out for themselves."

I knew then, and I know now, that I was lying to myself and others, that these were only excuses, and that, in fact, I would have gone on exterminating the Magyars even if they had not done anything in my village or anywhere else. Right up to the beginning of the war I had not suspected that anything of the sort slumbered within me. The war stirred it up, aroused it, and in such a way that I could not root it out. No seed will begin to sprout if the sun does not shine; so in me it would not have sprouted had there been no war. But it had existed within me, although unsuspected. What happened in our village had only brought into my mind what it was my duty to do.

An Eye for an Eye

I know now that there are men who cannot understand, still less approve, what I did. I know that there were and are many Serbs who would not have done what I did. I am a religious man, and I know what our faith commands: do not kill! But my conscience did not reproach me. Would I have been able to go on living if it had reproached me?

Now I recall that it seemed to me, when I was doing those things, as if it were not I but someone else. There was someone or something within me that gave me clear orders—"Do this or that"—and I did it. As if not I did it, that man whom you know and see, that man who I myself knew and saw, but someone outside me—some power, neither evil nor good, which I could not resist. They were my hands that held the knife, and the warm blood spouted out over my hands; yet it was not I, not my consciousness, not my mind. Often I said to myself: "What you are doing is a sin and a crime." It was as if I were not speaking to myself, but to someone else, perhaps to him who had given me the command. If there was sin, it was his sin and not mine. It so happens that these horrors torment me and that I recall horrible pictures when I am alone, and therefore I do not like to be alone. But it is the horrors that are unpleasant to me, not my conscience!

I have forced myself to forget many of those horrors—those I committed myself. But one of my deeds I remember today as if it had just happened. We believed that we had killed a whole family, and then in the stables we found a small boy. He was about eight or nine years old, with big black eyes. Everything was mirrored in those eyes, and he looked wisely out of them as from the depths of his soul. Mitar struck him on the temple with his knife, but the blade did not enter. The child's face twisted, tears and blood mingled. He clung to my arm. "Don't let him, Uncle," he whimpered to me, and to Mitar: "Don't, Uncle. It hurts!" I felt sorry for the child, but I was ashamed in my own eyes and before my comrades that I felt pity for any Magyar. There was no way out, so with the hand he was clutching I pulled his head back and with the other cut his throat. I cannot forget that boy and what happened to him. He comes out to me at night from the prison walls, wriggles through the bars, and entreats me in my dreams. I cannot even pray to God, though he might answer my prayers! But I do not regret even that—such deeds cannot be carried out without horror. I was angry with Mitar, though, for striking the boy so clumsily that I had to commit such a crime.

In the end war became insupportable to me, though not because of what I had done, since I had had to do it. I would have consented to do the same all my life and would never have tired of it. But a man wants his home and his village and a quiet life.

In 1946 Mitar and I came back to the Bačka, to our own land. We had sworn to kill our neighbor Janos if we came across him. But Mitar began to waver, as if Janos had not been a Magyar and was not now, in peacetime, still a Magyar. Mitar devoted himself entirely to his land and his family. I did not, even though at Baja I had left a wife and two small children by that wife, a Serbian girl I had lived with while I was raiding from there. I said to myself: "Enough of the Magyars. Now it is peace for them and for you. Get your house and land in order so that your wife and children may come." But in vain; the war between me and Janos was not over, and I could not apply myself to any kind of work.

I killed Janos and hid his corpse. The authorities had got wind of what Mitar and I did in Hungary, but they had not touched us. It had happened in wartime and in a foreign land, and not even the devil himself would bring it into the open. They did not know anything about the killing of Janos. If anyone suspected that one of us had killed him, there was no proof, and no one touched us. My wife and children came, and I began to work industriously and to live a peaceful life. Two years passed and Janos' death still remained a mystery.

Then workers' co-operatives began to be formed, and on that Mitar and I differed. He entered a co-operative and supported the authorities, and I was against them. I had told Mitar about the murder, never expecting he would inform on me because of a Magyar! Yet it was he who denounced me to the authorities. Time and circumstances had brought us into conflict. They sentenced me to twenty years.

Ten years I have already served. Ten more remain, unless there is an amnesty. Life, all that a man has from life, has passed me by. I am now an old man, decrepit and ill. Mitar, too, is old.

I am afraid that one or the other of us will die before I get out of prison. I must kill Mitar. I never thought that I would shed Serbian blood, but his I must. It seems to me that he is a Serb, and yet he is not; or if he was, he is one no longer. I must get even with him to be at peace. I have no other sorrows or desires in my life.

In prison, at Sremska Mitrovica
April 28–May 3, 1959

THE DOCTOR
AND THE EAGLE

Everyone in the village knew the doctor and the eagle. The doctor they loved, and the eagle they feared. There was no connection between them, for the doctor was a man, and between eagles and men, as we know, there is no relationship.

The eagle was a real eagle, probably a female. It was afraid of nothing and attacked without paying much heed to shouts or even to shots. It did not dare be afraid, for it had to feed its young, and if it had been afraid it would not have been able to seize its prey, which was guarded by men. It must have had some chicks somewhere up on the heights of the gorge, from which it regularly flew out and then back again with its prey. The village was at the foot of the bare and stony mountains, and only there could food for eagles be found. The eagle had learned this from its forebears, and when it soared over the hills and over the village it was aware of the least movement of anything living. It could always see poultry, silently choose its prey, and, unseen and unheard, swoop down upon it from the heights.

Nor was the doctor ever afraid, not of men, not of beasts, not of the night. He was not afraid of the authorities, for he was a rebel, and, as an atheist, he had no fear of God or the powers of darkness. Though he was not yet a real doctor—he was just completing his medical studies—everyone called him that, and he himself behaved like one and healed the peasants. The peasants loved him, for he treated them without charge and was not proud; he chatted with the old men, exchanged jokes with the old women, and played with the children.

When one day the doctor succeeded in catching the eagle, the news spread through the village, and the pair of them were always linked in speech and in story.

The doctor's house was isolated, just below the mountain, and the eagle liked to ravage the poultry around it. The doctor's mother often cursed it; it had carried off her best layer. When the eagle was captured, she was overjoyed and spread the news through the village, and the village was overjoyed and gave thanks to the doctor. The doctor deserved their thanks for saving the village from penury, and even more for the bravery and skill he had shown. The eagle, attacking the flock of hens, had gripped the broody hen in its talons, but the old hen in its struggles had managed to get into the house and drag the bedraggled eagle with it. The other hens, too, had fled into the house and were clustered around the hearth. The doctor ran out of the inner room and slammed the kitchen door. He then threw himself on the eagle, which was unable to fly and had nowhere to go. The eagle bit and tore the doctor's arms and hands, but the doctor overcame it and bound it.

Everyone thought the doctor would kill the eagle at once, as anyone else in the village would have done, but he threw it, still bound, into the outhouse for the night. The peasants were afraid that he, an atheist, might even let the bird go. But the doctor was a man who had been to school and wanted to think things over before he decided how to take his revenge on the eagle.

In the morning he did what he had decided overnight: he pierced the eagle's eyes with a red-hot needle, unbound it, and put it in the fenced garden. The eagle, morose and depressed, remained there peacefully until the cool of the evening. Then, at the time of day when the shepherds used to see it flying out of the gorge, something moved it to action. It moved apprehensively. But the fence hemmed it in, blood and pus dripping from its eyes and solidifying on its curved and powerful beak. The peasants made fun of it, the children hung over the fence and poked it with twigs, but it paid no attention, lost in a darkness that it had never before experienced. Suddenly it jumped up and flapped its wings. They were huge, wonderful wings, the wings of a great cruiser, with white feathers in them, and the leaves and grass quivered under their beat. It would certainly have flown away, but the branches of the plum tree hampered it. It folded its wings, and the crushed and battered feathers scattered. It fell to the ground like a thing, dull and stricken.

I asked myself: Where does it want to fly, when for it there is the same darkness everywhere?

The eagle tried again and again, stubbornly, till it collapsed, exhausted, wings trailing in the dust. All the while it was doing this the peasants were afraid it would indeed fly away and, even though blind, find some way to do them harm.

The doctor explained: An eagle has eyes that magnify, and from a great height it can see the smallest detail. When it wants to catch something, it closes its wings and plummets down from the heights, and what it sees grows smaller in its eyes until its prey reaches the proper size at the moment the eagle falls upon it. For an eagle the main thing is its eyes; without its eyes it is nothing.

The peasants all agreed that the eagle was harmless without its eyes, and they gave fresh recognition to the doctor. He was an educated man, he knew, and he had fixed everything as it should be. At last the peasants heaved a sigh of relief.

The eagle lived in the garden for a few more days, but the only things that took any interest in it were the hens, at first from a safe distance and from shelter and then boldly, ready to peck it. The eagle neither tried to fly nor to defend itself.

Perhaps in the end the hens would have finished the eagle off had not the doctor's grandfather decided that some use could be made of it. He seized it by the huge wings that dejectedly trailed behind it, put its head on a tree stump, and with a blow of his ax

The Doctor and the Eagle

cut the head off. The eagle's body twitched and grew still, and the old man said: "It's wings are strong. They'll come in handy to brush away the ashes and sawdust—at least they'll be of some use."

To me, a child, it seemed as if at that moment earth and sky merged in blood and darkness.

In prison, at Sremska Mitrovica
April 23, 1959

TWO WOLVES

The peasants knew it well, though no one had ever seen it. They knew when and how it attacked, recognized its tracks and the length of its stride. It was a young and powerful wolf that for two years had been prowling about the village, killing everything living that had not been shut up for the night. Its bold cunning was astonishing. It jumped over sheepfolds, burrowed its way into cattle stalls, snatched the dogs from their chains in front of houses. Men, too, began to be afraid of it and avoided going outside in the hours of darkness. Hunters laid snares for it, tethering goats to fences in such a way that it could not get out again, but all in vain. The wolf went on taking from the peasants, hiding in some lair that no one knew, if indeed it had one.

In the village there was a householder whose name also was Vuk (Wolf), a middle-aged man and a great practical joker. The peasants used to tease him: "That namesake of yours in the forest. Can't you somehow or other cheat him?" And Vuk, too, jested: "He's pinched something from everyone. But from me, no—my namesake spares me!"

But the wolf knew nothing of jests or of namesakes. It was hungry, insatiable, and the peasants, well taught by the damage it had caused them, kept everything living shut up tight. Hunger drove the wolf to desperation, until finally it fell into a trap that no one had laid for it.

Two Wolves

It happened one February. The mountain was still thick with snow, but near the village there were some open patches. That morning Vuk the peasant rose early, as he always did, to let the sheep graze for a little around the house before driving them into the fold. As he went toward the pen—it was on a slope about a hundred yards from his house—he noticed on the damp path the broad, rounded spoor of a wolf, the marks of the claws still filled with water, from which he concluded that a wolf had passed that way very recently. The peasant jested to himself about the wolf, saying: "Eh, namesake, it's not nice of you not to show yourself. I can't welcome you as you deserve." He was still cracking jokes as he drew near the door of the pen. Later, he recalled that he had wondered why he did not hear any movement or rustling of the sheep or the bell about the wether's neck, but, still jesting about himself and his namesake, he paid no particular attention.

As usual he removed the heavy crossbar—he kept his sheep well protected from the wolf—and opened the door. The sheep were lying motionless, with bloodstained fleeces and torn throats. In the farthest corner was the wolf, crouched and avoiding the man's eyes just like a dog.

Astounded by what he saw, the peasant Vuk did not immediately close the door; the wolf might even have escaped had it made a quick rush. But it seemed as if the wolf, too, was bewildered and perhaps ashamed. This was its first meeting face to face with a man. The peasant stepped back and once more fixed the crossbar.

It was at once clear to him what had happened. He had noticed a hole in the thatch on the far side of the pen where the roof met the steep slope of the hill. The wolf had torn away the thatch, leaped inside, and killed the sheep, but it could not get out again. At first Vuk could not think what to do with the wolf. What was more, with the passing of time he seemed to get further from a decision, and his thinking was hampered by the disaster that had overtaken him—twenty-five sheep in lamb and a twenty-sixth, the bellwether, had been killed. Naturally his first thought was to call one of the peasants who had a gun to kill the wolf; but the guns were all hidden, and no one would agree to come in the daytime when others could see him and perhaps betray him to the authorities. He thought of taking an ax himself and killing the wolf, but if he could not get a good blow in first the wolf would attack him. He thought for a long time and, having come to no conclusion, went home to inform his family and the neighbors.

The house filled with mournful crying, and the neighbors began to utter loud condolences. Everyone seemed to have forgotten about the wolf. When they finally realized that it was shut up, they rushed angrily to the pen. But no one could summon up enough courage to enter. After thinking it over, they began to withdraw, discussing what to do and each one promising to take a share of the meat of the slaughtered sheep and give Vuk a lamb. In the midst of this misfortune they began to crack jokes. One said: "In God's name, Vuk, your namesake has served you worse than anyone!" And another: "Now your wolf is a bellwether to dead sheep!"

At that jest the idea came to Vuk's mind of how to revenge himself on his namesake. "That's it! I'll make a bellwether out of him!" he said, and the peasants all laughed, still not realizing what he intended to do.

Without saying anything to anyone, Vuk took two long forked poles and with a younger peasant went to the pen. He slowly opened the door and peered in. The wolf was crouched in the corner, ready to leap, its hair standing up. They poked the long poles through the door, trying to pin it against the wall. The struggle lasted a considerable time, but at last they were able to pinion its neck with one of the poles and its loins with the other. Other peasants helped, and the beast was at last overcome. Then Vuk took the bell from the slaughtered wether and fixed it firmly around the wolf's neck with heavy wire.

Only then was it clear to the peasants what Vuk intended to do, and they wondered at his ingenuity. There were doubts about it, as there always are: the devil alone knows if it is for the best.

But no one could imagine a worse punishment for the wolf. Born to stalk and steal, it must announce its coming. One peasant even jested: "Vuk, your namesake is a crafty one, but he would never think you smart enough to do anything like that!"

The peasants huddled into Vuk's house, afraid to be in the open when the wolf came out. Vuk himself and the young peasant crept up to the door, pulled away the poles, and leaped into the branches of a plum tree in front of the pen.

The wolf did not dash out at once, but could be heard furiously shaking the bell. It continued to do so for a few moments after it came out in front of the pen. Then, convinced that it could not get away from that sound which had always attracted it to the flocks, it fled through the village to the accompaniment of barking and laughter.

Certainly it was not able to scratch the bell off; nor did it try, as if it were no longer a wolf. For a few days it could be heard from time to time in the ravines, now here, now there, ringing its bell. Then that, too, ceased. The wolf died of hunger—wondering what had happened to it.

In prison, at Sremska Mitrovica
April 24, 1959

THE AMBUSH

The captain knew they were watching him.

This was not merely intuition or his knowledge of the unpaid debt for his harrying of the outlaws and the destruction of their homes. There were also external and everyday signs.

They were sneaking around on those nights when the dog, Garov, barked loudly and deeply, telling him that it was men and not wild animals nosing around the house. The barking began moderately and anxiously, then became angrier and more intense, till the dog nearly choked, showing that unwelcome guests were approaching nearer and nearer, though they never announced their presence or knocked on the door.

The captain's house was isolated, for it was on his own property, not in the village—he had wanted to be apart from the common peasants. It was like a blockhouse, all of stone and with an upper floor; he had built it solidly at a time when he had to guard himself not only against vendetta but also against forays from across the frontier. On one of those nights when Garov barked, stones and cudgels rained on the walls, and the captain and his wife, awakened, listened with concealed anxiety to pebbles shifting and rotten twigs cracking under the tread of human feet outside the door. The captain took his carbine and pushed open the creaking window shutter, and his wife, as brave as she was anxious, cried out in a sharp voice, unfamiliar even to herself: "Who are you around the house by night who do not make yourselves known?" But all that was made known was Garov angrily straining at his rope and, from the lefthand corner of the house, the metallic rustle of beech twigs—the unknown had slunk away furtively into the night. Next day the captain's two sons, driving the cattle to pasture, searched around the house, on the slopes and in the meadow and forest, and found on the trodden grass cigarette ends and crumbs of cheese and bread that the ants had not yet managed to carry away. The ambushers had spent the day there, hoping the captain would come out to look at his beehives.

The most striking thing was the bearing of the peasants, especially those who were suspected of harboring the outlaws. They met the captain sullenly and silently and, it seemed to him, with concealed but unmistakable wonder that they were seeing him, that he was still walking on the surface of the earth. And the standard-bearer, an outspoken cripple who did not hide his sympathy toward the outlaws but was grateful to the captain for having saved his life and property at the time of the revolt, warned him, as a hero and a fellow villager: "Keep your wits about you— it's wolf time and the hills are green."

The captain could not hope for protection from the gendarmes of the nearby village, for though in his time he had hunted down the outlaws, he himself was now something of a malcontent, the new order had turned out differently from his ideals and hopes. Because of his discontent he had at first been transferred from his own district and then pensioned off, receiving as consolation an order and a higher rank. On his return to his district he found himself unable to settle down in peace. He was still at blood feud with the outlaws and was not trusted by the ruling faction. He could only rely on his own foresight and shrewdness. Though he had passed through many bad times, he was still only in his fifties, youthfully supple and agile.

He could not completely trust anyone except his wife, though he was not an outsider and not without brothers and cousins in the vicinity. He did not even trust his nearest and only neighbor, the miller, the more so because he knew from earlier times that the miller was hand in glove with the gendarmes, and he who betrays one side will betray the other. Furthermore, the miller had cast a covetous eye on the captain's meadow by the stream and perhaps suspected the captain's flirtation with his pretty and vivacious blond wife.

It would not have been hard for the captain to protect himself, to shut himself up in his strong blockhouse, except that he was afraid of being called a coward, and, too, he had to go to the village and the little town nearby for his pension and various other needs. Nonetheless, he had so far surmounted his difficulties and evaded all the snares laid for him, so that no one except his wife had noticed anything.

During the daylight hours he remained for the most part in the house, and if he had to go outside he avoided open spaces—the garden and the meadow. At night he went out only when Garov was dozing quietly in his kennel. He modeled his actions on those of the outlaws. Sensing that they would judge his behavior by their own, he would go to the village and town only when no one was expecting him, his carbine over his shoulder and walking sedately, but as soon as he entered the forest he would leave the path and steal through the undergrowth, eyes and ears on the alert, his weapon cocked and ready. He always returned by night, approaching his own house with stealth and entering it only after his wife responded to his signal.

The day before, he had received through the miller a summons to the local township, and that morning the captain had to set out. Accompanied by his wife, who, as if unintentionally, shielded his back with her body, he quickly passed through the garden and halted at the edge of the slope. About a hundred yards below them foamed the stream that burst out from the dark gorge into two or three hundred yards of wide thickets and then, slinking through the green denseness of the alders and willows, again fled into the ravine like a snake under a stone. From this point, on the right bank of the stream, stretched the captain's meadow, just mowed, and on the other side the blueness of the miller's potato storehouse against which shone white his little one-story house.

Twenty yards above the miller's little house leaned his water mill, a gray bird bending thirstily over the stream. He could see the miller in front of his house, busy with something white, carving a wooden bowl, as he did from time to time. The captain's gaze swept over the valley. Yes, the alder coppice between the meadow and the stream was thick, impenetrable; he must go that way. He quickly decided not to go by the path alongside the stream, but through the alder copse on the edge of the meadow until he reached the little bridge a hundred yards above the mill. That way, as at night, he would reach a point level with those in ambush in the thickets, would run into them face-to-face so that they would not be able to take accurate aim.

"Good-by," he shouted to his wife and set out. But she stayed squatting on the edge of the slope. Thus hunched up, dressed all in black, she reminded her husband as he looked back at her of a bird of ill omen, a crow, a raven. "Why don't you go? What are you waiting for?" he almost scolded her.

"Nothing, nothing," his wife replied, unoffended. "I am watching to see that you get to the village in safety."

The captain smiled and said to himself: "She's loyal!" And to all appearances carefree as usual, he laid his carbine across his shoulders, one hand on the barrel and the other on the stock. But his wife knew that his nonchalance was assumed. She saw how, on reaching the thickets, he held the carbine out before him like a glittering dagger and quickly, constantly turning to right and left, threaded his way through the bushes.

On his return from the village, the captain emerged in front of the miller's house as if in time with the moonlight. The miller's yard and even the roof of the mill had only just been flooded with bluish light, while the far side, the captain's side, of the stream yawned like an abyss of darkness.

The miller was sitting on his doorstep, his shirt unbuttoned, barefoot, and wearing dirty cloth trousers, as if ready for bed. With the unseasonable joviality habitual with him, he explained: "It's been stuffy all day, so you see . . . just to get a breath of fresh air." The miller's wife, too, was slopping around, barefoot and wrapped in a black shawl over a stained cotton blouse with rolled-up sleeves and a creased linen skirt that, the captain remembered, made her haunches seem wider and more provocative. She was moving constantly between the house and the mill as if urgently working at something or other—and that, too, struck the captain forcibly.

The jovial miller was even more jovial than usual. His thin face with long chestnut mustaches seemed still thinner in the moonlight, but his smile was wider, more ingratiating, and in the freshness of the night his voice sounded deeper, milder. "My wife," he urged, "has just baked a *pita,* because I was expecting my brother-in-law and his wife. The children have gone to bed, so why not wait a bit, and we can have supper in peace and have a chat. Perhaps we could even find a glass of plum brandy. It tastes better in the cool."

The miller's wife, too, stopped the captain, with a crafty expression in her voice that only the two of them could interpret. "Come on, sit down, for heaven's sake. Everything is not as it should be. But after all, we can scarcely see."

But the captain did not want to stay, though he would have liked to share the *pita* and have a chat. He was tired after his journey and knew that his wife was waiting for him at home even more anxiously than when she had seen him off from the edge of the slope. Therefore he went on, and the miller, yawning and disappointed, called after him: "A pity. No man likes to drink by himself."

The miller's wife, as if she had been lying in wait for him, stopped the captain just as he was passing by the mill. Standing on tiptoe, she whispered in his right ear, so close that he could feel the warmth of her breath: "Don't go by the bridge! Go around another way!"

The Ambush

Though her whisper had been so low, it was at once clear to the captain that there, on the bridge, an ambush was waiting, and that the miller not only knew something about it but had taken part in preparing it as well, and had tried to delay him until the moonlight reached the stream. The ambush could only have been staged on the far bank, in the bushes, for this side was open; the miller's meadow and small field stretched down to the water's edge above the pebbly bank. The captain quickly turned toward the miller's wife, to hug her in gratitude or to have a good look at her. Then, with a sudden movement, noticing that the miller had withdrawn into the house, he put his left arm around her waist. He felt the firm softness of her belly on his hand and gently pulled her back into the shadow of the mill.

"What is it? The outlaws?"

"Yes! Don't ask! Just get away!"

He went on holding her waist, but now with both arms around her. He drew her gently toward him, as a sign of gratitude and uncontrollable desire. With restrained warmth she welcomed him, beginning to tremble and to press her body against his. "Don't! Let me go! My husband!" she whispered enticingly, pushing him away with her hands. He let her go, and she quickly swung around and kissed him with moist fresh lips. Yes, that was her way; always moist parted lips before making love. Before he could recover himself enough to return her kiss, she had darted behind the mill toward her house and her husband.

The captain remained in the shadow, considering which way to go. The simplest, he finally concluded, was to cross the stream just where he was. The bends of the stream would hide his crossing from being seen by the ambush, and there were stones standing out of the shallows on which he could step and not get his feet wet. The mill wheel with its plashing and rumbling would drown all other sounds. He felt sorry that he had always been suspicious of the miller's wife, too. She was sly and crafty, oversaucy and overfree, but now, just for that reason, she was dear to him, dearer than ever before. It had all been nicely planned— his head full of brandy, his stomach full of *pita*. They couldn't have failed. In the reflection of the moonlight the smallest objects could be discerned: the rocks, the dense bushes, the squat stump of a dead alder, by day reddish and now obscure and rigid as a sentinel.

The captain was wearing an old but well-kept olive-green uniform and rubber-soled top boots—invisible and inaudible. It was fortunate that he had taken such good care of his uniform and kept his boots in good condition—the boots especially. He had not wanted to look like an ordinary peasant and wear sandals; in any case the soles would have given him away by their squeaking. Nonetheless, he had not explained to the peasants why he had had the rubber soles made—almost indestructible! And they had a good grip on stone, if it was not moist.

He leaped with care from stone to stone, and then, in midstream, afraid that his next step would land him in the water, he slowly put his foot down; the boots proved themselves suitable for walking in shallow water. The dried-up stream scarcely reached above his ankles, and in five or six paces he was on the far bank.

He was still quite near all of them, the mill, the ambush, the miller's wife. He even heard the miller shouting to his wife loud enough for those in the ambush to hear—perhaps it was the agreed signal for his, the captain's, approach: "Have you tied up the cow?" Nonetheless he was far away, as if by crossing the stream he had leaped into another, more familiar world, after the danger into which he had so nearly stepped.

He heard the gentle gurgling of the stream, almost the same above by the bridge as below in the thickets. The water dashing from the mill wheel foamed and plashed. But nothing else could he hear, and the miller's wife's reply to her husband was not intelligible. She had not betrayed him even now; she had not replied loudly to the agreed signal. As he stood in the alder copse, there on the far bank, it was for the first time clear to him how and why he was so dear to the miller's wife.

She loved his lean rounded head with the long upturned mustaches that smelled of tobacco and something still sharper—

something male and arrogant. She loved, too, his eyes, dark blue, keen, and honest, in some inexplicable way like his mustaches. Dearest of all to her was his body, bony and muscular, impatient and eager for life, as was the manner in which he made love to her, turbulently, hurriedly, and the more passionately in that remorse goaded him because of his wife and his neighbor. Perhaps what attracted her most of all was his aristocratic bearing, which peasants and uneducated men did not possess.

The miller, then, had come out of his house, shouted to his wife and to the outlaws what the captain had heard, and was impatiently listening for the sound of shots. Then he changed his mind; perhaps a stray bullet would come his way. He withdrew behind the corner of the house. His impatience grew. But nothing happened. The woman soundlessly went about her work in the mill, the stream swelled with cheerful gurgling, and the water mill clacked.

Uncertain if he had been mistaken about the time it would take the captain to reach the bridge, the miller, still concealed behind the corner, softly called to his wife: "What's up? He should be at the bridge by now!"

"Oh, he's on the far bank already," the woman replied calmly.

"Meaning—he's got away?"

"Yes, he's got away—he's a crafty one!"

The miller burst out: "And you—that means nothing to you! You're even pleased, you slut. Perhaps you've been playing about with him."

"I neither like him nor dislike him. As for you, you play about in front of your own wife with any skirt or tail in sight. Shame on you! He's a wise one, an otter—that's the guts of it!".

The miller knew just how far he could go in abusing his wife if he did not want her to curtail her tenderness and care for him. That frontier was usually marked by a flow of harsh, masculine words from her. "Shame," "guts," even if not spat out in a harsh, quarrelsome voice, could be regarded as such words. "Yes, an otter, an old fox," he agreed, conciliatingly. "And everything was prepared, so that it could not have been better done! No one could have spotted them—they took up their posts only at sundown. But go and tell them, so that they don't go on waiting in vain. Only take care that they don't mistake you for the captain. There's been enough trouble already. Remember what I said—take good care."

The miller's wife went quickly into the house and came out a moment later with a basket. "Bread and cheese," she explained to her husband in passing.

Knowing her husband well, she knew that he had on the tip of his tongue, "Bread and cheese indeed! What next?" But he indifferently remarked, still more malevolently: "Very well, very well."

The miller's wife slipped silently down to the bridge, her mind busy with what her husband had hinted and what had been discussed that morning: the outlaws must be sent downstream, for a gendarme ambush would be waiting for them in the gorge. Furthermore, she must, as she hurried, think up some signal to reveal herself to the outlaws, so that they would not mistake her for the captain.

Even without her intervention, the outlaws might be expected to strike down-river. From the crossroads by the mill, the path that led upstream was difficult for those unfamiliar with it to follow even in daylight, and the road to the village would only lead to a chance meeting with the gendarme patrol. The path by the captain's house was soon lost in the thickets and the barren mountain, and might even lead them into an ambush laid by the clever, audacious, and unpredictable captain. The one reasonable road, indeed the only way out, therefore led downstream.

The miller's wife decided what to do so that the outlaws would recognize her, but not how to induce them to go downstream. Nor had her husband told her anything definite. He had relied on her quick and subtle wits and her instinct to find the best possible solution to the most unexpected situation. On that, too, by habit, she relied.

The Ambush

When she reached the bridge, already lit by the moonlight, she started to hum a song she had been singing while gathering ferns for the cow's bedding some three years before when she had first made the acquaintance of the outlaw leader. She had later used that song as a summons and a sign between them. The song echoed in a whistle from the thickets on the far side, and a tall, slightly stooping figure wrapped in a long cloak emerged. She recognized the outlaw leader, a youth not yet twenty-five, famous for his audacity and notorious for his cruelty, with a high price on his head.

"What's the matter?" he asked, seizing her by the wrist with his left hand. He pulled her aside into the thicket, so that his two companions in the ambush could not see them.

"I've brought you something to eat," she said, as he halted.

"That's fine," broke in the outlaw. "But what's happened to him?"

"He turned up at our house a short while ago and went on somewhere or other. We listened and listened, but we didn't hear any shots, so I came to tell you not to waste any more time waiting."

"But surely there's no other bridge over the river?"

"Some river, some bridge!" said the woman scornfully. "Now you can cross it anywhere you like by jumping from stone to stone."

The outlaw, not very subtle about anything except murder, shifted uneasily from foot to foot. "True enough. And he's an old fox, such as we haven't come across before."

They were silent.

The miller's wife knew that the outlaw did not quite trust her, still less her husband. But she knew, too, that the circumstances were clear to the outlaw, and that her husband, where the captain was concerned, would have to keep his mouth shut and would help the outlaws either out of fear or in his own interest. Now, as the outlaw leader turned over his suspicions in his mind, she thought how to lead him into an ambush: it was enough if she told him not to go to the village or to the captain, for in those directions shepherds had that day spotted patrols. The outlaws would have nowhere else to go except downstream.

Still holding her wrist, the outlaw suddenly drew her toward him. Small, wiry, and taken by surprise, she was enveloped in the folds of his cloak and could smell his sweat and the scent of grass and earth from his broad breast. Yes, that was he!

At their rare meetings she had made love with him and recognized his rough, impulsive violence. She could not see his eyes, but sensed that their hard, keen green brilliance had been softened and tamed by desire. Only desire was able, for a few moments at least, to modify his savagery, his violent male aggressiveness, and make him submissive, childishly obedient. She loved that timid brutality of his and those moments when he forgot himself and submitted to her weak, tender limbs. But even more irrevocable was the presence of death, which was always with him. The whole district went in fear of him, and at any moment he might be killed. Every meeting with him was a terrible, final, mortal farewell.

Now, too, with unappeased and growing desire, he overwhelmed her. He crushed her in his strong arms and kissed her wherever he could, on the neck, the face, the eyes, with his huge, dry, hot lips, over which drooped still-youthful mustaches. "Don't, you madman! Control yourself!" she protested, in feigned anger. "Your companions are here, and there's my husband, too."

But he did not relax, and she put down the basket, threw her left arm around his neck, and pushed her right hand through his shirt, caressing his firm, hairless chest. Such caresses always aroused tenderness and submission in him. He bent down and tried to put his arm under her knees to pick her up and carry her off. As if she had been expecting this, she whispered to him, resisting him cunningly, without violence yet firmly: "Mad one! Don't you know that I might lose you, even tonight? Don't go downstream! Listen, listen, don't go downstream!"

"Why not?" he asked, coming to himself, his arm tightening around her waist.

"Don't ask! But don't go!"

"Why? Why?" His naturally harsh nature came once more to the fore, brooking no opposition.

Taking advantage of his momentary confusion, she got out the food, spread it on a dark cloth, and offered it to him, to give his disobedient hands something to do, then slung the basket over her forearm.

"I see that I must tell you everything! The peasants have seen gendarmes there, just before evening," and before he had taken this in she disappeared smoothly and silently in the thickets.

Her husband came out from behind the corner of the house and stopped her ill-humoredly: "Have you fixed it?"

"I have not," she replied coldly and unambiguously.

"You haven't!" he burst out, following her toward the house. "So now you're making up to the outlaws! You haven't, indeed! What did we agree?"

"Well, I haven't," the miller's wife said, stepping into the house. Then, after putting the basket on a shelf in the big room that also served them as a kitchen, she explained: "They wouldn't go that way. They want to strike at the captain." She had concluded that the outlaws would not go to the village now that they had heard about the patrols, and upstream by night there was in any case no path.

"At the captain? They're mad! Don't they know the sort of mountain wolf he is, and what a fortress of a house he has? Well, let them stew in their own juice! As for you, you lazy slut—I have put everything away and my head is aching a bit—go and tell the commander, so that he does not hang about all night long. And ask them to supper. But don't wiggle around the commander so much, as you usually do—may the dogs chew his carrion, God willing!"

"I will only give him something to drink," said the woman peaceably, wiping her forehead with the hem of her kerchief.

"Why are you sweating?" her husband asked, almost maliciously.

"Why shouldn't I sweat?" replied the woman, once again on

the alert. "Rushing here, rushing there—and some man about to lose his life at any moment!"

"Yes, but that's the way it is. What can we do about it? To help the captain means evil from the outlaws. To help the outlaws means evil from the gendarmes."

"I know," agreed the woman, then at once contradicted: "But we ought not to enjoy it."

"I don't enjoy it, either. But evil attacks from all sides—I can't exist without evil."

The miller used to justify himself in this way whenever something did not turn out as he wanted, or when he did something nasty. The miller's wife, irritated, wiped his beard and lips, from which the sweat was dripping, with the hem of her kerchief, and then on quick bare feet vanished into the brilliance of the moonlight.

Meanwhile, the captain slipped through the bushes, passed easily into the open, and reached his house. As was his custom, he approached the house cautiously. First he went over to the dog, which, overjoyed at seeing him, welcomed him with cheerful barks and leaps. Then softly, from around the corner, he called his wife. She at once responded and opened the door as if she had been standing behind it. After he came in, she double-locked the door and followed him into the room where they ate and slept when there were no guests. The captain's sons were already asleep on mattresses spread on the floor. His wife, too, usually slept on a mattress on the floor, while the captain slept under a feather quilt on a bed with a high headboard on which were painted bouquets of violets—such a bed was a symbol of the captain's dignity and aristocracy in a savage and backward land.

Sitting down on a beechwood chair, simple and hard, but with arms and a back, such as was not to be found in the village, the captain stretched out his left leg, which his wife, turning her back on him, straddled, taking the sole and heel of his top boot in her hands. The captain good-humoredly pressed with his other boot on his wife's bottom—that was what he had done in the army with his batman—and both boot and wife slipped off his leg together. He did the same with his right foot. Not taking off his gray cotton socks, the captain then stretched out, sighed deeply, and ordered his wife to bring supper.

The woman brought from the kitchen a plate of thick mutton soup, full to the brim with chunks of meat, a dish the captain especially liked, and after he had begun to eat, knowing his talkativeness at meals, she quietly asked: "Why are your boots wet?"

The captain did not reply at once, pretending to be busy with the bones, then muttered as indifferently as he could: "They were waiting for me."

"Who? Where? How did you know?" his wife urged him.

The captain said angrily: "As if you don't know! The outlaws! At the bridge." He again fell silent, sucking up the soup and chewing the scraps of meat from the bones with enjoyment. His wife went out and came back with a plate of sour milk and cream.

"You didn't say how you knew," she remarked, putting the plate on the table.

The captain took a mouthful, so as not to have to reply at once. Then, swallowing and without looking at his wife, he replied: "She told me. The miller's wife."

They both were silent, and the captain guessed what his wife was thinking: Isn't that proof enough that there's something between him and the miller's wife?

But his conclusion was not correct, not altogether. For even if his wife had thought something of the sort, she expressed aloud something quite different: "Whatever she may be—may she have every happiness. I will give her the finest of my blouses, that silk embroidered one you bought for me at Easter."

The captain listened attentively to what his wife was saying, was even overjoyed at her words, but went on thinking his own thoughts. Sucking down half the milk, he pushed away his plate, wiped his mustaches with a cloth, turned from the table, and pulled his wife, who had begun to clear away, onto his knee. "You are mine, my only one! The only one who would never betray me."

Leaning her head on his shoulder, the woman, almost weeping, whispered: "So long as you come back to me."

At that moment Garov began to bark, loudly, urgently—at a man. "They're here!" said the captain in a whisper, and pushed his wife away. "Put out the lamp!"

The woman leaped up and puffed at the lamp on the wall, then went back to her husband in the darkness. His right hand met hers in the gloom and pressed it, but not as before—as a faithful companion and fellow fighter. Wife and husband stayed silent in the darkness and listened. There was nothing to hear, and nothing could be heard except the furious barking of the dog in front of the house. The barking soon became frantic, as if someone were coming not only up to the house but into Garov's kennel. Garov was choking with short, sharp yelps.

"Give me the carbine," whispered the captain to his wife. She stood up and in a moment laid her hand on the gun in the corner above the bed. The captain pushed open the shutter, but unexpectedly in the darkness the little hand and the whisper of his ten-year-old son stopped him: "Tata, Tata, let me shoot."

The captain had been convinced that the boys were asleep. It seemed, however, that the elder had been listening secretly, quietly taking in all that was happening. "Good, my young falcon," the captain agreed, handing the gun to the boy. "But take cover along the wall."

A moment of tense silence, broken by the captain's shout: "Ha, Garov, my hero!" Then a shot, crashing through the house as if the walls would shatter, united those within with the night and with Garov.

The dog fell silent, but then, clearly understanding that his own people by their shooting were on his side, went on tearing himself apart with barks and yelps. The younger boy, awakened, began to cry and the elder to comfort him: "It's nothing, it's nothing, don't be afraid."

Then the dog began to calm down. His barking became less frequent and less harsh, more satisfied. He could no longer scent the unwelcome guests, now lost in the darkness.

"Go and lie down," said the captain, hugging and kissing his son, and clutching his wife by the arm in the familiar signal that as soon as the children were asleep she should come to his bed.

Meanwhile, the miller's wife, dancing along, crossed the field and the pasture and darted into the dark, stony gorge. She passed through so easily and cleverly that she did not even bruise her bare legs, though the path was strewn with large sharp rocks. It was hard to see in the gorge, but she did not stop for a moment, nor lose the path and stray into the coarse grass or down the slope. At the mouth of the gorge she whistled, not loudly but shrilly. She was answered by a whistle, also weak but deeper, and from behind the rocks emerged a corpulent figure that the miller's wife, as it approached her, recognized instantly by its bandy-legged walk as the sergeant, the commandant of the local gendarmerie.

"What is it?" he asked as he seized her by the arm, leading her back the way she had come.

They could not walk side by side along the narrow and uneven path, so the miller's wife went silently ahead, the sergeant clattering after her in wooden sandals. They came out of the gorge into the open and the moonlight and onto the slope, its rocky sides overgrown with ferns and old spreading thorn trees. The sergeant seized the miller's wife by her left hand and led her to an isolated thorn tree on level ground.

"What is it?" he repeated in his hoarse rough voice.

"They've gone."

"Where?"

"If only I knew! Bandits, the forest! I tried to get them to come in this direction or to say where they were going, but it was no good—they just shut up."

Though she was sure that the outlaws would have struck out along the path by the captain's house and perhaps out of spite tried to attack the captain, she kept this to herself, not only because her husband had concealed from the gendarmes that the outlaws were planning the captain's murder, but also because she did not like to talk too much about such things—it always

turned out unpleasantly later. Therefore she added caressingly:
"And for you, too, I felt a little afraid."

For the miller's wife had frequently had love trysts with the
sergeant. These meetings had given her a bad reputation among
the peasants, but it had not been hard for her to justify them to
her husband: it was necessary to give information to the sergeant
and to sell eggs and milk to the police station. More often, however, they met out of doors, because of the sergeant's overfrequent
and superfluous patrols around her house, and still more because,
especially in summer, she enjoyed giving herself to the sweets of
love under the trees and in the bushes and especially amid the
ferns, so she willingly met the sergeant in the coppice by the
stream and the outlaw in the forest above her house. In the green
foam of the stems and the lace of the fern leaves, she returned or
entered into the life that had flowed there before her or would
begin after her, in which perhaps there was no man, but everything was carefree sweetness and passion and everything smelled
of them—of those oppressive, sharp, intoxicating scents. And the
sky itself, through the green tracery that caressed her cheeks and
eyelids, would mingle with her loose plaits and cast a shadow
over her eyes, would become near, comprehensible, another, still
finer curtain behind that of the grass.

This was the thorn tree where they had met on several evenings.
Even had there not been the smell of the trodden ferns and the
seductive wild scents, it would have awakened in her memories
of excitement and desire. But now she went unwillingly, trying
to find a way to extricate herself. For she had refused the captain
and the outlaw, and now it seemed to her that she would be unfaithful to them if she gave herself to the sergeant. This was not
a night for loving and giving, something not one of them, or her
husband, had been able to understand.

"Pity, what a pity! Who knows when we shall have another
such chance," the sergeant complained as they went along.

When they got to the thorn tree, the sergeant assailed her with
his heavy, fleshy paunch, kissing her behind the ears with his

prominent, moist lips topped by a short, bristling, and ticklish mustache. She drew back, but he nailed her so tightly to the knotted trunk that it seemed to her he would squeeze the breath out of her.

"No, don't! Your men are down there and my husband might come," she protested.

The sergeant would not stop. "What are you playing at?" he said angrily, continuing to force her onto her back.

So he always did, without preliminaries or finesse, but also without violence, enjoying her with coarse and shameful words and forcing her, too, to use them, more and more furiously until desire completely absorbed him. In such moments these words assumed a different color and sense. Everything coarse and shameless left them, and all that remained was pure excitement and desire. This open shamelessness of his pleased her. When they were alone, or when he looked at her in the presence of others, she could clearly discern his insatiable longing for sexual union. He was experienced, worldly-wise in thinking up stimulating and exciting variations. A peasant, coarse and boorish, he was inexhaustible as a male. His power over several villages and his male violence had fused and become a part of him, and this combination had inevitably conquered the miller's wife.

But this time she began to resist almost roughly. "Don't, please —I'm all on edge tonight."

Since the sergeant pressed on as if he had not heard, she bent forward as if ready to kneel, to lie down, wriggled out of his plump soft hands, and rushed through the ferns, shouting: "Supper's ready—there's *pita, pita!* My husband is expecting you."

The sergeant hurried after her, trampling down the ferns. "Wait, wait! Are you out of your mind?"

She was already vanishing down the path. She could hear him puffing and panting after her and swearing. Then he stopped and blew his whistle. She slackened her flight and soon afterward heard behind her the clinking of weapons and the clacking of wooden sandals.

The sergeant and the gendarmes feasted on the *pita* and plum brandy the miller's wife served them. They did not mention the outlaws, for the sergeant had concealed from the gendarmes that the miller and his wife were involved in his plans, though they might well have guessed it. All of them observed the rule that there are things which are done and of which one knows, but about which one does not speak. Therefore they talked about village affairs, the harvests, and the weather.

Despite this, the sergeant's eager dark eyes often met the soft and humble gaze of the miller's wife, and she understood that he had forgiven her stubbornness that evening and he for his part understood that she would again, at another time, welcome him.

The sergeant had already risen and was brushing the crumbs from his trousers when the sound of firing was heard from the captain's house. Then it was recalled that the captain's dog had been barking more and more frantically for some time, but no one had paid any attention.

"The captain is at it again," the miller remarked.

"Ah, yes, the captain," remarked the sergeant, as if he agreed with something the miller had not said and perhaps had not wished or been able to say. "A strange sort of man. Worthy, intelligent, but so obstinate and arbitrary."

In prison, at Sremska Mitrovica
July 24–27, 1962

BIRDS OF A FEATHER

Existence itself seemed uprooted and dispersed in those flaming, passionate, lascivious dog days when Joka's body, freed from its heavy winter clothes, became one with the sun and the air, and her longings waxed as she looked at the maize on the slope below the house, at the meadow lying fallow with young grass on the right bank of the stream, and especially at the willow thicket, just sprouting in the stifling heat on the left bank, where she was then with Mladen.

More and more often she forgot all else in order to find enjoyment in her body, now plumper and fuller, conscious of its passionate energy and the certainty of enjoyment in love. Afterward, coming to herself after her passionate union with Mladen, she was angry at that forgetfulness, incompatible with the torrid summer and incomprehensible to her unshackled body, alien to the warm earth, the clear sky, and the greenery of the branches that offered themselves as a bower, boundless and most sweet. She was angry at herself and most of all at her daughter, Jela, and at her former lover, Boško, her neighbor and a schoolteacher, who also lived there on the left bank of the stream, in the little white house swallowed up in the greenness of its garden.

Ever since that link between Boško and Jela had become known, her own love affair with Mladen, her latest and youngest lover—which had just started—had seemed different, without that impatient, yearning readiness to seize him, to surrender to him, as soon as she saw him near the white house with the red windows, upstream above the yellow stubble fields. She had accepted just that relaxation, that extinction of Mladen in her, as a fateful presage of the rooting out and disintegration of her existence.

Now, as always in summer, she carried out her household duties barefoot, clad only in a rather thin slip of crepe de Chine and a loose dress embroidered with little flowers. Her darkened rough soles felt the warm, moist earth and her body the slightest chill or breath of wind. She enjoyed the exposure and freedom of her body, also because of Mladen, whom her sunburned rounded arms, muscular calves, and especially her rather full breasts and hips, seemingly more naked through the stretched silk, amazed and attracted.

Thus at her ease, ever since spring, from morning to evening, she had kept watch to see when Mladen would come down to the meadow below his house to fetch water, look after the horse, mend a bank or a fence, or immerse himself in a book under the elm. Then, usually without even pretending that she had anything to do, she would steal through the maize below the house, then between the acacia hedges down to the stream, and wade stealthily across so that the pair of them, she and Mladen, in the willow thicket, unseen but in full sight of the whole village, could snatch a few moments of hasty, naked, and frantic enjoyment.

The stream was near—one could reach it in four or five minutes. But since Mladen was capricious in his passions and only with difficulty could slip away, having to find a good excuse to make to his father and mother, who liked to keep their only child under their eye, she had always to be ready to go to the willow thicket. That expectation, tense and lascivious, deprived their union of tenderness and made it frantic and impatient. But one way or another she felt satisfied. Life was joyously fulfilled and she felt the tenderness within herself, before and after.

Only now and then did she succeed in inducing Mladen to

come to the willow thicket during the afternoon heat while his father and mother were sleeping and the workers and cattle were drowsing and taking their ease in the shade. On those occasions, spreading out a white counterpane on the fence as a signal, she would walk down to the stream to refresh herself in the eddy under the willow thicket and then, from behind the bushes, surprise Mladen just as he, approaching quietly through the undergrowth, was looking for her. She would firmly and eagerly pull him to her, smooth in her wet slip after bathing, with skin goose-pimpled from the cold and lips quivering with desire. Only then did their passion reach a mature, conscious peace, her body surrender to his hands, and their lips find each other's and unite in sweet and blissful oblivion.

Even had he not been her latest lover, Mladen was dear to her and attractive with his arrogant ardor, his still childlike, thin, supple body and strength, and his tireless and recently awakened curiosity. He was a seventeen-year-old student, only son of a pensioner, and the anxiety and strictness of his parents still bound him, so that he did not walk home with her as far as the little outhouse in front of the house, as Boško and others sometimes used to do. He was embarrassed that his liaison with her might become known, for though she was no whore she had the reputation of a divorced woman who was known to change her lovers often and without many tears. But the young man's desire, timid yet exuberant, drove him to her, and she, respecting his timidity, submitted to his feigned experience and attentively cultivated and developed his desires in order to bind him to her as closely as possible for as long as possible.

She was conscious that her passion for Mladen was crafty and deliberate, but she was absorbed in it and obsessed with it as never before. There was always some woman in the village who took special enjoyment in teaching young men the arts of love. But she was not one of those. She did not want to be, nor was she forced to be. She was pretty and still young, only in her thirties, in the full flush of her innate, conscious feminine powers, and men eagerly turned to her. Mladen was the first youth who had learned love from her, and she was drawn to him by his awakening, piquant, and flattering curiosity and her unrealized, concealed, and obscure desire for rejuvenation and renewal. It had first begun as a game, even as a joke. She had teased the tall, slim brown youth with provocative questions, and she herself had been unaware, right up to that spring, that she had been observing him for the past two years, waiting to choose the moment to seduce him.

Of all her lovers, most of them impersonal and chance-met, only Boško had remained rooted in her memory because of his crude frankness, his refinement in caresses, and above all his disdainful violence, which left her body exhausted, broken with satiated lust and transparent as eddies, aware of clear silence and almost passionate tremblings. She hoped that she would remember Mladen, also, though in a different way. Consciously surrendering to his inexperience, modesty, and immaturity, and imperceptibly drawing him into fresh and ever more shameless ways of love, she made him her male for that summer, one who would never forget her and who, even when he left her to go his own way in life, would return to her.

She had known all about him long before she seduced him—how he lived, why he got angry, where and how he passed every moment of his day. His parents had never been very intimate with her, though there had never been any quarrels between them, and Joka was sure that at one time there had been something between Mladen's father, a former tax official, and her mother, Doca, some love of which traces still remained: tired smiles in the wrinkles around their lips and their cool, almost familiar, attention and consideration toward each other. This had made it easier for Joka to meet Mladen, to stop and talk with him as if by chance. Though his father and mother kept a wary eye on him, it was not from fear for his chastity but lest he fall ill or catch cold or be attacked by someone. Remembering the strictness and harshness of his father, she succeeded in meeting him when his parents were not on watch, usually waylaying him on his way back from school. She rejoiced in advance at the uncertain victories of her unmalicious cunning and was thrilled to the marrow whenever she surmounted some new obstacle, passed some fresh stage, in the young man's moody and timorous intransigence.

Finally, in the spring, on the day after St. George's Day, she chose the hour, the manner, and the place for their total union.

She had noticed that Mladen was fascinated by the buds of spring and guessed that he would have been entranced by the St. George's Day vigil, the competitions between the young men and the dancing with the girls. As if unintentionally, having just washed with scented soap, she waited for him in the late afternoon on the road from town as he came back from school, and walked with him to the village.

It was not more than half an hour's walk to their houses. Usually they went by the main road, broad and level, from which, just below Boško's house, a path branched off toward her house. From that point to Mladen's house was still about ten minutes' walk. But there was a short cut to her house immediately after leaving the town, along the right bank of the stream, through a young oak coppice on the slope—a narrow footpath that branched off from the wooden bridge across which the main road led.

When they reached the bridge she said, smiling and gazing invitingly at him: "Let's go this way. It's nearer for me, and you will have a fine walk through the woods."

He seemed to hesitate, shifting his worn leather satchel from his left to his right hand: "But it's quicker for me by the road!"

Knowing him to be touchy and obstinate, she decided to excite him as she would a man, and smiled provocatively at him with her fine curved lips. "Are you afraid to walk alone in the woods with a woman? What if it gets dark? What will mother say?"

"No, no!" he shouted almost angrily, and followed her.

Now she had to thaw him out and get him into a good mood.

She had not much time left, but the circumstances were unusually good. Immediately after leaving the bridge, when they had gone about twenty paces and entered the leafy, clear green of the woods, she decided to put it to him with the least possible equivocation and yet in such a way that he would not be able to complain to his parents about her shameless assault if she should fail in seducing him.

"You know," she began, stripping the leaves from a broken twig, "I was not joking when I asked if you were afraid to go into the woods with a woman. You keep well away from me, and I— I am eating my heart out with desire to talk to you, to be with you, like this, alone. I often think of you, and I dream of you every night. I simply don't know what's the matter with me. I have never been so carried away before."

She spoke breathlessly, swiftly, to overwhelm him with their aloneness in the soft, pale, fresh greenery. But the young man said nothing, and because the path was too narrow for them to walk side by side, she could not see his expression. She turned to him. Mladen seemed to be paler than usual and his lips were trembling. She could not read anything special in his eyes, darkened by the sunset behind the green hills. What was more, he looked away as if scared, and stumbled. She steadied him skillfully and gently with her hands and held his, cold and agitated, for a long time.

They went on again till they were near her house, and since there was no open space where they could sit she decided to go as far as the wild pear tree and not to stop, but excite him and wear him down with words.

She was sorry, she said walking slowly and with tiny steps, that she was not as young as his classmates; surely he must be in love with one of them? She explained that she was still in her sweetest, fullest womanly strength and swore that all she wanted was his joy and happiness and that she was ready to give her soul for him. She implored him not to be cruel and merciless toward her and asked him to unite with her, promising that it would be wonderful and would give him delights such as he could never imagine. He remained silent, numbed and lethargic with astonishment or sweet expectation. But she, carried away by her own words, paid no heed.

When they reached the pear tree she slowly and resolutely turned around and took his free left hand into her hot palms. His fingers, too, were now burning, quivering. He did not draw away, and when she became aware that his fingers were at last searching for hers, she gently put her right hand in the collar of his open shirt and, drowned in his huge, burning, glistening, and yet frightened eyes, whispered softly: "Darling!"

He put his free arm around her, and since he could not summon up courage to kiss her, she stretched out, clinging against his immature and yet firm man's body, gently pulled down his head, and softly, without insistence, as if leaving everything to him, pressed her moist lips to his, dry and resistant.

She drew him quickly under the pear tree on the pretext that after all someone might surprise them on the path. She did not let go of his hand, though it was awkward for them, thus linked, to find their way through the bushes. He followed her obediently and, so it seemed to her, willingly. When she reached the pear tree she leaned against its dark trunk and again drew him toward her, to her lips and breasts.

"Put down your satchel, silly one! Why don't you come closer, when I would be everything to you, everything—and would give my living heart for you?" she whispered feverishly. Then, noticing some resistance on his part—he had almost angrily thrown his satchel away—she feared that she had overdone the tenderness and added: "How well and how sweetly you kiss!"

He did indeed kiss her, though feverishly and without that clinging which stops the breath and destroys the sense of one's own existence. He did not know what to do with his long bony hands, and seemed afraid of her breasts and still more of her hips. She concluded that he had already kissed some young girl, but that she would be the first woman to lie with him. She must take care not to embarrass him or repulse him, but must seduce him and lead him on, responding to his sudden, supposedly daring, but in fact fumbling and frightened advances.

The ground was moist, the grass still young and juicy. But she dared not bother about that—not now, not at this time. When he, overwhelmed, buried his head in her soft, perfumed breasts and his bony and supple body began avidly to merge with her full, strong hips, she concluded that she could confidently introduce the final act. She pulled him to the ground and, as if maddened and out of her mind, writhed under him, but never wriggled out of his embrace, and whispered to him: "Come, my heart, don't torment me any longer! But take care of your trousers."

She no longer had imperceptibly to help him, to feign surrender to his movements, to stimulate his manliness. "Ah, how sweet it is with you, my heart!" When it was over, he gazed at her without a word. In his eyes she could see herself, selfishly exultant and rejuvenated in the green flood of leaves and grass. She was afraid his secret remorse might make him run away, so quickly and deliberately she began to stroke his reddened, downy face, like a mother, like a sister. "How good you are, how wonderful, how tender. A real angel! She will be happy who gets you, who will enjoy you."

For now it was important, as important as the seduction itself, not to leave him to himself, to make sure that he did not slip through her hands, away from her caresses and her gentle embraces. She must compensate him for the loss of home tenderness and accustom him to the life now opening before him. The tops of the trees above them had darkened in the twilight, and from Boško's house—it was only then that she remembered she had given herself to Boško under this same pear tree—came the sounds of farmhands and cattle, and the mill on the stream below them clacked soporifically. In sudden feverish lament, he pressed his head into her shoulder, and she joyfully noticed his tears on her skin, chilled by the evening, and her own relaxation. She did not know, and for the moment it was not important, if he was weeping from shame or from happiness and ecstasy, but she went on stroking him, cooing, caressing him, provoking and stimulating him until the young man's face dried, and he began to kiss her all over with a fresher, still wilder fire, and his body lost itself in hers. Somewhere far away in memory, absorbed by the flames of enjoyment, was the knowledge that renewed delight kills the sense of sin and that it would no longer be so easy for him to resist.

Later, relaxed, they walked a hundred or so paces through the woods and halted in the dense undergrowth at the edge of the meadow, as if ashamed and embarrassed to be seen in the open. They waited there until it was dark, for fear someone would see them from his house or from the village. In his house the three windows facing them shone with a yellow light, and she, now a little sad, put her head in his lap, lamenting: "I love you as a brother, really as a brother. I have no brother; I am like a sister to you. I did not think that it would turn out this way with you. I embraced you like an elder sister. But what can I do when you are so sweet and dear that I can refuse you nothing? Tell me, when shall we meet, sweetheart? As brother and sister, if you prefer. Tell your sister, my dear one."

Raising her head from his lap, she noticed in his mocking man's smile that he did not believe her, but all the same his boyish face was shining with a blissful, sinless radiance. Her eyes really became moist with emotion when he kissed them, promising firmly and tenderly that he would meet her again the next day, in the willow thicket below her house, when he came back from school.

From that time on their love grew and expanded. They devised signals for their meetings and imagined all the rogueries of love, in which he became more and more shameless and she, apparently, more ashamed. That was something new for her. Through him she seemed to live her youth again, unknown, mature, and dissolute. She avoided, instinctively and deliberately, any meetings with former lovers, feeling that the lascivious purity of her liaison with him would become blunted, that the fire of his ever more frantic caresses would slacken. She swore to him, although he did not ask her, that she had been chaste ever since she met him and that she would remain so as long as he wished. That, she noticed, flattered him, and she was glad of anything that pleased him.

At first they met every second or third day. But as summer wore on, their meetings became even more frequent, and when his holidays began it was a rare day when they did not meet. Serene and rich, their love would certainly have lasted all summer had not Joka noticed that there was something between her daughter, Jela, and the teacher Boško, something that, had it not been her daughter who was in question, she would undoubtedly have interpreted as intimacy and passionate love.

It began in midsummer, in the flare of her love for Mladen, shortly after Boško's arrival on leave and the arrival five or six days later of Jela, who had run away from her stepmother. Joka, despite herself, began to watch her daughter and follow her movements, imagining changes in her and her intentions, and to watch Boško's departures from his house, but she also began to anticipate the summer joys of her own body. It even chanced that she twice rushed away tremulously from her lascivious desires, from the now mature embraces of Mladen, down there by the stream that gurgled around them as if with pealing silver bells, awakened from the fascinating dance of intertwined bodies or the still more passionate, fuller, and more feverish moments of union.

In the sleepless nights that followed she began to feel jealous of her own daughter. This appalled her and proved to her more and more that it would have been much easier to bear had it been any man other than Boško. For Joka had ineradicable memories of Boško and the experience of a lover to whom she had not only freely given herself over a long period of time but with whom she had shared every kind of love madness, often being so exhausted by passion that she became lethargic from fatigue. If she had in her passions any limit or frontiers, Boško had reached them, leading her almost to a sort of sexlessness and to blissful indifference. When she was alone she had a clear and shining realization that such a state was temporary and that she would awaken from it even more lustful, unexhausted and inexhaustible. She recalled, clear in her memory, the deliberately crude and shamelessly refined details of their ingenuities of love and their follies. All that summer of love with Boško, all that green, cool, amorous little valley, even the memory of herself, now lived in her like a red-hot coupling from which stood out the sweetest and maddest moments. In those memories were interwoven the orchards, fields, and copses in which they took or were taken, and everything seemed madder and more passionate since all took place, so to speak, under the eyes of the whole village and also under those of her mother, Doca, who, one evening when they were sheltering from the rain, herself made the bed and brought them snacks and soon transferred them to the feather bed in the only room of the house.

All this had happened only a short while before—the summer before last—and it was incomprehensible that now Boško, with his firm mouth, was kissing the delicate, untouched, rosy lips of Jela, straining her supple and resilient waist and heedlessly breaking the shoulder straps on her scarcely rounded shoulders, pressing her timid, only just glimpsed, breasts, and authoritatively, without hesitation, laying bare and separating with his bony weight her swelling and submissive thighs.

Inconceivable! Inevitable! For Boško had been the only lover who not only imposed on her a public liaison but also revived amorous passions.

At that time two years had passed since her divorce and Joka had only just recovered from the long and humiliating court case, in which her husband had bribed false witnesses to prove her unfaithfulness. During those two years she had confusedly slipped into chance and short-lived loves that left behind them a nasty satiety and a feeling of emptiness. She had also had to watch her behavior because of her mourning for her father, who died in the first year after her divorce. She had found it hard to settle down in the house and on the property from whose income she could live without too much effort, but of which she must take daily care.

It had been a comedown. Her husband, a wartime peasant speculator, had quickly risen to become a well-to-do merchant in the little town that grew from the ruins of the former state, and from the exchanges of goods, money, and men. At the same time she, too, had advanced, from a peasant girl tending the sheep in the fields to a housewife tied to her home and concerned with contenting her husband. It was an easy and comfortable life that lasted seven or eight years.

Though the peasant in her had never for a single moment been entirely driven out, even as some trivial ornament of national costume was never lacking from her dress, she began to behave more freely in that comfortable town life and to deceive her overly busy husband, to whom she had not been completely faithful even before this. Three or four times a year he had to go to Sarajevo to buy goods. The shop grew larger and their wealth increased, and she noticed that he had turned into a coarse and selfish upstart, eager for social advancement and insatiate of wealth and power. Though reconciled to this way of life, she noticed that there was less and less room for her in her husband's toadying to the rich men and the leaders of the town.

She drifted more and more heedlessly into unfaithfulness, and her husband took advantage of local gossip to exaggerate her transgressions and win his divorce case. Her daughter was left in her husband's care, and Joka went back to her father and village life, free, but lost and shamed, unable and unwilling to be a peasant girl again and sink back into heavy, and to her now almost animal tasks and into unchosen, peasant loves. Just as she was beginning to find her feet again in this new life, Boško appeared.

They had known each other slightly in earlier times, when she was an unmarried girl. Now he was a mature young man who, having finished his education and his military service, was waiting for an appointment. He was eight years younger than she was, but more experienced and more down to earth.

The first time he met her in the late afternoon on her return from town, he had escorted her across the meadow to the spring under the cherry tree below the house, and then halted and held her in casual conversation. As soon as it grew dark he had begun to kiss her so wildly and forcefully that, even had she wished, she could not have resisted. So he took her, just there, on the open field near the spring, before she had made up her mind whether to resist or to respond passionately; the dew fell, her eyes were filled with stars and her neck bathed with his hot breath.

Very soon, the following evening, in the woods, under the pear tree, on a thick blanket she brought with her, she had rivaled him and responded to him in amorous rekindling and invention.

Boško was her first really subtle lover who was ashamed of nothing. He never spoke coarsely, but would tell her to undress in front of him, watching her calmly and thoughtfully. Nor was she ashamed, but was always willing and eager to show herself to him and to draw him back to her, naked in body and desire. That was love without shame and without coarseness, in which both she and he expected and thought only of union. There was no lovers' tenderness between them, but through their passion and independent of it there arose a mutual affection, even respect; the lovers remained old friends and good neighbors. She was satisfied, radiant, warmed by a fire that until then she had only suspected. For what more could she, a divorced woman, older and uneducated, expect? She was flattered and rewarded. In passion, in the actual act of love, she gave—as she was well aware— as much as she took, and felt worthy and equal.

But the duality, the incompatibility of lover and neighbor, of scholar and peasant girl, young man and divorcée, remained to the end.

There was also something of that in the attitude of her mother, Doca, to Boška. She arranged the bedroom and welcomed them as guests, but in no way showed that she knew he was her daughter's lover. She greeted him and said good-by to him simply and naturally as to a neighbor and a young man whose family and reputation merited hospitality and welcome. Nor did she ever speak to Joka of her liaison with Boško; words were superfluous against the inevitable, and could only remind her of her shame and disturb the natural relationship of the three of them. Serious and quiet, after she had made the bed Mother Doca would appear smiling—and only in that amiable and pleasant smile on her harsh face was her enigmatic participation expressed—and announce, looking neither at her nor at him: "Now you can lie down." In the morning she brought them breakfast as soon as she heard their carefree conversation, smiling somewhat more clearly and widely, and saying "Did you sleep well?" They soon got used to her and called her if they needed anything, but always in such a way as not to remind her of what was happening and what in fact linked them.

So nothing disturbed Joka's liaison with Boško. It would have gone on just as it was despite the fact that when he came the following summer girls from the town and on the beach distracted his attention. Not expecting anything from him other than impetuous infatuation, she became resigned to being forsaken. That summer lived through with him in naked, invulnerable, and unforgettable passion would have lived on unsullied in her memory had not, this summer, the new relationship between Boško and Jela come unexpectedly between them, a relationship whose scope and content were not quite clear to Joka, nor could she permit herself to acknowledge it.

Though she easily enough overlooked the insult that her own daughter had, so to speak, stolen her lover, she could not reconcile herself to the fact that Jela, her little girl, was now experiencing those same passions and ways of enjoyment that only she and Boško knew how to bestow so generously on each other. That regret and bitterness would not have been so keen had she not known and remembered how Boško kissed, embraced, and overcame her, as if her body did not even now, whenever Jela was associated with him in her mind, recall with trembling the place and time and manner of its enjoyment. The liaison between Boško and Jela imposed itself on her through her own passionate delights with Boško. Pictures sharper and more passionate than they had been in reality kept coming into her mind, compelling her to look madly at her daughter's lips, neck, and breasts for the marks of Boško's lips and teeth. This hampered her in her revived passion with Mladen and drove her to introduce him to the ways of love she had enjoyed and imagined with Boško. It was as if nothing remained, not even her most secret desires, that did not involve the mad, turbulent eddies of Jela's and Boško's passion.

Nonetheless, very soon, some three or four days after she had first suspected Jela and Boško, she realized that those forebodings, those yearnings for Boško, were due to her own jealousy. She hoped, once she realized this, that everything would become easier and calmer. And so it did—at first. This impassivity lasted two or three days and then was transformed into something still worse, a frantic, gloomy opposition to Boško's and Jela's liaison. It was inexplicable and seemed to have neither roots nor buds, but flowered out of herself in an inevitable and terrible insomnia, filled with painful thoughts and wanderings between memories of her childhood and girlhood and her vain hopes of resurrecting and renewing her own experience with Boško. She tore herself to shreds between the past and hope for the future, now assuring herself that there was nothing between Jela and Boško, nothing terrible and irretrievable, and now, defeated, retreating before the accomplished fact.

She vacillated wildly between waiting for her daughter, if she had gone out somewhere or was late in returning home, and watching for some signal from Mladen, throwing herself aimlessly into love trysts or housework. She was aware of her undoubted jealousy and the disorder of her daily life, and her doubts impressed themselves on her at every moment despite Mladen and her relations with him, though in them and through them everything once more became clear and simple.

This year, as every year, on St. Peter's Day there was a church gathering by the mineral spring, on the open fields above the town. Joka arranged with Mladen that he would come back early from the festival so that they could meet in the woods by the pear tree, and therefore, but even more to still the jealousy within herself, she allowed Jela to go with Boško's sister, Milena—they were about the same age—to the spring.

About four o'clock in the afternoon Mladen, drenched in sweat, burst into the space under the pear tree. He at once drank thirstily from the water bottle and then stretched out wearily on the white blanket alongside Joka, barefoot, bareheaded, and loosely dressed. Only the dense shade of the pear tree resisted the shimmering heat. Joka liked the youth's sweat. Leaning over him with her whole body, she wiped his forehead with her black kerchief and then, unbuttoning his gray shirt to the waist, began to kiss him and caress his stomach and loins.

With half-closed eyes and outstretched limbs, the young man gave way to lazy enjoyment and to the downpour of her fresh kisses and the firm, insistent caresses of her hand, precursors of accumulating depths of desires. But she knew him even better. The quivering surrender of his loins, the growing though drowsy radiance of his eyes, and the trembling compression of his dark-red lips she welcomed as intentional restraint, as a refinement of lust. In order not to hinder the growth and maturity of those desires, she did not want to be aggressive; she held back from passionate embraces or crudely provocative touch. Her thin, short plaits—her hair was fine, soft, and a bright chestnut color—dangled on his chest, and her lips and whispers refreshed his face, lips and eyes and ears. "Little one, dear one! You are tired. You need to rest. So rest, take it easy, heart of my heart!"

But Mladen was aware—and she knew it—that she was warming him up, luring him to passion, to union with her body. By those supposedly motherly and sisterly caresses she fanned her own flame, too. Nothing could take the place of her enjoyment with Mladen, and therefore she did her best to solace the dear, clumsy, lonely boy. So that their relationship should last the longer, she clothed her longing more and more in that pleasant motherly-sisterly form, which seemed to the young man acceptable and even dreamlike.

Now, as her plump, firm body began to embrace him in its soft contours, he, seeing close above him her eyes and her rounded lips which opened and called on him trembling, suddenly came to himself, gripped her with his right arm, drinking up her lips, and slowly turned her over. In a moment he was transformed into a firm, strong, and impatient male and she into a female supple and desirous. The earth beneath her disappeared and the bushes around her; only her eyes, looking over his head, which she was holding with her right arm, kept looking through a strange, fantastic mist as in a dear and distant memory at the impenetrable roof of shining green leaves. "Dear man of mine!" she whispered, hugging him tighter and finally closing her eyes.

Then he was once more tired, but with a sweet relaxation, which she could transform by her careful, now almost wifely, caresses into a still more fervent heat and a more naked passion. Still filled with desire, she covered him with soft, moist kisses and stroked his sweaty, thin, yet already muscular thighs, no longer as a boy whose lustful regret must be calmed but as a lover who must once more be kindled and awakened. But that, she knew, was not enough. If those gentle and seemingly involuntary caresses the youth's passion once more awoke, so also did his return to reality, to a world in which those two knew that they were lovers but were not compelled to be so again. In order that he should once more be gripped by passion, it seemed that he had to alienate himself from the act of love of a few moments before, and especially from her fresh desires, which she was no longer able to conceal. She helped him, as always and in every-thing, to return from that melancholy brown study to reality, though not to that world in which every movement of her body, every quiver of her lips or flash of her eyes, revealed the insatiability of her desires, but to that other, everyday world in which they seemed no more than acquaintances and friends.

That hungry yet uninsistent caressing had to be completed by some reasoned, almost cold, conversation about no matter what. Therefore she began to talk to him, to ask him how it had been at the festival, to tease him that he had been looking at the girls and had forgotten all about her—getting old, simple, and ugly.

Mladen had at other times defended himself weakly from her teasing. That had not offended her. If not this year, then next, he would leave her, and certainly even now he was in love with one of his schoolmates or some girl from the town. But now there was something reserved and exceptionally silent about him, as if something had happened at the festival that he wanted to conceal from her or that it was difficult for him to tell her. Inquisitive and uneasy, thinking that some harm might have come to Jela, she assailed him with questions.

"Well," he admitted at last, "Jela! She went off with Boško into the woods, supposedly to the upper spring. We all went there, and she was nowhere to be seen. Everyone was talking about them."

"Why?" Joka began, pretending to be astonished, ceasing to caress him. "Other girls go with young men—outside the woods and in them." Mladen remained silent and she, encouraged, went on: "You immediately think the worst."

"But no, that's not the same," Mladen replied, almost angrily.

"Why not? Why shouldn't it be? Look! She's been a young woman for some time now. Of course, she's young, but she is mature. Many girls of her age get married. Perhaps she liked the young man and he her," she spat out, more and more unconvincingly.

Withdrawn into some unspoken knowledge, Mladen did not interrupt her. But when she, excited by his silence and reassured by her own loquacity, cried out: "You should be ashamed to think anything of the sort," he did not deny it, but cut her short. "But everyone, even those who do not know you, knows that you and he were lovers. They even say that you have been the go-between! They all kept their eyes on her and were whispering about her."

Joka had suspected that Mladen must know about her and Boško, though they had never spoken about it. But the unspoken truth did not have the sharpness of pain and insult. Furious with herself, she had before this thought that there was something ugly in a love affair between her daughter and her former lover. But now, when Mladen had almost palpably exposed the certainty of this liaison and her own uncertain, perhaps even equivocal, role in it, she realized how monstrous, how atrocious, it must seem in the eyes of the world. She was astounded. It was clearer than it had ever been that any marriage between Jela and Boško was impossible, even if he were willing. Filth breeds filth. What would happen later, when someone should refer to Jela as Boško's mistress, if indeed someone had not already done so? Her lips sagged and her words died on them. Her hands remained forgotten somewhere on the young man's body, in which they seemed to have lost interest.

Mladen, as if searching out some hidden and insistent thought, remarked: "There's no reason to wonder at it. You know, she's a little like you, but much younger and prettier."

He did not go on, checked by her horrified look and astonished at his own sudden realization. The look in his eyes, the harsh, alarmed firmness of his lips, made her think, convinced her, that he, too, if not before then certainly at that moment, longed for Jela's vital beauty, already known to him, already tasted, through her mother, through her, Joka.

But he soon recovered himself. Raising himself on his left elbow, he began with slow tenderness to brush away the loose hair straggling over the rather low, smooth, sweaty forehead and dark, plumpish face, restoring her courage and stressing his words with kisses: "Don't worry. That's how it is. You are dear to me. Sweeter than ever. I hadn't intended to tell you but you dragged it out of me. Come on, laugh! Won't you kiss me? Won't you give pleasure to your little boy?"

He had never before spoken to her with such tenderness, or

been so forward in his caresses. Not only did she scarcely notice his passion; she also thought with horror that it was inflamed not just by her but, in some unknown and incomprehensible way, by Jela, too. Now all she knew was that she must respond to his caresses and give herself to him; the half-conscious demands of her ardent, unappeased body were quite separate from her longing for love, for the tenderness of loving and being loved. Something deeper and more ominous than her jealousy of Jela and her hunger and regret for Boško was concealed in her bitterness; it hampered, too, her enjoyment of love with Mladen even at the moment of ecstatic and complete surrender.

She began to blame herself for behaving too casually, lulling herself with infidelities. Everything, from the very start, had confirmed that a love affair had developed between Boško and Jela. Now, as she tried to correlate the movements of her lips with Mladen's and to unite with him with hips and hands, she recalled details and concluded that Milena, Boško's sister, though not fully aware of the nature of the relationship between him and Jela, was the go-between. She was consumed by a fury until then unknown against Boško, the spoiled, selfish little upstart, and against his flat-chested, washed-out, secretive, and apparently passionless sister, who called for Jela, went with her into the town, and kept her at her house until darkness fell.

"I must keep an eye on Jela. I must never let her go out alone," she concluded, seizing the youth by his shoulders and spreading out before him. But he did not seem to have heard. He was preoccupied with passion and the warm, moist, incomprehensible depths of her body.

This time there were not, nor could there be, those unrepeatable passions she had felt the first time she had been intimate with him. Fear and worry about Jela and her own fate chilled her, and as soon as the young man lay back she stood up and began to tidy her hair and tuck it under her kerchief.

"Where are you going? You're surely not going to leave me now, when it's best for both of us?" the youth protested, not rising from the blanket.

"I must, I must," she replied, decisive and businesslike, and then, shocked at her own coldness, kissed him on the neck and added: "Don't be angry, my sweet!"

She pulled him up from the blanket almost by force and, brushing him off, began to explain: "Can't you see? The sun is just below the peaks. It will soon be night. I must find her before darkness falls. And I must get dressed. I would have gone sooner, but I could not, because of you. How could I leave you unsatisfied, my sweet one?"

As he combed his hair, Mladen grumbled: "Where can I go now? What can I do till it gets dark? I shouldn't have come."

"But, my dear, we have had a good time anyway," she went on in the same cajoling yet businesslike way, folding the blanket. "It's true we didn't have as long as we could or as we wanted, but nonetheless! You must realize, I am a mother and she is all I have. She is inexperienced, naïve, still a schoolgirl. And you, you are my heart! Another time, whenever you want, whenever you like, I am yours as often as you like and as often as you can. What does she know about life, about men? Her future will be dark if I do not help her. It's easy for us two. We'll make up for it when we are in the mood, my young man."

Though pacified, he seemed not to hear, but stood leaning against a tree trunk, gazing out over sunlit but graying hillsides and the deep valley. She came close to him, kissing his lips with quick dry kisses and stroking the curls of his freshly combed hair. "I'm sorry, I'm sorry," she whispered. "I could eat you up, all of you, all! Only now do I see how sweet you are to me." Then she added, unrelenting: "But I must, I must, I must go to Jela!"

The youth moved away from the tree trunk and sighed: "Now I'll have to go back almost as far as the town, so that the people in the village don't see where I have come from," and added after cold reflection: "But I think it's all a waste of time. She's fallen blindly for him. Nor can one wonder at Boško. She is very beautiful, all gaiety and vigor, and as mature as you are. At the fair there wasn't a girl like her. Perhaps there were some prettier, but not one so young, so ripe, and so attractive."

"Don't you torment me, too, my dearest!" Joka reproached him sadly and with forced good humor, putting the pillow and blanket on her right shoulder. It would be quite natural if he, Mladen, a youth, should cast an eye on Jela, but Joka as she went away severely admonished him: "You would never be able to do anything like that—she is my daughter!"

"No, no, I couldn't," the youth replied with conviction. "But I was watching her while Boško was paying court to her. There's something wild in her, provocative, and yet she has your—how can I put it?—your good-humored generosity and gracious strength. Her dark eyes cut one like a blade, her full lips smile at one as from some great depth. She seems scarcely to touch the earth, and her breasts are firm as apples and threaten one like horns!"

Jela was an attractive cross between her father's sharp, fine features and her mother's soft plumpness, and though Joka had always been aware that her daughter was beautiful, only now did she realize that the girl's beauty was an unbridgeable gulf between them—as if she had been born again in that beauty, and yet had died in it.

It was a full hour's walk from the town to the mineral spring, but Joka met her daughter and Boško about halfway, amid the scattered crowd, in the twilight that smelled of dried leaves and was fresh with bluish shadows.

Joka was embarrassed at finding herself among the crowd, which, carefree and tipsy, tottered along the path, and began to make excuses: she had happened to be in the town and had walked out to meet them. Boško was not drunk; he drank rarely and little. He began to tease her before everyone. Then he added softly and mockingly, twisting his lower jaw, but loud enough for Jela and Milena to hear: "You remembered too late. Anyway you, too, were amusing yourself with someone else."

Though he was not inconsiderate, he always, if anyone crossed him, became sarcastic, enjoying his own sarcasms: thus he had never been able to be reconciled if she, for any reason, cut short his enjoyment of love. But it was only necessary to smile at him and show a little tenderness, and he would at once cease his sarcasms and become merry again, forgetting all his misunderstandings and mishaps. He easily lost his temper, but also, as soon as he had vented his anger, he was quick to repent.

This time Joka, even had she been inclined to break down his bitterness with jests or entreaties, could not do so before Jela. She retorted angrily: "What a mess! No wonder I'm worried!" and took her daughter by the left arm and pulled her away.

Boško stood for a moment as if he wanted to say something, but only clenched his teeth angrily, shook his head, and went on his way, his broad shoulders swaying more than usual and his thin, white fingers twitching. Milena remained standing there as if making up her mind, but when Joka ill-humoredly brushed past her, she ran and caught up her brother. Jela, not looking at her mother, broke away from her grasp and remarked harshly and bitterly: "You'd think I was a cow! I'm grown up now. I can look after myself!"

Joka thought of snapping at her: "Be quiet, shameless one! Is that the way to talk to your mother?" Then she remembered that her daughter not only knew why her father had sought and obtained a divorce, but might also have heard rumors that Boško had been her mother's lover, and so, feeling herself in the wrong before her daughter, she restrained herself, muttering: "We'll talk of that later, when we're alone."

They walked on for about half an hour in tense silence, toward the new moon rising over the valley in the greenish freshness of the hills, each wrapped in her own rancor and indignation.

But beyond the bend, at the crossroads where the path led to Boško's house, Boško was waiting for them, eager to spit out his anger: "You're too late, Joka. Have you forgotten what you were like when you were sixteen?"

"If I'm too late, or if I've forgotten—Jela is not going to follow my path," Joka retorted without stopping.

Boško went on up the path to his house, whistling to express his self-satisfaction, and Joka turned and hastened toward the little bridge hidden among the alders.

"Jela is not going to follow my path." Those words, spat out in fury, now seemed to her the most fateful and decisive in her opposition to Jela's and Boško's love. Though it was probable, after Boško's mocking words, that she was too late, that what had passed between Boško and Jela had irrevocably set Jela on her mother's path, those words, once said, gained a special, until then unsuspected, significance.

Though she had not previously thought too much about her way of life, it had seemed to her more and more, even when there were difficulties, as about the divorce, that it had been bearable, even enjoyable. Even when they had been in the village and in penury, she had been able to live comfortably and, though she was no whore, had always been able to satisfy her desires. It helped that she was of a tolerant, even mild, disposition and, though she was not a liar, did not strive too hard to keep to the truth—for insistence on the truth poisons friendships and embitters enjoyment no less than taking refuge in lies. She avoided clashes, except when there was no other way out, and cheated in love, though not overmuch—according to circumstances. Often her lovers had deceived and abandoned her. Words of love are not in any case to be taken seriously. Passions express themselves in sonorous and unreal phrases so that they may appear more beautiful and more passionate. Sometimes, to be sure, she was seized with a sense of sin because of her adulteries, but it was neither deep nor lasting, and she quickly found a remedy, usually in confession. For it was strange but incontestable that after prayer and confession everything was sweeter, even though, or even because, it was more evident and unambiguous. So whenever she began to lose measure, whenever her passions became transformed from pleasure and ecstasy into rough and forced orgy, when it was hard to put a brake on her sins, she would pray wholeheartedly to God in the old church at the end of the town and ask Him to forgive her. She would make her humble offering and go to confession to the old priest who would by habit and almost jestingly remark: "You, my dear, once again for sins of the flesh?" and she frankly and humbly would reply: "Once again, father. What can I do since God so created me?"

Thus she had weathered her difficulties, and life was what life is—joys and sorrows intertwined, ebbing and flowing like the tides. The best thing in life was that evils and misfortunes could quickly be forgotten and that always—just for that reason, for she never asked from life more than life could give—there arose new, deeper, and more final joys and sweets.

So not even now, despite the harshness and conviction of her words—that her daughter, Jela, must not follow the path she had trodden—did Joka, looking back over the whole of her life, regret that it had not been better or wish that it had been different.

Comparing herself with her daughter, she had to confess that she had lost her virginity consciously, eagerly, and joyfully, in her sixteenth year, to a big, heavily mustached captain, a widower three times her age, who had come home on leave and had spied her—as he wandered about the pastures hunting—a shepherd girl eager to be led astray. Her mother, her suspicions aroused, had become angry and embittered, perhaps even more so than Joka was now about Jela, and had forbidden her to go out again with the sheep. Perhaps her parents' suspicions and the gossip in the village had been the main reasons her parents had hastened to marry her off in another village. She recalled now that she had been secretly resentful of her parents because they had stopped her association with the captain, the more so as she suspected that there had been some love passages between him and her mother; in truth, Joka when still a little girl had seen her mother, Doca, tenderly brushing dust from the captain's gray military greatcoat.

Nonetheless, despite the similarity between Jela's destiny and her own, and the beauties and values of her life which Joka recalled and summed up as she walked the hundred yards across the meadow, as soon as she reached the little bridge she almost burst out once more: "As long as she does not follow my path!" Even after crossing the bridge and walking with her daughter across the fallow field, her obvious lack of logic and the similarity of her destiny and her daughter's drove her to repeat to herself: "As long as she does not follow my path!"

Jela walked behind her with head bent, but obviously neither humble nor ashamed. She looked neither at her mother nor straight in front of her, but now here, now there. She walked firmly and easily, with a noisy tapping of her shoes. In the greenish mingling of twilight and moonlight, Joka suddenly noticed how strangely, terribly beautiful her daughter was. She was more like her father as a youth. With her clear-cut, finely drawn features, she seemed to be hovering and soaring in the heights, whereas Joka's compactness and heaviness had grown out of the earth. Jela did not have anything sharp, bony, or harsh about her; her father's features had been rounded and softened by her mother's feminine fullness. She was supple but not unusually tall, and her firm and, for her years, rather full breasts swelled proudly in her white silk blouse. This evening her lips were dark-red, clear-cut, and full. They stood out sharply on her long pale face. Her dark eyes were made still darker by the night, and perhaps also by rancor—she was of a violent, capricious temper, in contrast to her mother's mild and peaceable nature and her father's cunning and resolution.

From the bridge to the house was no more than ten minutes' walk, first over the level meadow and then up the stony stubble field, beside the spring under the cherry tree. Bewildered by her own confusion, astounded by her daughter's beauty, and fearful of a clash with her, Joka, walking in front, remained silent and forced herself to concentrate on her thoughts and memories.

Her recollections flowed smoothly on and condensed into memories of her youth, of the big, sullen, and rather unskillful captain at the moment when she gave herself to him in the thickets above the village. The morning dew was still glistening, and she could smell the tobacco from the captain's black mustaches, the berries, and the moist earth. The gleams in the sky kept disappearing and reappearing, the leaves quivered on their long stems, and the huge tufts of grass brushed around her face, so that they and the scents became a part of her, were transformed into her painful, inquisitive, and sweet ecstasy. Now she trembled in the moist night and felt shame for her daughter, so indescribably lovely, so indestructibly young, whom she had forbidden to follow her own, her mother's, path.

The memories came of themselves, and thinking of them did not worry her. But it was hard to find words to draw her obviously rancorous and obstinate daughter closer to her. So, without words, they reached the cherry tree and the spring. It was now only a stone's throw to the house. Panting as if from fatigue, recalling with displeasure that it was right here, on the meadow, that she had for the first time surrendered to Boško, unprepared and more curious than excited, she sat down by the spring to talk things over with her daughter. Jela stood on her left, looking back the way they had come, perhaps at Boško's house, from which a single lighted window shone through the darkened garden.

"Give me some water," Joka ordered her daughter, though she herself was nearer the spring.

Jela passed silently in front of her, took water, and handed it to her mother in a tin cup. The chill of the water aroused Joka's thirst and she drank it down, and while she was doing so Jela began to wash herself.

From above, from Joka's house, the old house dog barked two or three times. Jela straightened up, shaking her wet hands. Silver drops rolled down her face and hands, and though the impression of that first love meeting with Boško was still ineradicable, Joka burst out—or so it seemed to her—with those so long pent-up words: "I have no one under heaven but you! And you have no one but me! I alone worry about your happiness."

Joka, too, had been an only child. Or, rather, she had become an only child when two younger brothers died of the Spanish flu. But it could be said that her mother, Doca, had become more indulgent to her daughter's peccadilloes just because of her brothers' deaths. No, that had happened later, when Joka's deception of her husband had been hard to conceal and Mother Doca had grown older. Nonetheless everything was different for Jela. Jela was still a girl, young and pure, and for her it was too soon to follow her mother's path. Furthermore, Joka as a girl had obeyed her parents, especially her mother, having inherited all her ingenuity and cunning, whereas Jela was unbending and obstinate and could—that was the worst!—always return to her father or run away, leaving ruin and desolation behind her. Now Jela was listening, her face still gleaming with moisture, but without a smile, without a movement, with a hard, resolute face, as if her mother had not tried to draw closer to her.

Joka went on: "You should tell me yourself, as to a sister, if something troubles you—so that I could help you. Who could be dearer to you, who could be more true and faithful to you than your own mother? I don't know what there is between you and Boško—I can see that something is hatching, and already people are beginning to gossip about you. But you can lose your reputation. I do not believe that his intentions toward you are serious—an educated man, son of a landowner, he will be looking for a better catch. Perhaps I was wrong, am wrong, but you must take care, keep your eyes open. A reputation can be lost in a minute. Who will take you if it is rumored that you have been playing about with other men? Tell me what he wants, what he says to you. What is there between you?"

The girl at last looked down, but replied with ill-humor: "What should he promise me? I am not a baby."

When she was a girl, Joka would not have dreamed of talking so to her mother; she had had to choose her words, put a brake on her tongue. Even now, at least outwardly, something of that subordination remained in her relationship with her mother. Jela, however, was of a new generation, a girl grown up without a mother's care according to her own wild, independent moods. Joka decided not to stretch, not to break, the delicate threads she had woven with such care between her and her daughter.

"You are not a baby—and yet you are. What do you know of love, of life?"

"What is there to know? I like Boško."

"You like him? And does he like you?"

"He likes me. At least he says he does."

"At least! He says so! Does he like you or doesn't he?"

"He likes me, I think."

"And what else? What is there between you? What happened today?"

Jela made no answer, still gazing vaguely about, drawing a vizor over her face.

"Did he promise you anything? Since he told you—that he likes you? What did he mean?"

Jela shifted, gazing rigidly at her mother. "Why do you ask me so many questions?"

"Why? But I am your mother! I want to help you."

"Well, that's it . . . he said he likes me."

"Did he touch you? Did he try to kiss you?"

Jela's face hardened, and that invisible armor became harsher and darker. Joka went on relentlessly: "You must tell me everything. I can't let you run around wherever you like and meet anyone just like that." She rose, carried away by her own words. "What will your father say, if he comes to know? You are everything to me—my life and my happiness. You mustn't meet Boško again. If he has anything to say, let him come to me—I am your mother."

Jela said: "I will still see Milena," but Joka cut her short: "No, not her!"

"But whom can I see?"

"No one. Me. Milena—is a procuress."

As if searching for the right word to provoke her mother, Jela turned and, looking straight at her with her dark eyes icy in the moonlight, sarcastically interrupted: "Perhaps you're saying all this because you are jealous."

At first Joka was bewildered. Yes, her daughter must have heard of her flirtation with Boško. The meadow in front of her, just to

the right of the spring—the place of her first union with Boško—
oppressed her with a sullen, insuperable, abysmal weight. This
was no longer a sin that could be absolved by confession, for it
had begun to have a life of its own independent of her, in space
and things, and her daughter's suspicions and reproaches whipped
and goaded her. She was filled with fury, so unfamiliar, dark, and
uncontrolled that she longed to tear off all her clothes together
with pieces of her living flesh. She seized her daughter by the
shoulders and, shaking her, shouted: "Pfui! Shameless one! Just
because of that you must not go with him! You should sink into
the earth, shame on you!"

Jela remained silent, inscrutable, slowly freeing herself from
her mother's hands. Joka's fury began to lessen. She was sorry for
it and was filled with fear that her daughter would run away. She
seized Jela by the elbow and dragged her toward the house. "From
now on you'll not take a step outside the door! Do you hear? I'll
soon deal with Milena—I'll put her tail between her legs! Whatever has been has been. I am your mother and it is my duty to
look after you and preserve your reputation. As for you, you
ought to be ashamed!"

When they got near the house, the dog greeted them with
yelps. The dog loved Joka most of all, though she never patted
him or stroked his head. As she arrived in front of the house, she
grew angry with herself and decided that for the moment she
would say nothing to Mother Doca.

As they entered, Doca—perhaps she had heard the quarrel near
the spring, or perhaps she could read something from their flushed
faces—looked at them questioningly with her small green eyes
beneath broad black brows and remarked with icy preoccupation,
as her mother had certainly done before her, or her mother's
mother: "There are bad people everywhere! I was worried. I
didn't know you two were together." Neither daughter nor granddaughter made any reply, but went inside.

While her mother was busy with supper, it occurred to Joka to
strip off her daughter's blouse and look at her breasts and

shoulders for the marks of Boško's lips or teeth. But she refrained, because of Mother Doca's peace of mind, because of her daughter's resistance, because of herself; no one, not even she, the mother, had the right to do that. Driven once more to fury by these thoughts, she clenched her fists, pressed one into the other, and shook them over her daughter's head, scarcely touching her heavy raven-black curly hair, which fell in thick tresses over her smooth, tender, rounded shoulders. "Woe is me, unlucky one! I could kill both you and myself!"

Yet she was only speaking sinister and threatening words as in moments of passion she spoke fiery and endearing ones. She herself knew that she was not able to do anything to her daughter other than forbid her to leave the house. Joka even refused Milena's invitation, two days later, to sit one afternoon with her in the garden. That day, for the first time, afraid that her daughter would find out, she did not slip away for her meeting with Mladen, leaving him to look for her in the willow thickets in vain. She tried to be as considerate as possible to Jela, to woo her with food and with words, to bury their quarrel in oblivion.

But nothing could repair the broken threads, weak and uncertain on her daughter's side. Jela remained withdrawn in silence and sulks, and her sullen tenseness was even transmitted to Mother Doca, who moaned more and more openly, foretelling misfortune and hinting to her daughter to tell her what was the matter. So the week went by and another one began.

On Saturday, which was market day, Joka had to go into the town, and she was of two minds about what to do with her daughter, whether to take her or leave her at home. Thinking it over, she decided to take her daughter along in order to keep an eye on her. Mother Doca still did not know anything for certain, and was so lenient with her granddaughter that she could refuse her nothing. Therefore Joka ordered her daughter to get ready to go with her to town.

While Jela was dressing and getting ready, Joka stood in front of the house and looked at the village and the road, along which groups of men and animals were passing. There was no signal for her in front of Mladen's house, no invitation to a love tryst, and down below, on the edge of Boško's garden, someone was sitting in the shade and reading a newspaper—certainly Boško. For who else knew how to read? He must be watching, over the top of the page, to see when she, Joka, would be going to town and whether she would take her daughter with her. That annoyed Joka, and as soon as Jela was ready she hurried off through the woods, so that she could at least avoid a meeting with Boško or Milena, and so that they would not be able to give a signal to Jela.

There is always something that every mother, and Joka among them, when meeting friends or acquaintances, does not want her daughter to hear; also, Joka had to haggle over the sale of her produce. In the crush Milena or someone else could whisper to Jela or she to them. Joka therefore thought it would be best if her daughter stayed with a relative, whose house in a secluded garden was on the outskirts of the town.

But that evening, when she went to the relative's house, Jela was no longer there. They told her: "She got bored with waiting and left for home with one of her girl friends two or three hours ago." So her daughter had outwitted her.

Tired and sweaty, Joka hurried to the village. When she reached the crossroads by the bridge, she thought that Jela might be in the garden at Milena's, so she went by the road and not the path through the woods. The road, dusty and mud-caked, stretched out before her, and she could not decide what to do about her disobedient daughter. She felt instinctively, both as woman and mother, that Jela was even then at a love tryst with Boško and was giving herself to him, while she hurried along the path, which seemed as if it would never end, stubbing the stones with the toes of her heavy, clumsy shoes. She tried to convince herself: perhaps it was not so, perhaps Jela really had been bored and had gone with Milena just to spite her mother; after all, Milena was her girl friend, she wanted to be with her, and for the last ten days she had been as if in prison. Though in life nothing

ever turned out as well as one hoped, misfortunes were often not
so bad as anticipated.

Once again the details of love trysts appeared before her eyes,
not her own this time but Jela's and Boško's, without yearnings
and caresses, transformed into crude, naked couplings. Somewhere
in the depths of her conscience she felt ashamed to think this way
of her own daughter and to see her in such a role. And even as
now she was not thinking of her own experiences with Boško, he
seemed to her, though she could still feel vague and inextinguish-
able tremors in her body, a strange and alien male, one scarcely
known to her, who lusted for and incontinently fell upon the
modest, inexperienced beauty of her daughter.

She was choked and blinded by the yellowish dust churned up
by the flocks of unsold lambs in the stuffy heat of the valley. She
looked forward to those moments when the midday heat gives way
to the freshness of evening, when the mind is still clouded with
desires and the tortured body looks forward to the breezes from
the mountains and the coolness and sweetness of the night. Her
blood beat in her temples and her limbs felt heavy in the heat,
but she knew this was not due to yearnings and passions, but to
worries, heat, and anger.

When she reached the end of the path that followed the dried-
up stream toward Boško's house, Joka stood on a mound and
called to Milena. But no one replied—perhaps, she thought, because they could not recognize her voice, suddenly tense and
hoarse. She called again, more loudly, this time in her normal
voice. Milena, in a white dress, came out in front of the house and,
turning toward Joka, stood as if thinking.

"Were you calling me?" she asked at last.

"I was. Is Jela there?"

The girl answered after a pause: "No. She didn't come."

Joka went on standing there, uncertain what to do next. It
seemed to her that what she had been thinking was not only ex-
travagant but stupid, that Jela could be with Milena and not at a
love tryst with Boško. But since the girl remained standing in

front of the house, as if she wanted to say something more to her, Joka asked: "Did you come back together?"

The girl was again silent, longer than before. "We did," she replied, "but she didn't come in to see us. Why don't you come up?"

Joka did not reply. In her haste to get away she almost slid down the steep slope. She hurried across the meadow, but at the little bridge had to slow down. As if she had picked up the scent, she concluded that Jela and Boško must be somewhere in the vicinity. Coming out onto the meadow, she stopped and almost without meaning to called her daughter so loudly and shrilly that once again she did not recognize her own voice.

She listened, gazing around at the yellowing and darkening fields, at the hills rich with greenery, at the white houses and the already violet gardens. But no one replied, no one came. She called once more, with the full force of her lungs and in her own voice.

Her mother came out in front of the house. But she did not reply either. She did not ask her daughter why she was calling Jela. Her appearance nonetheless told Joka that Jela was not at home, and her silence reminded Joka that she, too, must remain silent.

Joka broke off. There came from her only a strangled cry. She knew in a flash; there was no use calling, the worst had happened. Even her own mother would not answer. It must be that the old woman sensed, perhaps had noticed, where her granddaughter had gone and remained silent, motionless and voiceless. Against the white wall of the house she seemed like a raven, a bird of ill omen.

Joka had to do something. Weak, helpless, peering around, she suddenly saw the pear tree with its rough, dark bark in the soft green thicket, that same tree under which she had exchanged caresses with Boško and under which she had seduced Mladen. It was there, too, that she had become aware of her opposition to the relationship between Jela and Boško, only a few days before, when she had left Mladen unsatisfied and unsatisfying and had hurried home to find her daughter.

Lovers—she knew from her own rich and long experience—caress each other and give themselves to each other at any time and in the most incomprehensibly unsuitable places. No one knew better how to choose convenient and hidden corners. And nowhere on the steep slopes, overgrown with bushes, was there any better place for a daily love tryst than under the pear tree. One could get to it unseen, either by the path from the town or through the alder thickets at the edge of the meadow till one reached the bushes about a hundred yards from the little bridge over which Joka had just passed. Joka herself used to go there with Boško. As they went along the path and over the open field they could be seen from the village, but after they reached the meadow the only person who could see them as they went downstream was Mother Doca, since Joka's was the only house on that side. The meadow was subject to floods and was not a suitable place for a meeting by night, except on the slope by the cherry trees, and by day the two of them had gone under the pear tree, right up to the time when they ceased to hide from Mother Doca, when she accepted their liaison and prepared the bedroom for them. They even had their own path, along a ditch where the bushes were bigger and yet more open so that their clothes did not catch on the thorns or get tangled in the twigs. But that was a roundabout way. In a straight line it was not more than three hundred yards away—rather less than to the house. And just as the house welcomed and summoned with its whiteness, so now the pear tree, just above Joka, threatened and excited her with its twilit, dense greenery and wide, seductive strength.

Joka rushed madly across the meadow, straight toward the pear tree, stumbling into the ditch while trying to jump over it. She was assailed on all sides by the dense thickets of hazels, beech and oak scrub, dog roses and blackthorn. She saw at once that she had made a mistake. She would have reached the pear tree more quickly had she gone the roundabout way, down the meadow, by the familiar path. But by going back she would lose many seconds, and each second was vital and unbearably long. She forced her way through, paying no heed to hundreds of thorns and branches that pierced and pained her.

Boško and Jela would certainly have heard her call, could have seen her as she drove straight at them across the meadow, and could not have failed to hear the rustle of leaves and the crack of rotten twigs. But she did not care. She only wanted to get there as quickly as possible, to reach her daughter and prevent Boško from taking her virginity, so that Jela would not follow the path that she herself had trodden and that had become unthinkably, inexplicably terrible as soon as she realized her daughter might follow it. She no longer had any doubt, as she wrestled with the thickets, that Boško and Jela were under the pear tree; it was as if she could see them, as if she were already fighting, wrestling, to defend Jela.

She at last broke through to the path, about ten yards to the left of the pear tree. She rushed toward it along the well-trodden path.

There was no one there. The sparse rough grass under the pear tree told her nothing. She could not hear a sound; no one was hurrying away. There were no traces and no signs. Joka began to sniff the earth, searching for the strong, bitter, male smell of Boško. She went over it on all fours and then sat down under the pear tree, leaning against its rough, dark, knotted trunk.

From the village she could hear the usual calls and bleatings, the mill clacked, the twilight thickened around her, the sunset flamed red over the hilltops. Tired, frustrated, ashamed, she went home as soon as she had recovered her breath.

She saw Jela sitting on the little bench by the wall in front of the house, her head resting on her right palm, watching as Mother Doca milked the cow, pushing aside the calf trying to reach the udders. They did not notice Joka, or, in enigmatic silence, pretended not to notice her, until the dog made her arrival rapturously known.

On the way into the house, Joka touched her daughter on the brow, to awake her from her trance and find out if she were sweating. The girl remained motionless, but her forehead was moist and her face flushed as after running or after the act of love.

"How dare you leave town without asking me?" Joka asked, panting heavily.

The girl remained silent, frowning sullenly as usual.

"Who was with you?" Joka insisted more and more furiously.

"You know very well," Jela replied provocatively, then rose and went into the house.

Joka turned to her mother, who was standing with the milking pail in her right hand, her left clamped to the small of her back, as she did when she expected a change in the weather and complained of aches and pains. Mother Doca behaved as if she had heard or seen nothing. There was no sense in involving Doca in her misfortunes, especially if it were a question of Boško, of Boško and Jela, about whose liaison she perhaps knew nothing. But this time she must have it out with her daughter, and Joka went resolutely into the house.

But before she had stepped over the threshold she heard steps behind her and, turning around, saw Boško, in white canvas shoes, swaying his broad shoulders in that teetering walk of his, coming from behind the outhouse and moving toward the house. He called out a greeting to Mother Doca and then, sighing as if tired and angry, sat down on the bench, crossing his legs. "Light the lamp, Joka," he shouted at her in his usual commanding manner. "I want us two to have a talk."

At that moment Joka would have liked to kill him, even wondered if it were not her duty to snatch the ax from behind the door and drive him out into the courtyard. But that would be ugly, the whole scandal would break, and not even she herself would be able to understand her action. He had come to her house, and she, she had assailed him with harsh words and an ax! After all, how was he to blame? Wasn't it said: till a bitch wags its tail a dog will not worry it? Jela, after all, was more to blame.

After standing a moment, almost calm, Joka obediently went into the house to light the lamp. At the door she collided with her daughter and, astonished, stood aside for her. As she went into the room, she looked out from the darkness through the court-yard window to see how Jela behaved toward Boško. The girl sat down on the little bench beside him, though there was scarcely room for two, and he did not move to make way for her. There was something slavish, humble, and yet unashamed in Jela's atti-tude, something ingratiating and compulsive. It was only because her mother and grandmother were there that she did not sit on his knee. It showed that something had taken place between those two to make the proud and arrogant Jela dependent on him and humble toward him. So are all women when they have given themselves to the men they have chosen, and modern girls are also arrogant and insolent. Now there was nothing Joka could do, especially with Boško and her mother there. She suddenly felt that she had no more strength. She could no longer do anything, so she busied herself with the task for which she had gone inside.

At first she could not remember where the matches were, and when she found them on the shelf behind the door, she noticed that there was not enough oil in the lamp and that its chimney was far from clean. In the summer they used the lamp only long enough to eat their supper and prepare for bed, so that it re-mained for a long time untended. The oilcan was in the anteroom that served as a kitchen. Going in there, Joka noticed from the doorway how those two on the bench were smiling and whisper-ing, while Mother Doca tethered the cow to the fence below the outhouse. Feeling still more helpless before her daughter, Joka went back into the room.

But just as she had lit the lamp and was kneeling down to con-trol the height of the flame with a litle screw, Boško came in with-out a word, as at one time when he used to come to her. He did not sit on the bench under the window but on the high iron bed, into which he sank so deeply that his legs scarcely touched the floor. As she was hanging the lamp between the windows, he asked her, as if continuing their conversation, in his familiar slightly mocking manner, she knowing though she did not turn around that his mouth had relaxed into a grin: "Why are you angry with your daughter? Have you gone crazy? As if you don't know what youth wants!"

"But she is innocent!" Joka turned, looking angrily at him. "She is still a girl! She will have to get married. Would you marry her tomorrow?"

Boško took off his black-rimmed glasses and, rubbing his eyes as shortsighted people do when their eyes are tired or dazzled, went on, needling her: "I'm not yet thinking of getting married. And as far as her innocence goes, she is as innocent as you were when you bore her."

"What! Surely you didn't . . . ?"

"No, I didn't. She was no virgin when she came to you. But that is of no importance in this case. There is no sense in persecuting her or getting angry. Look at today. We two were hidden in the alders, there at the foot of the meadow, and you kicked up as much row as if the house were on fire. Jela had to run as if the devil were after her to reach home before you. You of all people, who knows very well how men suffer without that, even monks and nuns."

Joka stood in front of him, in the center of the room, her hands dangling. She waited until he put on his glasses. When he had done so, smoothing his dark bushy eyebrows, she said: "But she is my daughter! Have you forgotten what there was between us and what we said to each other? How can you now, with her? Aren't you sorry? Aren't you ashamed?"

Boško jumped up from the bed and stood close to her, putting his hand on her shoulders in a friendly way. "You of all people should understand. You must! You will understand! I know you. With her it was as it was with you. Only a little fresher, more innocent—always unexpected. Perhaps her likeness to you first drew me to her. In the beginning it was more or less a joke, a sort of fiendish curiosity. I began to tease her, to kiss her, and suddenly

I discovered you in her—unknown, as if you were a young girl.
Now there is no way back. I will take care that no one finds out.
But if you persecute us as you did today, then all hell will break
loose. For we two will go on meeting, even if the whole world
knows."

She looked up at him, at his smooth chin and rather wide nostrils and somewhat thick, bony nose. His face was pale. He had
never given way to any passion, except that of love. Now she
realized this more strongly than ever and could see from his well-
known yet nonetheless new face that he had no ability, no wish,
to hold himself back.

"And she?" Joka asked. "How will she . . . when she knows
all that there was between us?"

"I myself noticed that she knows all about us, though we have
never talked of it. It would be no use denying it. It even attracted
me. Once she said: 'I am my mother's daughter.' I don't know
what she meant by that unless 'You attracted me as you did her,
and I must live as she does.' And she suspects about you and
Mladen. She said: 'Mama now loves youths, and I—more mature
men.' "

Joka was silent, overwhelmed not so much by the revelation
that her daughter was not chaste—that no longer seemed to her
so terrible, for many girls married unchaste, and she herself had
gone to her bridegroom after her love affair with the mustachioed captain—as by the abundance and certainty of her daughter's
experience, and above all by the incontestable similarity between
her own and her daughter's youth. Certainly there were differences: perhaps the captain had not been her mother's lover, or
at least Joka had never known for certain; and she had had to
conceal more than Jela did. But the resolution to try out love in
all its forms and to the utmost—that was the same for her and
for Jela. Boško had not told her that in so many words. But she
had known it from his determination not to give up Jela; Jela
had bewitched him with sweets and juices sweeter and fresher
than hers, Joka's, had been. Still more definitely was it confirmed

by the sense of Jela's words, which Boško had inadvertently quoted to her a few moments before: Jela, her daughter, so young, now preferred more mature men. As if Joka up to that moment and until that realization had forgotten her girlhood, the whirl-pools of passion among the scents of the hayfields, the bellowing of the bulls and the moist paleness of the moonlight, the tension of her body and the swelling of her breasts, her entrails which opened and summoned the mysterious, all-embracing world and the unknown and uncomprehended masculinity. Now her daughter was experiencing the same thing—it would have happened with no matter whom if she had not come upon Boško. Perhaps it was better that it had been him. He was neither boastful nor malicious; there was no danger that she would learn anything bad from him—she would learn only the enjoyments and skills of love.

"I feel lost," Joka uttered at last. "What do you advise me to do?"

Boško smoothed his silky, chestnut hair with his right hand, as always when he was undecided. "I can't tell you exactly. You are expert enough in these matters. Only—don't interfere with us."

Then, as if some new thought had flashed through his mind, he walked two or three times up and down the room and, halting by the window and looking out on the darkness of the valley, remarked: "Why don't you lend us a hand?"

"What are you thinking of? Me arrange the bedroom? I, here, before my mother, who did the same for us?"

Boško did not reply, continuing to gaze out into the darkness. Evidently he had been thinking much the same. Outside, in front of the house, there was silence, and Joka, through the open court-yard window, saw Jela in a white blouse, motionless, gazing into the valley, her chin in her hands as if waiting for her mother's judgment. From the anteroom could be heard the clinking of tin plates and spoons; her mother was preparing supper.

"Would you like to stay for supper?" Joka asked, in order to break the silence.

"No, I won't. I could, but I won't," he replied, not turning toward her.

She looked at his neck, over which curled locks of his hair; she remembered that many, countless, times she had smoothed her hand over that broad, stubbly neck. Now there remained something unfinished, unsaid, between them. He did not go away or turn around, though he irresolutely refused to stay to supper. She looked once again at her daughter there in front of the house; worried and angry, Jela had buried her head in her hands. Clearly Joka was an obstacle to those two, able to embarrass them but not to turn them from their desires.

"Nonetheless, I'll go and see what Mother Doca is preparing. Perhaps it's something you like," she concluded in a conciliatory tone.

Boško, fiddling with his fingers behind his back, did not reply.

Mother Doca was pouring out sour milk, and on the table a plate shone red with thin slices of dried ham, both of them Boško's favorite dishes. There was, too, a bottle of golden plum brandy; though he was no drinker, Boško would willingly enough toss off a couple of glasses while sampling the ham. Mother Doca was silently and relentlessly preparing a supper just to his taste.

"Mama, I beg you!" Jela called beseechingly and angrily, bursting into the light of the open doorway.

Joka stepped irresolutely across the sill, half closing the door behind her. Her daughter unexpectedly and with unrestrained and savage tenderness put an arm around her waist and, laying her head on Joka's shoulder, sobbed: "Do whatever you like, Mama, but I can't, I can't live without him!"

Joka gently put an arm around the girl's shoulders and led her back to the bench in front of the house. "Don't worry, joy of my heart. You are all mine, blood and body and all my happiness. Your mother will never do anything to hurt you." Little by little she appeased her daughter, drawing her to her breast and kissing her hair. Then, as when Jela was little, she combed her hair with her fingers and began to sing her a funny nursery rhyme. Once again a child in her mother's lap, the girl at last smiled, screwing up her eyes and wiping her face.

Through the window Joka watched Boško, who was still gazing into the night, and listened to his nervous whistling. Kissing her daughter on the forehead, she got up and went resolutely into the house as if she had remembered something important that could not be postponed.

Going into the anteroom, she remarked to her mother: "We will take the food for those two into the outhouse," and then went into the room, not shutting the door behind her. Boško turned, leaning with his hands on the window frame. She did not look at him, but slowly and deliberately took an armful of cushions and coverlets out of the chest, taking great care that they not trail on the floor, and went to the outhouse.

She noticed that all of them were watching her in silence. But no one looked directly at her, not even when she went back a second time, carrying pillows and a sheet. Returning a third time, she said to Boško, looking at him calmly and wearily, as if speaking to a stranger: "Go and get some rest."

He did not look at her, but smiled shamefacedly and went outside. She heard his sharp, harsh whisper and Jela's in reply, and then the footsteps of Mother Doca, carrying a tray with plates of food and the bottle of plum brandy, a little tin lamp in her other hand. In the mad dance of light and shadow, the three of them made their way to the outhouse. Joka threw herself face downward on the bed and burst into sobs.

She did not know how long she lay there, and she heard nothing until her mother's hand on her head aroused her. She got up, wiped away her tears, and said: "I'm getting old, Mother."

Mother Doca smiled sadly and wisely. "That is a woman's destiny. Come to supper. I must take them a jug of water. They'll be thirsty."

In prison, at Sremska Mitrovica
July–August, 1963

THE OLD MAN
AND THE SONG

To the young man from the Rovci tribe everything was new, and his friend Šćepan, the same age as himself, said: "Nowadays everything is getting younger in Montenegro. The Great Powers have exiled Mirko, the prince's uncle, and now the young prince has taken the reins of power into his own hands and is surrounding himself with younger men. Soon Montenegro will be revived and strengthened, after this unfortunate war. We up here on the heights have somehow or other managed to wrestle the Turks for a fall. But down there, among the lower Piperi, those who are nearer Zeta, everything has been burned down, and men are still living in lean-tos and cow stalls."

"I see, I see," Vuk agreed, though he could distinguish only wisps of smoke down where the yellowed meadows and dark fields ended and the bare stony land began. He could not see the lean-tos or the cow stalls, but was assured that they belonged to the Piperi, the neighboring tribe, with whom the men of Rovci, the Rovčani, from time immemorial had fought and made peace about the borders of mountain pastures, for the most part desolate. The Rovčani, immured in the distant Morača gorge, would not even have noticed that there had been a war, except for their casualties.

Vuk had never seen so wide a stretch of cultivated land as the expanse below him. In the golden, misty early autumn dusk, the gray-green cliffs and stony hillocks down in the swimming depths lost every harshness and roughness and looked like children's sand castles. As far as eye could see they merged with the mist and sun and the waters of the distant lake in the endlessness wherein Šćepan's finger pointed out shapes and places shimmering like water among the stony mountainsides, dark indigo in the dusk. "Do the Turks hold all that?" Vuk asked, stretching his arm toward the scene below.

"Well, how can I put it? They do and they don't," Šćepan replied. "They hold only Spuž and Podgorica. Those dark patches behind that low hill are the houses and walls of Podgorica. Spuž is far away to the right, a rock like a haycock in the fields; you can't see it from here. It is five or six hours' march from one to the other, and caravans pass only by day, with a strong escort, and that rarely. They have fortified positions on those two outcrops, Trijebač on that side and Velje Brdo on this. They guard the gorge that runs past Podgorica down to Zeta. But their life is harder than ours. They tremble at every bush and dare not stick their noses outside the walls except to raid the villages for cattle. The war devastated us, but it brought even worse terrors and troubles to them. Our sirdar, Jole Piletić, though he's getting on in years, brought back heads from Spuž itself, and the Kuči voivode, Marko Miljanov, has the Turks so shut up in Podgorica that they have to sit on each other's heads and shut themselves up before the first stars can be seen. You, too, will have to find somewhere to spend the night. It is getting late, and someone will have to row you across the river in a safe place, so that you don't run into a Turkish patrol or an ambush. You will be able to cross with one of our men tomorrow evening. Here even a madman does not act blindly."

Vuk knew he would have to spend the night somewhere, though he had hoped the crossing would be easier. He was bearing a letter from the Rovci voivode to the prince and hoped that he would be able to enroll in the *perjanike*, the prince's bodyguard. Except on the mountains he had never before been outside Rovci, away from the poverty-stricken rocks that seemed as if they would at any moment close and cover the cleft between them that was the sky. Though to him, young and eager and buoyed up by hope and by the task with which the Rovci voivode had entrusted him, everything seemed easy and possible, he had to pay heed to Šćepan's counsels. So the young men waited for the evening and supper, sitting in front of the house in earnest conversation that wiped away the Turkish evil and harshness and swept worry and fatigue into the darkening gulf of the plain.

Nonetheless, later, inside the house, the young man from Rovci found himself forgetting the impulse he had felt that afternoon looking down from the mountain heights and began to question Šćepan about the journey before him and the conditions of life among the Piperi. For though the house and property of Šćepan's father, Mašan, might have been considered poor, they were unexpectedly well stocked and comfortable by comparison with the reed hovels and stone huts on the precipitous ravines where the people of Rovci lived, often along with their cattle. The house was roofed with shingles and had an inner room as well as the wide, stone-flagged hearth by which they had had supper. On the soot-blackened shelves were countless copper and earthenware vessels—among the Rovčani, food was served only on wooden platters—and garlands of onions and all sorts of other things that Vuk had never seen before hung on wooden pegs. At table they had been served with sweet fruits, grapes and figs, which Vuk knew only from tales. The numerous members of the household, though in coarse and mended clothes, were gentler, more considerate, and—this he noticed especially—cleaner. Even the weak and helpless old man on the felt rug by the fire—certainly a dependent relative who had come here to die—was clean and well groomed, and, though he was almost blind and hard of hearing and paid no heed to the conversation or what was happening, he was treated with a courtesy that, while cold and habitual, was rare among the harsh and penurious Rovci even to their born fathers.

The Old Man and the Song

Though he racked his brains, Vuk could not call to mind any-thing in which he could take pride—nothing but the empty and naked Rovci heroism. After supper, in the bitterness of his be-wilderment and the Rovci poverty, he began to boast of the only thing he could, of the men of Rovci who alone had never paid tribute to the Turks, and of Rovci as the haven of refuge for haiduks and rebels from all Bosnia and Serbia.

They listened to him attentively, not reproving him, though they themselves had passed their days in struggle before the mouths of Turkish mortars and in the shadow of Turkish strong posts and standards. What was more, Šćepan's father, Mašan, black-browed and heavily mustached, rather similar in appear-ance to his son, began to praise the heroic fighters of the Rovci, whom hunger, penury, and isolation had never caused to waver but had strengthened in renunciation and sacrifice. It was pleas-ant to hear this from a man of an alien, even rival, clan with whom the men of Rovci had until recently been in vendetta and with whom there were yet many minor debts unsettled. But it also shamed Vuk, as if all this Piperi comfort and courtesy be-mused him, even as he had been stupefied by those boundless plains below him and Šćepan. The young man remained silent, realizing that the Piperi were in no way inferior in heroism to the Rovčani, though they had many times been forced to pay tribute, even though they had sometimes barred the way to the men of Rovci so that they could not go to Cetinje and Montene-gro. And so, as time passed and supper drew to an end, he found that there was less and less about which he could boast.

Looking carefully around him, he suddenly noticed that he could not see a gusle. It would have been hard to find a Rovci home without one. In the isolated shepherds' huts, in the winter, far from God and man, there had always been skilled guslari among the Rovčani. Their skill had become richer and more perfect thanks to the haiduks and refugees who brought with them new sounds and songs. Vuk himself was already a skilled guslar, and when supper was over and he had given thanks for the good food and hospitality, he remarked that he was surprised not to see a gusle in the house.

He nearly added, "And there is no real Serbian home without a gusle." But now wary in his judgment of the Piperi, he kept that back, allowing Mašan to reply: "Among us, gusle and guslari are getting rarer, though we are all eager to hear them. Do you, by chance, know how to sing and to play the gusle?"

Still wary, but eager to distinguish himself in some way before a strange and more civilized tribe, Vuk admitted: "Well, I can play fairly well—in the manner in which we of the Rovci play."

"All the men of Rovci sing well. Your speech is softer and is better for verses," Mašan said. "So, if you are not too tired . . ."

They brought the gusle, and about a dozen neighbors, with a horde of youths and children, came into the house.

Vuk knew many fine songs from ancient and from recent times, but he set aside the little-known song about Vuk Lopušina, which had originated and been perfected among the Rovci or the tribes nearby. At first he had thought he would sing that song and charm the men of Piperi with it, convinced that its vigor would please them as it pleased and excited him whenever he heard it. But as he was tuning the gusle and getting used to its tone, he remembered that in that song the Piperi leader Paun Šušović did not appear in any too favorable a light. To tell the truth, it was only a song, to which all sorts of things had been added to make it more beautiful, and it referred to long past times, but nonetheless it might offend his hosts and their neighbors, the more so since they, like the Rovčani and, indeed, all Montenegrins, were more sensitive to the words of a song than to any insult in everyday life; words remain, but in time other slights are carried away like water. While he was thinking it over, he realized that he could best repay the courtesy and praises of his hosts, and show them that not even the Rovčani were as bad as they were painted, if he sang them a song about the Piperi hero Savić Spasojev.

He began his song, carried away by his wish to excel and to repay such hospitality as he had never before experienced. They listened with almost religious respect, and at the same time looked at each other significantly and smiled uncertainly. Vuk interpreted this as recognition both of his skill as a singer and of his broad-mindedness in the choice of his song. Only the old man stirring up the ashes of the fire took no part. Warming his thin, almost transparent, hands at the fire, he turned from time to time toward the singer as if his weakened hearing and darkened mind had suddenly realized the marvelous, distant, and unknown past which was nonetheless still worth hearing about.

The song told how, in some long past time of bewilderment and terror, when the Turks strolled at their ease about Zeta and Morača, collected dues and tribute, and assaulted young women and girls, the hero Savić Spasojev rebelled against them and against the majority in the clan, and began to seek revenge and to root out the Turks in the name of justice and honor and of Serbia and Christendom. Around the solitary and outlawed hero, who had renounced home and property and even marriage, and every sweetness and joy, slowly collected a little band of madmen determined, to the death, to achieve their hopes, redeem their pledges, and win through despite the times in which they lived.

The song went on to tell how that little band of seven or eight comrades, by night and disguised, went to Podgorica to wipe out a notorious oppressor. On his way Savić left first one, then two, in hiding, until at last only he and one other crossed the Morača, slipped into the town, and approached the courtyard of the oppressor. Since his comrade did not dare to scale the wall and draw the bolt of the courtyard door, Savić ordered him to kneel, leaped on his shoulders, and drew the bolt himself. Then he rushed into the great room of the house and killed the oppressor. Tumult arose in the city. That comrade of his, frightened, fled toward the Morača, and Savić remained alone in the walled town, with himself and death, always terrible and different, no matter how many times a man faces it. His way back to the river was cut off, and he had nowhere to go except to the Vizier's Bridge, where the guards, now aroused, were awaiting him. Savić attacked the guards. One he cut down, another he wounded, a third he threw into the Morača, but a fourth slipped under his *handžar,* or long knife, and attacked him with a pistol. Missing the guard, Savić's blow struck the parapet and broke away a piece of it—and now the Podgorica Turks call that the Stone of Savić. But the guard hit him and broke the haiduk's leg. Nonetheless Savić dragged himself across the bridge. His band then entered the fight and caused confusion among the Turks, and the comrade who had been with him at the courtyard, hearing the noise of battle and overcome with shame, swam back across the Morača and bore off the wounded hero.

The song ended with the usual praises of the hero, the lament that such things had once been but were now only a memory, and a pledge for the health and good cheer of those who were listening.

But the praises did not come at once, as Vuk had hoped. It seemed as if the listeners wanted to take breath, and they once more began to look at each other. At last Mašan broke the silence: "You sing well, man of Rovci. It is wonderful how you have learned so young. Our thanks for the song. It is good for every Piperi to hear how one of our heroes is so well known among the Rovci. I have heard that song, but you men of Rovci have, I see, embroidered it and made it even finer. It is as if I were hearing it for the first time."

Then praises began to flow in from all sides. Only the old man remained silent and went on stirring up the fire. At last he sighed as if some long-forgotten sadness was rising from the embers, turned, and with inflamed, colorless, and lackluster eyes looked at those listening. Then, moving with difficulty, as if afraid he would break, he lay down on the felt and turned his back to the fire. The old man's face merged with the shadows, and from those present rose a sort of sad embarrassment, as if everyone had been expecting the weakened and ill-humored old man to say something; but he had disappointed them by his silence and his withdrawal to his usual place beside the fire.

The Old Man and the Song

Unexpectedly, Šćepan went up to Vuk, who, carried away by the exaltation of the song and the praises, had almost forgotten him, and asked him, taking the gusle from his hands: "Good, Vuk! And would you like to see Savić Spasojev, since you have sung so fine a song about him?"

Not sure that he was not being mocked, Vuk retorted: "How? Who knows when all that happened? Anyone seeing so great a hero would feel as if the sun were warming him."

Once again those present exchanged glances and smiles, but now more openly. Mašan even laughed aloud: "Eh, since you want to so much—this is Savić Spasojev!"

He pointed at the old man who was lying motionless, his face expressionless in the shadow.

Only then did Vuk look more carefully at the old man: dried-up, thin shinbones sticking out from the yellowed cloth trousers, caved-in bony shoulders, ugly and pitiful as if twisted and distorted, showing under the faded and mended jacket. The old man was bald and had scaly patches on the crown of his head, but long tresses of sooty hair fell over his neck. His sparse mustaches rose and fell as he breathed heavily and asthmatically. Most terrible of all was the old man's neck, wrinkled, rough, bare, and crisscrossed with tendons, as thin and fragile as that of a newborn babe.

Vuk looked in disbelief first at Šćepan, then at Mešan and the others. Their expressions confirmed that this was indeed Savić Spasojev, the man of the song that the man from Rovci had just sung. "Uncle Savić," Mašan said, in order to break the silence and also to reassure Vuk. "Did you hear how the men of Rovci have garlanded you tonight?"

The old man was silent, as if he were not listening or because he did not wish to be disturbed. At last he muttered, coughing, but not moving from his comfortable position: "I heard some of it. They've added and made up all sorts of things!"

Mašan waved his hand and smiled mournfully: "He's very old. He has lost interest in everything."

As if to console the old man, Vuk, and themselves, the men of Piperi began to recall Savić's exploits and his services to the clan, describing his onetime speed and beauty, his strength and courage. They recalled his winter loneliness, his many wounds, and his thirty years as a haiduk—up until about twenty years before, when he had been laid low with rheumatism and some cursed sort of asthma, so that from then on he could not go out of the house, still less think of bearing arms.

All this time the old man said nothing, as if he were not listening or as if they were talking about someone else. At last someone, perhaps in order to stir him from his lethargy, said that even he, Savić Spasojev, was unable to overcome fear; before a battle his teeth would chatter, and in order not to scare his band he would put his cap between his teeth. He knew himself better than anyone else did, and therefore he had been such a hero.

Then, finally, Savić spoke, with bitter ill-humor: "In those days I had some teeth." Then he raised himself with difficulty on his elbow, and, gazing vaguely at the men as if they were strangers, he went on: "Why are you repeating all that tonight? Let me rest! Then it was easy to be a hero. Guns did not carry as far as they do today. Now they have guns that are not loaded by the muzzle, but you can put a whole cartridge into them. They will kill both heroes and cowards."

Obviously accustomed to Savić's ill-humor and indifference, the Piperi began to disperse, a little offended and disillusioned, but still praising the singer and the song, as if it had not referred to the frail and worn-out old man beside the fire. Šćepan in a whisper asked Vuk, with the intention of putting him at his ease: "Are you glad to have seen Savić Spasojev?"

Eyes brimming with tears, Vuk replied: "No! It were better for me if I had never set out on this journey, or if I had broken my arm!"

In prison, at Sremska Mitrovica
March 1–3, 1966

A MONTENEGRIN JEST

Later it seemed even to me as if I had planned it all beforehand and carried it out according to the minutest detail. But I had not, or at least not really. If I had, what I am telling now would turn out somewhat different from what I wish, namely, to entertain and make my friends and comrades laugh. The fact is, men of my sort have a keen nose for possibilities and rush into everything pell-mell. Those who succeed, succeed; they are wise and farsighted. Those who fail, fail; they are stupid and cannot see beyond their noses.

That, in truth, is our job, if you can call it a job—to know what one must do and what one must not do; or, in other words, one must speak what one does not feel and think things that not even a madman would ever dream. But most important, at least while one is speaking and thinking, is to believe what one speaks and thinks, to believe in one's own sacrifice for the highest justice and the happiness of those whom we believe we represent. In our work that is a fact. If man is a living thing and life is always different, there is surely always something to be done, something to think and to speak. For that is politics—a profession that one chooses in spite of oneself and that a man is no longer able to renounce once he has tasted its sweets and its bitterness.

It was difficult to forge ahead. First of all, one was hampered by job seekers and upstarts from one's own party and, at the elections,

opponents who were not choosy about their methods, from brib-
ery and lies to beatings in the dark and theft of votes. If one was
an opposition candidate, as I usually was, then to hell with honor
and good repute when facing such dangers and troubles! I have
no love lost for the authorities, and they even less for me, though
I have shouted myself hoarse proving that I and my party alone
meant well to the state. On the other hand, there are always too
many authorities for the people; a politician must shout louder,
but he must make it clear that he stands for the people and is part
of them. It was especially difficult and impracticable for us of the
peasant party; one had to be a peasant, which one was not, and
dared not be a townsman and a gentleman, such as one would like
to be.

Though I have never been hungry or poor, I have tramped
about for months in peasant sandals, visiting Godforsaken hovels
and wolves' dens to which a raven would not bring its bones. I
have been a godfather more than two hundred times, have gone
uninvited to weddings and spoken funeral orations for men whose
names I did not even know. I have promised schools where there
were no children and church bells where there were no churches.
I have helped widows at harvesttime and presented cakes of soap,
combs, and mirrors to peasant women who never even washed with
lye or did their hair to make more splendid a beauty they did not
possess. I have become as austere as a monk when pretty girls
passed my way, and have been gentle and appreciative of bleary
eyes and curses from hags and spinsters.

Whenever and however, with whomsoever and in whatever task
. . . For one may think of everything and yet never be sure of the
people; no one knows what they are cooking or what is in the
pot. . . .

But I had never been able to get a toehold in the hamlet of
Vučje Zdrijelo, not merely because it was isolated and off the
beaten track but also because there was only one clan in it, so that
I could not even rely on what was nasty but easiest for me—stirring up clan jealousy and old rivalries by my derision. And there

were more than a hundred votes there, with the prospect of more to come, even as there were poverty, continual disease, and—without lights—going to bed at dusk.

It was just before the May 1 elections of '35. The dictatorship was at its harshest and was perverse and ruinous. Every vote was important; we must wear out and rip to pieces the threadbare and rotten sack of the dictatorship.

In Vučje Zdrijelo every man was for the government, as a flock of sheep follows its ram. They had, in fact, their ram—Commander Bajo, an old-fashioned blockhead whom no one had been able to move from his place though he had already passed his eightieth year and had a pretty good officer's pension—he who had never been an officer. For, as everyone knows, every Montenegrin, even if he has no right to a pension, considers that he has. Just for that reason every pension in Montenegro becomes an object of suspicion whether or not it has been deserved. Bajo's right to one could not be denied and nothing of the sort could be said of Bajo, seeing that he had been a leader of the Montenegrin home guard and later, after about three-quarters of these leaders had died, those remaining had been granted military ranks according to the size of the units they commanded. As a fighter right back to the war of '76, he might well have missed the old Montenegrin state and King Nikola, from whom no authority had ever kept Bajo whenever he wished to approach the king or had any cause for complaint. And surely Bajo would complain, since above his gospodar there was no one except the Lord Almighty Himself! But he, like the majority of the Montenegrin leaders, accepted a pension from the new state willingly enough, reconciling himself with the thought that he was growing old and that the very memory of the old state and its all-powerful but easily approachable ruler were gone forever.

I already new Commander Bajo by sight, though I had never been to Vučje Zdrijelo. My way had never led in that direction, and in recent times I had been repelled by the fact that all the men of Vučje Zdrijelo were supporters of the government. In the first years after the war, Bajo had ridden into the town every market day. But in recent years I had not seen him, probably because he had at last won his right to a pension and because of his great age. Perhaps I would never have heard of him again until the announcement of his death had not the elections intervened. Rumor had it that, in his hamlet, not only was there no opposition, but also the men of Vučje Zdrijelo would not even greet a supporter of the opposition if they met one on the road, much less allow any opposition candidate to hold a discussion with them or a meeting in their village.

Then, ten days before the elections, when it was already pretty well known who would vote for whom, my path led me not far from Vučje Zdrijelo, and I began to think: Who is it who holds the men of Vučje Zdrijelo together? What is it like among them? It was, of course, clear to me that what held them together was the old clan isolation and the habit of following their leader, in peace as in war. As the day was drawing to its close, it occurred to me to go there, even though my party comrades tried to dissuade me and not one of them would go with me. "Another of Markiša's follies," they said among themselves. "He will find his night's lodging among the wolves on the mountain and not in Vučje Zdrijelo."

But I knew that the doors of Vučje Zdrijelo would be open to me. Men of an older time, they would never refuse a night's lodging to no matter whom—if I did not stick my finger into the wasps' nest and start suggesting that they vote for me. So nothing of the sort even entered my mind, except perhaps in jest. I wanted to see what sort of men they were, and at least soften them a little for the future and let them see that I was neither wolf nor werewolf.

In the tumbled wilderness of stone, in the spring dusk that smelled of sun-scorched rock and fresh greenness, Vočje Zdrijelo, a tiny green valley that merged into the sky and the mountains, was more beautiful than I had expected and than its name—the Wolf's Gorge—suggested. The little one-story stone houses, with terraced gardens and outhouses, seemed to me pleasant and clean in the fiery rays of the sunset. For though, in my calling, one can work without song and without beauty, it is better with them. The girls at the spring were clean and pretty, as if they had just come out of the water and were basking in the sun. I could see from their curiosity that men rarely came there to ask for a night's shelter, but they welcomed me modestly and gaily and pointed out Commander Bajo's house—just the one I had guessed it would be, since it was in the middle of the village, the largest and finest house, and the only one with two stories.

I made my way toward it. Since I had already decided to enter the wolves' den, then it were best to go to the leader of the pack. On my way I noticed that the village was more compact than the usual Montenegrin village and thought to myself that their unanimity might be due not only to their clan exclusiveness but also to their need to remain closely linked with each other as a defense against the wolf and the haiduk, the tax collector and the harsh weather. Therefore I wondered how Bajo and the people of Vučje Zdrijelo would welcome me. I was not even sure they would recognize me, and wondered how I could appease them and put them in a good mood with my first words. But, as always, things turned out quite differently.

As soon as I turned into the little street by Bajo's house, there was a rustling and I heard my name mentioned. Someone had recognized me and was rushing to tell the news and give them time to recover from their wonder and embarrassment. I lengthened my stride, and as soon as I was in front of the house shouted: "Are the doors open to a good Serb and a wayfarer in a noble Serbian home?"

Within the house I could hear the sound of an old man's footsteps dragging on the flagstones and Bajo's voice, weak but still firm, though interrupted by coughing: "This house has never been closed to a Serb and a wayfarer." Then there was some whispering, and the old man added: "If he *is* a Serb, a good Serb, and a wayfarer—one who wishes us well." Unbelted, in threadbare clothes, with boots clean but unbuttoned on his bare feet, the old man appeared in the courtyard. He put his hand over his bushy brows, shielding his small, washed-out eyes, although there was nothing to dazzle them. "Who are you? What good fortune brings you to us tonight?"

Though I had always known him to be harsh and inflexible, even when at the height of his powers, I now realized that he was also cunning, with the inborn and ineradicable cunning of the simple peasant who considers that every townsman and every representative of authority exists only in order to deceive him. So instead of speaking simply, I broke into my spiel: "So your falcon eyes betrayed you that you did not know me, though we have emptied so many glasses together." I started thus against my will, for, as far as glasses went, we had neither drunk nor mourned together. But old men forget, and it is always pleasant to simple people, especially when younger men are present, when well-known men recognize each other.

I had just opened my mouth to say who I was when a dark youth leaped out of the house, one of those who go to school and who—even as I myself—are never tired of reforming the world. "Grandfather," he shouted, "I told you! That is Markiša!" And he added, more in earnest than in jest: "Take care! He's already beginning to win you over."

I at once felt, by that sixth sense which only men with a real gift for leadership and deception possess, that my most serious opponent would be this immature youth, and I called out: "What luck for me were I able to turn an old wolf from his path! I was overtaken by the darkness and my footsteps led me here, and I have always wanted to see how you live. But I will not force myself upon you. It would not be the first time I have had to spend the night under a beech tree. I came for no other reason—not to risk my reputation before men. But I see that among you everything is topsy-turvy; eggs have begun to teach hens."

The old man seemed irritated with his grandson, but lost nothing of his cunning. "There's no need to give me advice, child! I remember you, Markiša, of course I remember you, but I am getting blind and beginning to forget. Since you are here, you will not have to spend the night under a beech tree, as you have not come to sully my reputation or to divide Montenegro even more than when the Turks ravaged it and made the people turn to Islam."

It would have been senseless to argue with the old man, to prove to him that Montenegro under his gospodar had been still more bloodstained and tormented. To old men everything seems worse than it was in former times, and Bajo was obviously already living in some far off, mythical past from which he could not be brought back. Even had I wished to deceive the people of Vučje Zdrijelo with fair words, there seemed no prospect of gaining any advantage, so, in order not to drag matters out, I agreed with the old man that the divisions in the country were great and I would not think of plunging neighbors and clans into hatred and confusion, one against the other. But I added: "We are still all of us Serbs, and should it come to the moment of decision we shall be found united against the oppressor and the enemy of our union and of our state." So we went into the house, jesting and asking after each other's health and the spring crops and pastures.

In addition to two rooms facing us and a room to one side, the house had a wide hearth around which the householders of Vučje Zdrijelo quickly began to collect, partly out of curiosity and partly to down a glass or two of plum brandy. As if by agreement, no one mentioned the elections or politics, except that the youth—I learned that he was the old man's grandchild, a student teacher in his last year at school—kept making snide remarks, to which I retorted jestingly.

Unconsciously, as we toasted each other and exchanged jests and anecdotes, which as usual touched on long-ago battles and heroes, that other side of my character, always awake, collected and set in order my impressions, not ignoring a single word of the most innocent phrases.

Besides the grandson, Djole, there was the old man's son, Krsto, a peasant who obviously did not wear himself out with hard work. The old man had no other male children, since Djole's father, an officer, had died while in prison in Austria. Krsto had a whole flock of children, who peered at us inquisitively, forgetting to wipe their noses, while he behaved with noticeable reserve, smiling behind his twisted black mustaches, like a man who has something to say but will not interrupt the conversation between his touchy father and an unknown guest. He served the plum brandy and gave instructions to the womenfolk by winks and nods. Quite different was the behavior of Bajo's brother, Mrgud, so young that one might easily mistake him for a son, and in appearance also quite different, thin, dark, and toothless, whereas Bajo was stocky, heavily built, rugged. Mrgud seemed to be keeping watch on his elder brother, supposedly to correct him and interpret his words, but in actual fact he kept contradicting him and mocking him cunningly. He was obviously dependent on his elder brother but respected him only in words. But whenever Bajo grasped the sense of Mrgud's words he would burst out in sudden unconcealed anger, and the younger brother retreated quickly and hypocritically.

The old man could not stand being contradicted, and one could get the better of him only by cunning and ingenuity. Like all men who have at one time been outstanding, he considered that even now he was superior to others, the more so because he lived better and was wealthier. And as far as sense is concerned, no one will ever complain that he has too little sense, and to him especially nothing of the sort could ever occur, seeing that he had been the leader of the clan. His weakness was not so much in his obtuseness —he had an inborn peasant wisdom of the sort that is handed down unchanged even to the most unlettered—but in his assumption that he understood the new times and the new tensions better than anyone else. This had created a certain tenseness, in truth mild and transient, since everyone was submissive to the old man, both by tradition and because of his greater wealth and the reputation he had enjoyed even outside the clan.

A Montenegrin Jest

His grandson, Djole, was obviously the old man's darling; even when the old man was irritated with him, it was more in sorrow than in anger. Just because of the old man's tenderness, Djole was more and more opposed to me, despite the fact that he could not agree and did not agree with his grandfather's old-fashioned ideas, but clearly leaned toward the newer ones that were then spreading among young people. Every defense was good enough to use in such circumstances, so Djole made use of the old man's often muddleheaded and comical obstinancy. All my efforts to draw closer to the youth and to appease him were in vain. Even my allusion, at a moment when the others were not listening, that all the opponents of the dictatorship must agree and unite, for to create an opposition meant to blaze a trail for youth and new viewpoints and movements, did not make any special impression on him, though he did not contradict me. It was as if he wished to say: "Agree among yourselves by all means, but I will not allow you to outwit Grandfather, even though I do not agree with him." In truth the young man's sharpened awareness was of no significance, since there was no talk about the elections. And I noticed that he was considerate to me as a guest and helped me to get to know men and conditions in the village. Nonetheless, he was young and inexperienced, and considered that politics could be kept separate from hospitality and perhaps also from anything else.

So I passed the evening and before supper the peasants, except for the brother, Mrgud, and five or six householders, all withdrew. They laid the table in the big room, in the corners of which were two beds, clean and neat, where the old man and his grandson slept. We ate supper more quickly than is usual in such circumstances, partly because we had already sated our hunger with snacks and partly because I was tired and my hosts were not accustomed to long night sittings.

I myself do not know how, but, just after supper, the event happened that is the subject of this tale. I had already noticed the old man's obsession with death and had seized on it, but the episode began quite spontaneously. Someone made an allusion, or perhaps I myself asked, and the old man, sighing, informed us: "I have made all preparations for my burial, so that no one will be put to any trouble or expense on my account."

"He has even set up his tomb," added the ubiquitous brother, Mrgud. "And that, by God, more expensive than the houses of many of us."

I discreetly approved the old man's whim, and said: "So it should be. He will be there a long time, and in a house one lives only for a lifetime."

"You speak well," remarked the old man. "But he doesn't understand. He has not yet one foot in the grave."

"And tombs are not made for everyone," I commented.

Commander Bajo drew himself up and looked proudly at his brother and the peasants as if to say: "Do you hear what my opponent says?" but Mrgud broke in: "One must think also of the living."

The old man responded brusquely, with crafty bitterness: "Eh, had anyone else said that except my brother, whom I . . ."

"God save us," Mrgud went on hastily. "I meant nothing bad. I only wanted to say that the tomb is a very fine one, a very fine one."

That seemed to settle the dispute, but I, seeing a chance of stirring up the brothers and entering more intimately into the affairs of Vučje Zdrijelo, asked: "Certainly, old friend, you have, as becomes you, made ready your burial clothes?"

Djole, not without sarcasm, remarked: "What should become him more?"

The old man paid no attention, but retorted: "Yes, indeed, six years ago—the best that could then be found in the market."

I jested: "And surely you have found mourners, to sing your funeral songs? But, Commander, you should find some younger singers, so that your heart could rejoice when young lips and fine eyes mourn your passing."

Mrgud smirked and said: "You are joking. He is so old now that two of those he chose have already died."

"It was not I who chose them." Bajo, all ears, turned on his brother. "But there was some talk of that. You belittle everything that is mine! So what, even if I had chosen them—they have grown old and died." Then, paying no heed to his brother's excuses, he turned to me, smiling through his sparse white mustaches. "I am too old, Markiša, to rejoice in young women. This shortage of mourners is not important. There are more than two good ones even in our own clan. But I am worried about a speaker, an orator. It must be someone from outside, and I cannot think what to do about it. To tell you the truth, it is unpleasant to me to have to ask someone. . . ."

"That would mean that he wants to praise himself," Mrgud broke in inevitably.

The old man went on with irritation: "It's unpleasant, I say, to look for an orator myself and still more unpleasant that someone from my own clan should praise me."

I leaped up, impelled by an unsuspected and unseen, but already familiar, power. "That is the most important thing of all, and there must be much to say about you."

"That is so. There is!" the grandson flashed at me, and then turned to his grandfather: "Someone will be found, Grandfather."

"Perhaps a teacher, or a priest from some nearby village?" broke in Mrgud.

"Teacher, indeed!"—I began to wonder at myself—"Mićun? But he is scarcely more educated than Bishop Rade's Pop Mića,* and the priest hardly knows more than to bleat when he reads his service from a book."

"He couldn't do it." Bajo shook his head sadly. "And the teacher is one of our own kin."

"Yes, that is so. I hadn't thought of that." Mrgud began to withdraw.

But the old man, now angered, cut him short: "Why should you? You are not dying. I am!"

In a moment everything changed. Everyone would have burst

---

*This is an allusion to Njegoš' *Mountain Wreath.*—TRANSLATOR.

into laughter had they not been afraid of the old man's anger, and I stood up in the middle of the room and, putting my hands on my hips, shouted: "Indeed, there must be much to say of this gray falcon! Indeed there must! Let us not look at him now when he has grown old, his eagle's wings folded, but when he flew over these mountains and his sword flashed as far as Travnik and Skadar, filling the enemy with terror, so that their women frightened children with his name. How, indeed! Why do you, young man, look on me so suspiciously?" Carried away by the impetus of my own words, I darted a glance at Djole. "Know then that, though Commander Bajo and I are today opponents, I will say what there is to say. Those whose swords were more flashing than his can be numbered on the fingers, and there is no Serb to whom it would not be an honor to say farewell to such a man as he!"

The old man, obviously moved, withdrew into slow and profound meditation, which began to worry the others but which secretly rejoiced me. I remained silent, to give him time to arrange his thoughts, but his grandson would not admit himself beaten. "You think that you would . . ."

"I think nothing, young man, but, since it has already come to that . . . I say what is and what should be said. I do not wonder at you for not knowing what an orator and a funeral oration mean to an old Montenegrin. You are too young. But you ought to know what sort of grandfather you have and to be proud of him before all the young men of Montenegro. Is there anyone here—there are five or six of the most prominent householders and clansmen who have known him in both good and evil—who can refute what I have said, I, an outsider who speaks only of what he has heard?"

"You speak well, but all that about Skadar and Travnik . . . you have gone too far. . . ." Mrgud began.

"Perhaps I have, perhaps not," I interrupted him. "Whence came the Turks with whom he fought and shed his blood but from the viziers of Skadar and Travnik? Even if he did not strike as far as Travnik or Skadar, you can be sure that he, the haiduk, the mountain wolf, came very near them."

"Eh, Mašo," Bajo called out, "you have taken note of everything! But my brother who is no brother . . . he was messing about in the ashes, while I was fighting and spilling my blood in Hercegovina. . . ."

"Therefore, Commander, he cannot understand you, even though he is your brother," I shouted, displaying a greater excitement than I really felt, more than I should have displayed at the beginning, and paced up and down the room, wrinkling my forehead as if thinking.

In fact I was not thinking of anything special, but was seeking for an excuse to go on, if not to win him over, then at least to soften the old man. For the ice had already begun to thaw and the steppingstones to show. The increased malice of his grandson, the frequent envy of his brother, and the still deeper reserve of his son confirmed that. Bajo had even begun to call me Mašo and I called him commander. Not one of them, perhaps not I myself, though I could see farther than they and could see what the result might be, realized the significance heroism and eloquence had for the old man.

Not only will no Montenegrin ever renounce his heroism, but also no one is as blind as he toward flattery of his courage. Among warriors, even when they are not Montenegrins, belief in their heroic exploits and fearlessness increases as their memories grow weaker and the farther away they get from the happenings of war. I therefore did not expose myself to any danger by stressing the old man's heroism, even though I knew nothing about it and could be sure only that Bajo must have been above the average, since he had advanced to the rank of commander. But he still belonged to the times when heroism in Montenegro was a way of life and a viewpoint on the world and on his own destiny. The stressing of his heroism was like the exposure of those facets of his personality that he regarded as the most outstanding and most lasting and that from ancient times were regarded in Montenegro as the greatest of human qualities.

As far as belief and record were concerned, this had continued into our own times and was very close to all those present. Eloquence and oratory in those long past and immutable ages of Montenegro had been the inevitable companions of heroes and of heroism, had cleansed them from the mire of everyday life, transformed them into timelessness, and sown the seeds of heroism in the generations to come. So it had always been, even though in recent years it had begun to die out and lose its power.

I knew this without having to think about it, suspecting that in it lay my own possibilities and the weaknesses of my opponents. So I paced the room in silence, prolonging it and keeping all who were present tense, convinced that the grandson would not have the patience to remain silent, sure that I would weaken his influence on the old man.

And, in fact, the grandson's patience gave way. "Imagine what you like and flatter Granddad as much as you like, but you will never induce him to ask you to speak over his grave—so that he will have to pay you while he is still alive!"

Instead of replying, and as if reconciling myself to his mood, I shrugged my shoulders and sat down as if discouraged, and the old man said sadly: "Don't, Djole, when you can see that he wanted to say something fine."

"I did want to," I said, "but I don't want to impose. I am not angry at his youth and I pardon his ignorance. But if anyone thinks that I have come because of some politics or cunning, I can retrace my steps and go back where I came from! But let this fine old man remain convinced that I wish him well from a pure heart and am speaking the living truth—the enemies of Serbdom know his martyred bones better than all of us."

I had risen as if ready to go, but his son, Krsto, beseechingly barred my way, and the old man shouted: "Don't, Mašo, I beg you as a son! Speak, as I see you know how. My heart, lonely and grown old, is eager to hear fine, heroic words."

Once more I stood up, this time really thinking of a funeral oration for the old man, sure that no one would interrupt me. I strode up and down, in thought, until I felt that the expectation was tense to the breaking point, and then, serious as over a bier and emphasizing my points with my right hand, I began:

A Montenegrin Jest

"Are you taking your rest, Commander Bajo, are you over-thrown, rampart of our marchland? Has men's hope, women's hope, been quenched at last? Are you going to your flock, O eagle of the mountain? Are they mourning you, O true and loyal friend? Have the hands fallen that drew from the scabbard the Serb sword unrusted, and does the Serb fame remain unsullied? O fateful curse without mercy! Serb loss without recompense! Why have the mountains groaned and the heavens been clothed in darkness? The lightning strikes among the rocks and the centuries-old pine tree is at last cast down—the Commander, pride of heroes, the honor of his clan! . . . Sad brothers, stricken company! We are one in a vast, single sorrow, for we accompany to his final resting place one of the last heroes of old Montenegro, one of the few who shed luster upon the Montenegrin name and with their blood and sacrifices washed away the stain of slavery and brought once more to life the Serb empire, wider and more beautiful than ever dreamed of by our martyrs dying without a cry upon the stake or on the gallows. . . .

"It is the custom to speak well of the dead. But Commander Bajo asks no more than the bare truth, half the truth, even a crumb of truth, and he, now dead, stands proudly before that flock of falcons which once stood before Prince Nikola and with bare hands cast down the Turkish towns and fortresses and laid the foundations of our great state and the happiness of future generations with their blood and bones, their sufferings and sac-rifices. And among that glorious flock there are no wings brighter than his! These archheroes will make an honored place for him today when he appears among them. I will not number the fights and tourneys, the Turkish heads he has taken, or all his sufferings and wounds, so that I do not delay his noble and tormented soul on the eternal path upon which it has set out. It is enough for me to say there could be no famous battle in these parts in which he did not play his part from the time when he could lift a gun, and it would need three retainers to follow him in battle to gather all the heads he has cut off. For in battle he paid no heed to aught save his own good name and the destruction of his enemies—to the resurrection of Serbdom and to the glory of Montenegro. And as the hero so, too, are the hero's torments! For half a century he has kept Serbian vigil in this bloodstained marchland, usually hungry and thirsty and, by God, naked and barefoot . . . but warmed and sated by the thought of Serbdom and the blood of his enemies. . . .

"Do not think that he has been rewarded a hundredth, nay, not a thousandth, part for his exploits and his sacrifices. Medals do not cover his wounds or lessen his torments, nor would his ungrateful descendants have thought to erect for him a worthy memorial had not he himself, modest hero that he was, set aside enough to assure himself a worthy tomb. For a long time past there has been no place for him in this shameful world and corrupt Serbdom, which only too swiftly forgets its testaments and its heroes. His place is among the bands of Kosovo and the Montenegrin knights, with Nikac of Revina, Vuk Lopušina, and Sirdar Jole. . . . Heroes and martyrs, this heroic martyr will today be covered by this icy tombstone and this black earth. But his heroism will be known to fame and his sufferings will be recalled as long as Serb blood flows in our veins and the Serb ideal shines before the world!"

This speech and eloquence carried me away, too, as so it should if one really wishes to achieve something. Now it was time to bring it to an end; every exaggeration militates against itself. I had to pause, to see the effect on my listeners, especially on the commander and his grandson, and to weigh up and foment the greatest flight—the final peroration.

The old man, flushed and openmouthed, gazed at me ecstatically and as if rejuvenated. His grandson, Djole, suddenly cried out, waiting his chance: "He's deceiving you, Grandfather! He's only talking like that!"

His grandson's words reached the old man, but he, not realizing their sense, shouted excitedly: "Every word you say is true and blessed, Mašo! You are the first who has told and recognized my services and my sufferings. I might have transgressed terribly against you tonight and been shamed as I have never been before any man!"

But his grandson did not give up. "Grandfather, Grandfather! Come to yourself!" he shouted, snatching at the old man's hand across the table. The old man began to look around him uncertainly, while the young man went on like a machine gun. "He only talks fine and empty words! He promises golden hills and valleys everywhere and to everyone. Yes, yes, you promise—but do not perform! You cannot keep your promises, you don't even want to. Though you are in our house, I will tell you, since you want to change Grandfather's opinions, I will tell you how they showed you up in the town. He once, yes, he, this Markiša, came into a café, and someone there asked: 'Markiša, what did you do about my affair when you were in Belgrade?' And Markiša replied: 'Just before I left I went to the ministry and they promised me that they would finish your business very soon.' And he: 'I didn't ask you anything, Markiša. I was only testing you.' Everyone in the café burst into laughter, and even today they tell the story with a laugh," the young man ended, smiling with victorious malice.

Even if everyone in the café had laughed then—for what Djole said was quite true—no one in the room laughed now, but they all looked at each other in perplexity. Even the old man, disbelievingly, began to look around and at last looked questioningly at me. I, too, was confused, though I must, and could, conceal it. Having no other way out, I myself started to laugh loudly, until finally, supposedly brushing the tears from my eyes, I said: "Even I have to laugh every time I think of that, though it didn't happen in quite that way. Some ne'er-do-wells and urchins thought that one up at a time when I had so many petitions and complaints on my hands that it would have been a real marvel if I had been able to remember all of them. I knew they were joking and went halfway to meet them, as if I had forgotten what that fellow had asked me. For as long as men are alive they will joke, and opponents are always on the watch and exaggerate every slip. But let any man find any mother's son to whom I have made a promise that I have not kept!"

My statement and my bearing calmed those present, and pleased the old man, as if he wished to say: "I knew that Mašo was not so bad." But nonetheless some shadow of mistrust remained, and I added sadly: "But the young man interrupted me, just when I wanted to say the best and the most important."

Only then was it clear to me that it was a good thing I had not risen to my peroration. There were still possibilities for one more assault on the old man, though my head was emptier than when I had broken off my speech. But an empty head need not be an inconvenience for a man of my calling; all that is needed is to know the right moment for suitable thoughts and words, for which life always provides the occasion. Such an occasion must now be awaited—and prepared for. If today my profession may not seem to me the very finest, or even the most honorable, then, as always when something has to be done, everything seemed natural and attractive in its novelty. In any case, man cannot always be honest, and I again began to lay in wait for the old man, so as to put my ideas in order and sharpen them.

"Djole, you shouldn't interrupt with these trivialities," the old man finally reproached his grandson. "I shivered all over while you were speaking, Mašo, as if I saw myself already dead. No, I cannot be calm, since you have still finer and truer and, may I say, more moving words to speak."

The old man's last sentence could be understood both as a question and as a request to finish my speech. But I prevaricated, still unprepared and uncertain how to go on, remarking: "But now it is not important, Commander, since no one will ask me to come to your funeral."

"It is important, surely it is, Mašo," the old man said sadly. "A man does not know who he is or what he is until he hears it from a good speaker. You see, here are my relatives and my household —and they would never have realized my sacrifices had you not spoken of them tonight. Won't you come and speak at my funeral, Mašo?"

"I had wondered, Commander, how I could answer that. Since we are, so to speak, in opposition to each other, you will have to pledge your people to permit me to speak."

The old man remained silent, thinking. But his brother said: "You spoke well. No one can deny that, although—he did not leave behind him such a harvest of heads."

"Nor will anyone's flesh creep hearing Markiša's exaggerations," added the grandson.

"It is not you who see yourself dead! It is I who am dying!" shouted the old man. "But speak, Mašo, as best you know, so that I who am dead may hear you to the end."

The old man was not only angry, but deeply moved as well, and it flashed across my mind that there was something deeper and more inconsolable in him than merely unrecognized heroism. I stood up and preened myself in the middle of the room, waiting until everyone was tense with expectation, and then began, emotionally:

"Say farewell to your strength, O hero, and scatter the black earth about you. Listen, O Montenegrins! Have pity, O manly strength, on emotional women and on the darkened garlands of the girls. Has darkness become dear to you, the fair world heavy upon you, O Commander? Can you without your flock of falcons not regret your brothers and your comrades, your favorite grandson and your only son? There, there is eternal darkness without dawning, cold earth without warmth, your brothers without consolation, your comrades without reward. O dark abode, true comrade!"

Suddenly, from the abyss of darkness that yawned through the open door, the sound of women mourning filled the house. Though I had been carried away by my own words and my own enthusiasm, the lamentations startled me and I looked around. The old man was weeping silently, and the wailing of the women, which had been caused by the last words of my peroration, smothered his tears. Some of the clansmen began to breathe heavily, and the old man's son, Krsto, weeping wildly, crouched in a corner and covered his face with his hands. Only the brother and the grandson were unmoved, the former crafty and the latter smiling maliciously. Even I myself was overcome by a sort of grief, as much false as sincere, and a hope, as much instinctive as deliberate, that I would finally break down and win over the old man.

While weeping and wailing spread through the house, I lamented: "O Serbian earth, pure and free, embrace your hero and your martyr! It, Commander Bajo, is all your world now and forever! Heaven will give you refuge, it will divide you from your brothers, will take from you your home and Serbdom. Your eyes will be quenched, that they do not see the world at dawn or the heroes under arms. Your wise lips are chill, your manly breast grown cold. Look around you, hero! Turn, Bajo, brother! Do you no longer yearn for the sun or have pity on your brothers? Why do you not break, O white day, why do you not arise, O hero? Who will outlast eternity, who will console your heart? Grief to the home, mourning to the kin! Stay, sun, do not set! Comrades in battle, do not go away! Here are torments—but for a hero torments are real life and joy. Here are your brothers and colleagues, here your lands, here your white house, your youth. O foundations overturned and heroes cast into oblivion, brother Bajo! And there is empty darkness, black lifeless earth, O good grandfather and incomparable hero!"

Weeping and moaning drowned my words. The old man was overcome by sobs, and on my face, too, flowed tears. I noticed that only the brother and the grandson did not weep, but remained silent, gloomy, and depressed. Despite my tears, I remained calm and collected, as I had to be, so that what I had achieved with such trouble would not slip away from my grasp. The relatives must be allowed to weep their fill, but the speech must end otherwise—in hope and clarity. And so I ended, in a calm voice and with moderated words:

"But if we are here burying the tortured and outworn body, his noble soul hovers above us, serene and free, before it makes its way into eternal light and glory, into the heroic circle of the

Serbian martyrs. His heroic name will be remembered and his heroic exploits recalled as long as these hills hear the Serb speech and glisten with the Montenegrin hearth fires. May the earth rest lightly on you who have unstintingly poured out your blood and sweat for the happy life of new generations. Eternal be your memorial among Serbs and heroes, Commander Bajo!"

When I ended, I crossed myself and approached the old man and kissed him on the forehead, as is the custom when one says farewell to the dead. Tears still flowed down the old man's face, dripping onto his jutting mustaches and his dry, quivering hands.

But he was radiant with peace and hope. "You are my orator, Markiša," he croaked with deep emotion. "God's justice sent you to me that you should accompany me when I depart this earth. Listen to what I tell you: whoever of my clan does not vote for you, let his name be black before the world and his hearth be quenched."

Even today it is not clear to me all that the old man felt and imagined while I was speaking. He had prepared everything for his burial—tomb and graveclothes, even candles. Only an orator he had not found. It was necessary that I weep for him in my speech and that he see and experience his own death in his lifetime.

What was important was not what he thought and felt, but that the men of Vučje Zdrijelo should one and all vote for me, as befits men and sons of the people led by the enlightened manliness and heroism of Commander Bajo.

In prison, at Sremska Mitrovica
February 21–26, 1966

TSAR DUKLJAN

It was terrifying, in waking hours, over the dark eddies, in the gloomy depths of the forest, and in the moist ravines. For one day Tsar Dukljan will break his fetters and once again rule over the world and me. It was still more terrifying in dream. Then, everything that menaced, everything that I could not resist, everything that filled me with horror, would summon me before the almighty and inevitable tsar of evil. He did not exist, and yet I could not escape him, whether waking or in dream.

Today there is no more terror, none of that emotion evoked by the legend about him as someone who once existed and who still exists. There is no longer that presentiment, that almost sensual awareness, of Dukljan in things and in people and in myself. But the legend about Tsar Dukljan is not dead; it has been transformed into something even more terrifying, into the intellectual realization of the eternity of evil. The live Tsar Dukljan was equally inaccessible; he lived as he lived, and no man could evade him as long as he was alive. Everything changes, and the legend, too, has changed within me. But it has never left me, appearing implacably in ever new forms. Now I know that it will outlive me, imperishable, inexhaustible in all its facets.

Perhaps the legend makes no sense, but in it I seek for and discover a meaning, as men do with everything, in the hope of justifying their thoughts and their deeds, their very existence.

The legend of Tsar Dukljan is an ancient one. Sometimes it seems to me that it must have begun with the first man, and undoubtedly it was my earliest full and terrible realization of the world and of human destiny. But also of every human being! For a man, first of all, is confronted by good and evil; perhaps that is one of the reasons he is a man. Everyone has his own Tsar Dukljan, his own Snežana and the Witch, his own Red Ridinghood and the Wolf, which accompanies him to the grave. No one knows when Tsar Dukljan began—that is to say, the legend about him. Therefore it imposes its own, my, her, your, meaning. Tsar Dukljan appeared with man, and human existence is indivisible from him.

Dukljan, the tsar of darkness and of evil, lived in very ancient times and ruled over men. He built a strong fortress where the Morača and the Zeta meet, and no man could stand against it. Then God, the tsar of good and light, sent his elect, Ilija, to master the tsar of evil. But St. Ilija was unable to overcome him, though he fought him on the land, in the waters, and in the air. He was neither stronger nor wiser than Tsar Dukljan. Then God Himself moved against the tsar. He razed his fortress to its foundations with a terrible thunderbolt, sparing only the innocent serving girl, Moračanka. The angels took her, with her milking pail and the cow she had been milking, and lifted her into her own homeland, and the tsar they fettered and plunged into the deepest whirlpool of the river Morača. They could not destroy him altogether, for the tsar is immortal. He is constantly twitching, and one day he will break his fetters, once again to rule over the world and men.

The legend, as may be seen, took shape in time and place. It was Christianized and linked with Montenegro and the Roman city of Dioclea, the present ruins of Duklje, and the name Dukljan is derived from the Roman emperor Diocletian. But the Slav tribes, in all probability, inherited the legend from the peoples they found in the Balkans, that is to say, in present-day Montenegro. The struggle of darkness and light, between the god of good and the god of evil, is pre-Slav and is, we know, the first explanation of the world and of human destiny. Expressed in other ways, the theme of the legend of Tsar Dukljan appears in prehistory, in India, Mesopotamia, Persia, and the pre-Columbian Central American civilizations. That the legend of Tsar Dukljan remained and took root in Montenegro is due—or so I would like to think—to the extremes of my country, the senseless extermination of life and the most unselfish renunciation. But these are desires! Tsar Dukljan knows not death and will never forsake my land. Nor can he; without men he would not exist, nor would he have anything to conquer.

I trembled and went in terror of his immortality and the impossibility of escaping from him. And since I could not escape from him, it seemed to me that he was essential in the nature of things and men, that he was the supreme law, the inevitability of all things. If he, according to the legend, is the other and invincible side of God, that is to say, of goodness and reason, it is not merely a poetic and mystical form of truth that evil is inevitable in man, that man by the very fact that he exists—and a living being cannot not exist, and a reasoning being has no reason to destroy his kind—must take refuge from evil. Dukljan is indestructible; good is transformed into evil as soon as it becomes a barrier to human duration. And so long as men are a blend of good and evil, then all one's life is a wrestle with Dukljan, since one bears him in oneself. But life is also divine, a confirmation of the power of man over him, that is, over himself.

I marvel at Dukljan and I hate him. I cannot be without him, yet I would like to free myself from him. Eternal is his kingdom and eternal the struggle against him.

There is no fear that the legend about Tsar Dukljan will die; it will appear again in a different form, to terrify and inspire. I am not writing about it in order to save it from oblivion, but so that, in a moment of boundless duration, I can say something about my, about human, destiny and about my land.

It is the most terrifying, the most beautiful, but also the truest, legend that I have heard. Without it I would not exist. It must be hoped that we shall change its form, if we cannot and will not erase it from memory and existence.

Tsar Dukljan is man and man's fate and, because of man, man must be his most pitiless opponent.

When the legend of Tsar Dukljan began is not known, nor will there be any end.

In prison, at Sremska Mitrovica
October 1, 1959

ABOUT
MARKO MILJANOV

The only way by which man can keep himself from being alone and capitulating to evil when schooled by oppression and poverty is by a return to, and a reliance on, moral principles and spiritual values. When society expels a man simply because he has come into conflict with the ruling system, he can only adapt his ideas, that is to say moral norms, to another world, his own world, which, if no more, promises to be more lasting than the real one. For anything of this sort a man must be above reality and outside his own times, must renounce his own existence.

Marko Miljanov, of the Drekalović clan and the Kuči tribe, confirmed this by his own life, though it never occurred to him that by doing so he was revealing a great truth: renunciation of life is also a form of existence, exclusively human; for other living creatures gather the fruits of the earth, build homes, and live in communities, but only man by his skill and reason is able to renounce all this. The lesson of Marko's life and character is that a man can do the impossible. What is more, it is a man's duty to do just that, for only such behavior is in accord with moral and other principles, with what is essentially human in man's nature. As Marko thought, so, too, did Njegoš: "Who wishes to live eternally is a martyr in this world." Marko Miljanov did not expound this wisdom, but it is evident in the course of his life and his actions. What is most interesting and also most significant is that he did not regard his renunciation as martyrdom, but as something so natural and inevitable that he could not imagine behaving in any other way. For him it was simply the only possible manner of existence.

But I had wished to say something else, to speak of my many and imperishable contacts with the voivode and of what he involuntarily expressed in his literary work and in his life, for in his case these two can in no way be dissociated.

His life, in short, ran thus: He was born in 1833, the son of an undistinguished father, Milan, and when he was fifteen years old he began to kill Turks and take part in raids against them—his tribe was then under Turkish rule. The Montenegrin leaders at Cetinje relied on him in the hope of extending their principality over the Kuči territory, and he relied on them in his efforts to liberate his district from the Turks. He became the favorite of Prince Danilo and Prince Nikola, and by his own efforts rose to the highest rank, that of voivode. He accompanied Prince Nikola to Vienna and Italy and undertook important foreign missions for his country. For the sake of the Serb ideal, he even reconciled himself to the horrible devastation that the Voivode Mirko Petrović, brother of Prince Danilo and father of Prince Nikola, wrought in 1856 upon his Kuči, among whom still prevailed the desire for tribal independence. And because the Kuči, by the decision of the European diplomats, remained a part of Turkey, Marko spent most of the time from 1859 to 1862 in the Mala Rijeka ravine, raiding and awaiting the great moment for a settlement of accounts with the Turks. This came with the war of 1876, in which it was he, Marko, who won the great Montenegrin victory at Fundina.

But no sooner had the war ended and Montenegro obtained its independence and the recognition of its prince at the Berlin Congress of 1878 than discord arose between the more important military leaders and insurgents and the recently created camarilla, or council of advisers. Voivode Marko, too, came into conflict with the prince, more harshly and irreconcilably than any other, so that he renounced all his ranks and privileges—he had in any case been stripped of them—and withdrew to his own tribe, on a Turkish property that had, it is said, been presented to him by his own soldiers. This happened in 1882, but before that, in 1879, the famous hero and general had to lose one more battle: The Moslems of Plav and Gusinje refused to abide by the decisions of the Berlin Congress, even though the sultan had agreed to them, and Cetinje sent Voivode Marko to settle accounts with them, not giving him enough men and, more important, stirring up against him the powerful Serb tribe of the Vasojevići on whose territory the fighting took place. In such circumstances the voivode lost the battle at Novšić, only to begin another and a different one— against the prince and the system of government, a contest that he had even less likelihood of winning and in which he could not rely on anyone or anything except his own force and uprightness.

If one excepts two trips to Serbia, the last one due to illness, he lived all the time on his own property, not much better or larger than a peasant's, tending his bees and pruning his vineyard and, incidentally, though he was scarcely literate, taking up his pen with the aim of saving from oblivion the heroism and sacrifices of the men of his district, Montenegrins and Albanians. At that time, Austria, relying on his popularity and also aiming at undermining the authority of Cetinje, offered him the rule—and, according to some accounts, even the crown—in Northern Albania, but he, true to himself and to the Serb ideal, unhesitatingly rejected it. He died in 1901 at Herceg Novi, in a foreign land. But he was buried at Medun, a fortress at the entrance to the Kuči lands, which he had won from the Turks and which—he may never have known—had existed before Turkish times and perhaps even before the coming of the Slavs. The prince's authorities forbade speeches over his grave, but it appears that they could not prevent the participation of the people, at any rate those from his own district.

He had lived long enough to see the first printed proofs of his works, which, as soon as they appeared, aroused wonder and respect, as the famous critic Skerlić puts it, for the writer as the most expressive representative "of what is best and most essential in our race and of the works themselves as works of art," full of life and vigor, both moral and physical. So they still are, to the present day.

My first acquaintance with the voivode, as with other Montenegrin legends, was in my boyhood. Luka-Mujica Danilović, a merchant from Nikšić and the father of Stefa, Voivode Marko's second wife, was *kum* to my family—at the time this relationship as a sort of godfather was the most complete and hallowed of all —and this was a sufficient reason for my father, even had so famous a personality not been involved, to stress his almost family kinship with the voivode in every tale he told about him. At the same time, my mother's grandfather, born in the Plav district, had been an insurgent in the fighting in the Lim valley and after the unfortunate battle at Novšić had been forced to fly into Montenegro, so that his leaving his centuries-old homeland was closely bound up with the disgrace of, and injustice to, Voivode Marko. Tales of that battle were my first introduction to perfidy and betrayal. No one specifically stated that the voivode had been betrayed in that battle or that the men at Cetinje had purposely arranged for the Vasojević reinforcements to arrive late, but everyone, describing the events of the battle and the other facts in connection with it, came to that conclusion. In their accounts, the battle lived again as something fateful, and Voivode Marko played the role of a knight, vainly striving to turn destiny to our, the Serb, side. There was something in him, in that battle and especially in that betrayal, that terribly recalled—in my eyes and in those of men living at the time—the Serb tragedy at Kosovo.

Then the course of life and the tasks it involved separated me from Voivode Marko, though in every phase and every decisive moment of my existence I turned to him, finding fresh encouragement and discovering values hitherto unobserved. At one time it was the heroic side of his personality, at another his national role, then his poetry, and today his relationship to the world and society. To quote Skerlić again: "Marko Miljanov is one of the most brilliant men of our race. This is a man about whom could be written whole psychological and philosophical studies." I would have liked to write such a study, or something similar, had I been in a position to collect the material for it. Of all my works that I fear may remain unpublished or be destroyed, I am most sure that this would be among them. Nonetheless, the urge drives me on to save, by these lines, at least something of my intentions.

My impulse is neither simple nor unique. I want to speak as much about myself as about the voivode, to identify myself with him. Conscious of this, I would like to talk about myself as little as possible. However, since I am not writing, nor have I the conditions to write, a study of Voivode Marko and yet I feel an irresistible urge to write something about him, I will speak about the Voivode Marko whom I bear within myself, even though it may turn out immodest and affected, as must every linking and comparison of differing realities and destinies. This means, in fact, Voivode Marko as my ultimate inspiration, my inner truth, and also my solace and encouragement. For that reason these lines aspire to only one truth, the expression of what I have in myself of Voivode Marko in my utter and most hopeless loneliness, or, more accurately, of what I would like to be.

But if now and in this place it is at least partially clear that recourse to Marko Miljanov is a search for encouragement and revival, it remains enigmatic why I have so many times and in so many ways turned to him. Why have I, even without thinking of him, inevitably been with him? For he, openly or secretly, has been such an ineluctable reality of my life and my everyday existence, as also of the great ideals and struggles of my times, that he is finally manifested as truth, as a summons, after which there is nothing till the grave in which all passions are stilled and all accounts settled.

The war of 1876 meant for Montenegro a revolutionary and fateful transformation. It brought her national independence, put an end to tribal separatism, and, what was perhaps the most important, introduced a monetary economy and incorporated the cities in her everyday life. The cities had existed before, but as a Turkish and for that reason alien way of life, hostile to her arbitrary and self-willed tribes and peasants. But that revolution devoured its own children without paying the least heed to the fact that it had arisen from the greatest ideals, from the centuries of sacrifices and exploits of heroes and the profoundest national aspirations. Though unexpected, everything ended as it was bound to end, by the legalizing of absolutism—in this case the prince's—by the formation of a camarilla, and by the disillusionment of the leaders of the insurrection. The heroic, mythical, period of Montenegro was destroyed. The most resolute and, until then, the most important leaders came into conflict with the conditions that were the fruit of their own efforts.

Peko Pavlović, the legendary commander in Hercegovina, and the Sirdar Jole Piletić, who transformed the plain of Zeta, the garden of Turkish pleasure and power, into a battlefield and a heap of embers, left Montenegro in 1879, and the Vasojević voivode, Miljan Vukov, despite the fact that in thirty years of fighting he had won for Montenegro almost half of her territory, was degraded and expelled. In one way or another the same thing happened to the rest; dramas of conscience and the sweets of power and enrichment escaped no one, be he ordinary soldier or high-ranking chieftain. Among the prince's closest kin dissentients appeared—for example, Voivode Sako Petrović. There were even some in old Montenegro, the area around Lovćen that had lived by war and pillage for two centuries past, and in the newly won districts, in Upper Kolašin, in the Montenegrin Hercegovina, and in the coastland.

But among them all Voivode Marko was exceptional. Involved in the fighting in the Lim valley by duty and conviction, he came into conflict with the prince rather later than Jole Piletić and Peko Pavlović. But the camarilla did not delay; on the suggestion of the prince, or of someone of his suite, a fellow tribesman, the priest Ilija Spahov, in October, 1877, wounded Marko in the arm. It was rumored, and the rumor has even reached us, that the priest Ilija fired at Voivode Marko because he was flirting with the priest's wife. Marko was a hero and a prominent man and also he had a golden tongue. He was at that time a widower, so it would not have been strange if he were smitten with some young woman, though report has it that he was very considerate to women. But reports say even more insistently that the priest fired at Marko by arrangement, and that the whispers about a love affair between Marko and the priest's wife were only a pretext to get rid of the favorite and self-willed voivode. For it is on record that Voivode Marko begged and beseeched the prince to let Ilija out of prison and, what is more, said: "It was you who tried to kill me, gospodar, you and not Ilija!"

That Voivode Marko was an outstanding personality well before his clash with the prince was evident even to those who had not the penetrating eye of the writer Matavulj or the journalist Holeček. All of them, though without Matavulj's picturesque conciseness, spoke of his quick-wittedness and deep reasoning power, and they never tired of listening to him as a storyteller.

Marko Miljanov was also a handsome man. Some sketches of his face, true even if not good, still exist from the time of the 1876 war, and there are also several photographs of him when he had passed his sixties. Both sketches and photos show well-defined and clear-cut features, and especially a certain intensity of gaze and a high forehead. Marko Miljanov turned gray early, and his wide mustaches fell like broken wings over his firm lips and strong chin—although when he was younger, as can be clearly seen from the sketches, he did not let his mustaches fall freely but twisted their ends up a little. He was of medium height, not especially broad in the shoulders, but obviously muscular and heavily boned.

There is a photograph of him shaking hands with the Voivode Lazar Sočić; it must have been taken immediately after the 1876 war. From it one can see that Voivode Marko had begun to broaden out and that he dressed elaborately. This was at the time of the sudden enrichment and advancement of the chieftains and their separation from the people, which did not completely by-pass even Voivode Marko. Usually the chieftains, on various pretexts—most frequently in the form of a present from the gospodar or from the fighters under their command—seized the best Turkish lands and properties. Voivode Marko obtained less than others—a Turkish house and some land at Medun, and that as a present from his soldiers.

This house and land no one interfered with, not even when he fell into disfavor. Since they were within the walls of the old Medun fortress, it may be that their position on the jutting cliff leading into the Kuči lands pleased Voivode Marko, more than their comparatively modest value. On the stony hillside and above the plain, that house was a lonely eagle's eyrie. At the time of his victory, his power and reputation were so great that he could easily have obtained more fertile and extensive lands on the Zeta plain and a town house in Podgorica. It is said that Prince Nikola at one time accused his chieftains of being plunderers and that Marko Miljanov, without contradicting him, retorted: "We are very petty plunderers compared with you, gospodar!" Though it could not be said that Voivode Marko plundered anything—the Turkish houses and lands were in any case shared out—it seems to me that with one side of his nature, even if not for long, he did become involved in the tendency of all conquerors to seek luxury and ease. At that time he was often seen entertaining lavishly at Cetinje, and it was at the same time that he married the beautiful Stefa, twenty-six years younger than he and not from a chieftain's family.

But those were only momentary incidentals, and as soon as conditions crystallized, all the fatness and gold, all the luxury and ease, all the longing for banquets and power, in fact, all that was not a part of his inner nature, fell away from the harsh mountaineer in proud self-denial. Thus he appeared, especially in his old age, in a different form, pure and self-disciplined, moral and idealistic, well but not ostentatiously dressed, looking inward to values that were not material but eternal, a noble who cared nothing for nobility, a peasant not tied to the soil he worked. As if he were not a vigorous and robust old man but a youth, he resolved to die for honor and his good name, to live for his word and deed and the good of others.

It can be seen from all his portraits that he was a fighter and a warrior, but of an older and special kind, a fighter and warrior in the name of humanity and for humanity. Marko Miljanov had allowed the distribution of food to the Turkish garrison at Medun, the windpipe of his tribe, for despite everything he considered that fighters should fight and not win battles by starving one another. That was the countenance of inner purity and courtesy, incredible and even terrible to those who lived as people were then living, squabbling over tidbits, larger houses, better positions, and more lucrative reputations. I know of no face that has so revealed its inner side—heroism and humanity—and its past —fighting against oppression for an ideal—and its remarkable manner of existence—on little bread and much honor.

What especially set him apart and will always be a cause for wonder was the manner in which Voivode Marko broke with the gospodar. Most of those who broke with him did so silently, secretly, flattering the gospodar and expressing their loyalty to the hallowed and distinguished house of Petrović. Voivode Marko did so openly and publicly. The boldest and most resolute, like Peko Pavlović and Jole Piletić, left the country. Unlike them, Marko remained; if Prince Nikola was a prince, then let him be prince in his own principality. This land and people, Montenegro, was not his dowry. In this way Marko afflicted the consciences of the ruler and his camarilla so that they could not put him out of their minds, how much less stifle or forget this constant reminder proudly existing in the midst of their tiny state.

Voivode Marko had no clear and definite ideas about replacing the despotism of the prince and the system he had himself created. He did not have a program or an organization on which he could rely. Furthermore, he had no intention of becoming the leader of any opposition. Conditions in Montenegro, though they seemed unjust, were in his view the only possible ones. Even had he sought, he would not have been able to find any external support. In Serbia there was King Milan, whose dissoluteness had become the main problem of the state and his Austrophilism the betrayal of his own country. There existed another Serbia, intellectual and democratic, which Marko Miljanov, much later, was to rely on, and which was to accept him as a literary and moral influence. The Great Powers, insofar as they paid any attention to the dispute, were on the side of the prince, and any support they might have offered to Marko would have been at a price he was not willing to pay.

The clash with the prince broke out at the time of the unlimited strengthening of the princely powers and was the fruit of a long and troublous conflict. The power and reputation of Prince Nikola were then at such a height that even such spirits as Laza Kostić and Sima Matavulj wondered at it. The prince was the incarnation of the Serb ideal and the resurrection of the nation, before which everything else seemed petty and unimportant. There was no sort of opposition except the dissatisfaction of the chieftains—and that had calmed down. Marko alone stood out against the prince whom he loved and to whom, untaught but inspired, he sent letters in verse filled with sincere hope and adoration. Montenegro was in truth a despotism, but one to which, apparently, not many were hostile. Everything still seemed fine and harmonious. Everyone knew that it was possible to meet the prince personally, that he could be convinced to put right what ought to be put right and to give freedom the more quickly and easily since no one had the slightest intention of contesting his power.

It was at this moment that Voivode Marko rebelled, apparently without visible or significant reasons and in a manner that no one had anticipated. He renounced rank and titles, power and pelf, and returned to the village. Stronger than he and the very nature of his existence were, there moved within him the primeval, human, and natural sense of justice, or, more accurately, that inexorable conscience which goads a man to compare words with deeds, to dissociate lies from truth, to measure promise by performance, to compare the idea with the reality. Voivode Marko asked nothing, but he as a person could not become a part of or agree with the circumstances that had inevitably been created. His conscience came into conflict with what had been the fruit of his bloody efforts. Who knows, perhaps he dreamed of withdrawing peaceably from everything without harm either to himself or to the prince. But that was impossible. Despotism would not be what it is if it could allow its opponents well-being and an unsullied reputation. And Marko was not an ordinary, undistinguished man, but a voivode, and the most outstanding of them all. He could not leave the prince and the camarilla in peace and bow his head to the world. It did no harm to the prince if Marko did not love him or agree with him, so long as he obeyed him. For if the prince paid heed even to secret thoughts, how much more did he pay to words, and especially to deeds. He wanted subjects who did what he wanted them to. Able in most things, Voivode Marko was unable to do what others do most easily—conceal his thoughts, swallow his words, and tread his conscience underfoot.

Marko acted according to his conscience, and that was the best and greatest thing he could do. And the most mistaken. Prince Nikola rose to the title of king and ruled for more than thirty years longer, but the resistance of Marko Miljanov, even after he died, could not be ignored or wiped away, seeing that it was made up of something immaterial and by that very fact immeasurable, and therefore eternal and ever-present. Among the mass of the people the popularity of the voivode grew, despite the fact that he could not harm the ruler's authority, still less shake it. The voluntary exile on the rock of Medun gained a mystical power and attraction; human conscience confirmed his irreconcilability, his incorruptibility, and his indestructibility. There was a worm at the heart of the prince's apple.

Marko did not become the leader of an opposition; he did not live to see the kindling of a democratic, constitutional movement against the prince's more and more autocratic despotism. But even after his death he was the inspiration and stimulus of all the genuine liberating movements in his land. From Prince Nikola he took away nothing; despite his despotism and his pusillanimity in the First World War, Prince Nikola remained a ruler of outstanding achievement, just and wise whenever he was not forced to fight for his own holy lordship and dynasty. In such circumstances he set aside wisdom and justice when he did not dispense with them altogether. Nonetheless, the prince was never healed of the wound that he inflicted himself by his persecution of Marko Miljanov, and his conscience forbade him to call Marko voivode or to summon him to the counsels of the chieftains. He took away Marko's pension and threatened all who went to visit him. The clash with Voivode Marko was the first indication that the prince and the Serb ideal were not identical and that despotism was still less identical with sacrifices for that ideal. More and more clamorous celebrations made that fissure ever more difficult to gloss over. Marko Miljanov was the wound to the prince's conscience, and just for that reason it could not be healed.

Successes could not overshadow it, nor time efface it. It was a blow that would accompany the prince and the prince's Montenegro even after their departure, as long as they were remembered. Perhaps Voivode Marko was not fully aware of his great influence. The prince must evade it if he were not to endanger his princely power and break his bonds with the camarilla and the new and all-powerful class of chieftains. It was easy for the prince to win the day-to-day battle with Marko, but he lost the battle with eternity. And Marko, desiring little or nothing, withdrawing with honor into the everyday life of mortal men, achieved everything—and immortality.

Marko Miljanov is a strange example difficult to explain, of detachment from his times and his social milieu. Having reached the topmost summit of his times in Montenegro, he behaved as if he were there temporarily and by chance. Even when the prince and Marko were at their most intimate, the prince felt an aversion to Marko's curt words and frank, inexorable thinking. The chieftains who owed their positions to their loyalty to the prince, as well as many who had no aim beyond chieftainship, ground their teeth and rejected the self-willed and apparently undisciplined voivode. Marko did not seem like a man who has a definite aim; in truth, he had not. He was simply a man to whom bootlicking, flattery, and the pillaging of national property under any pretext had become abominable and repellent. With him it was simply a revolt of human conscience, or whatever there is in human conscience—if such a thing exists—that is outside time and place.

The clash developed in the Montenegrin manner—insults to parents and family, personal abuse and unbridled calumny. It was answered by the sharp, outspoken, and always dignified words of Marko, who never laid any stress on his own services. It was as if he had wiped out his own past, or paid little heed to it. As if he wished to say: No matter how great, the past is insignificant compared with what I think, what I bear within me. And this, too: The future is insignificant, seeing that it is formed by what we bear in ourselves as a moral, as an eternal and unrealizable, truth. Warring from moral impulses with the Montenegrin reality, with the government that then existed, Marko Miljanov made himself independent of time and place to the greatest possible degree. He had never been servile or uncertain, but now he was free. It was not easy to achieve; he had to renounce glory, honors, wealth, even life. He had to stand up against his own ties and realities. It was not by chance that many, most frequently those of the camarilla, said that he had gone mad. From their viewpoint this was not entirely inaccurate. Who had ever heard of anyone renouncing power and lordship of his own free will? But Marko Miljanov had turned toward eternity, toward enduring human and moral values; for there are no other eternities, nor any truth more final and infallible.

When he withdrew to Medun, Marko could foresee what

awaited him—poverty-stricken Montenegro was rich in experience of this kind. Nonetheless, in reality everything must have been still more painful and more offensive. There is no information about that. It is known only that for years he remained alone at Medun. His wartime friends and comrades rejected him, his *kums* forgot him, boors from the village insulted him, intentionally not addressing him as voivode or even addressing him as exvoivode. He was not invited to feasts or *slavas,* and his own table awaited guests in vain. They named him Kasomović or Kasomo, for the smallest and most undistinguished clan, though he always called himself Drekalović—the Drekalovići were the most famous and widespread Kuči clan, and men used to say "the Drekalovići and the other Kuči." When the Vasojević voivode, Miljan Vukov, died, Marko went to the funeral, but the prince's voivodes did not want or did not dare to speak with him. Enemies plotted to kill him. So the years passed, not one or two but nineteen. Even when the pressure was at its mildest only a few persons came to Marko Miljanov, the bravest, and they for the most part on nonpolitical work.

The lonely voivode had, however, one great joy, his wife, Stefa. She was twenty-two when he ceased to be a voivode. That blow, even had it not been sudden, must have been unexpected for a girl who had married as much a glorious personality as a handsome man. By his first wife Marko had had three daughters and a son, all of whom had died soon after birth. Not a single child by Stefa—his little son, Sava, did not survive. Those two lived alone, in the stony Kuči wilderness.

Stefa herself is a special, lyrical, and in her own way epic theme. If not the most beautiful, she was certainly one of the most beautiful girls in Montenegro, slender and harmonious in everything, with thick black hair and milky white skin. She remained devoted to Marko until his death and for long years afterward. Right up to the eve of the First World War, every afternoon could be seen through the wide windows of the Hotel Moskva in Belgrade a tall and upright Montenegrin woman—she always wore a veil and some trace of national costume—slowly sipping her coffee and conversing seriously. All Belgrade knew this woman of modest bearing and historic, almost medieval, beauty. But few knew that she had been the wife of Marko Miljanov. The voivode had already been forgotten and his name was no longer spoken except by those familiar with history and literature and the more obscure records of Montenegrin tradition. But for her the voivode was still alive; by her unaffected poise and severity, by the distinction of her movements and her striking composure, she expressed a serene, self-conscious grandeur, the voivode's grandeur. When he died she was in her forty-first year. There was something youthful and at the same time spiritual about her even thirty years later, a quality found in nuns and women devoted to literature or science. She had closed the voivode's eyes and alone accompanied the corpse across Montenegro, facing a desolate, unpeopled wilderness. She had raised a tombstone to him at Medun, neither better nor more beautiful than those of other chieftains and with far simpler, more modest words.

The voivode was fortunate in Stefa. Misfortune showed that they had not met by chance and that he, in marrying her, had not been influenced by her beauty alone. She, too, was fortunate in him. The Montenegrins wondered at Marko's consideration toward his wife. They said that he had given her a fur jerkin and that he let her enter a door ahead of him, like some Frenchman. Such courtesy no other Montenegrin of his background or his times would ever have permitted. But Marko Miljanov paid little heed to what anyone said, knowing that one should never show fear of what people say. In his last letter, just before his death, he called on his friends in Serbia: "I entrust to you my Stefa and my honor. Farewell!" How much there is in those half-dozen words! Love and gratitude and a whole lifetime of two beings in loyalty and solitude, in exile and in constancy, and the inevitable thought of the voivode for his honor, which he knew she would not, could not, sully.

When he left Cetinje so madly and suddenly, Voivode Marko

did not know either what he would do or how he would live; this was, to him, obviously of little importance. He had to do what he must. Least of all could he have hoped to find an aim and a consolation in writing. He had had no schooling and had only picked up a little knowledge from friends and acquaintances. But he had done some reading—national ballads and history, not scientific but mystical and anecdotal—and had already composed some national ballads to be sung to the gusle. He must have felt within himself, if not the power, at least the obligation—and that is the true and inevitable power—to say something of man's heroism, of the men and the country that were his own, for future generations. In the very first year of his exile he began to write *Examples of Manliness and Heroism,* a book without which the brilliant and universal facets of the Montenegrin and Serb people would never have been so well defined and irrefutable.

For the fifty-year-old illiterate—for that, in fact, he was—this must have meant a terrific effort, whether new to him or not. His writings have no punctuation, nor did he know any of the rules of spelling, and his manuscript is tragically peasant and self-taught. Even taking his excuse of inexperience and his stressing of his unliterary ambitions as intentional modesty, the picturesqueness with which he describes his own efforts—on one side of him the paper, on the other his thoughts and his pen—leaves not the slightest doubt of the tribulations of his undertaking. In fact, he dictated one part of what he wanted to say, and to that is largely due the unevenness and uncertainty of his storytelling. Still, dictation itself is an achievement for an uneducated man unused to literary work.

What drove him, what force impelled Marko Drekalović to write, and on top of all his other troubles to undertake the greatest of all? I would say that, primarily, it was an endeavor to find some new aspect of life more constant than he had known until then, more constant than authority and power. This corresponds with the spontaneous action of every deposed man of power, and Voivode Marko was that, even though he had renounced power for ethical and enduring values. Finding himself, so to speak, with nothing to do except to worry about bare existence, Marko Miljanov felt it to be his duty—he expressly stresses this—to save from oblivion men notable not because of their titles and wealth, but because of their ethical qualities and exploits, their humanity and heroism. It was certainly also a continuation of his opposition to the prince and the camarilla and the established order, in a direct and general manner. The voivode came to realize that not all Montenegro bowed the knee at Cipra (the open space below the Cetinje monastery, on which the prince's palace was built), and that there were men even more distinguished than the chieftains of the time, if not in power and wealth, in uprightness and heroism. But it was at the same time an expression of the voivode's spiritual existence: If I no longer have money and position, I still have something to say that will defend me against oblivion.

Yet I hold that something much deeper and more inevitable was working within Voivode Marko Miljanov Drekalović. To put it simply, he possessed the poetic gift and felt its irresistible urge. The power and originality of his storytelling confirm this. Having broken away from the ruler and the ruling casts of chieftains, he certainly did not think he could save himself by writing. Voivode Marko never and at no time saved himself; his conscience and his honor brought him to that step, and he was brave enough to listen. There were others who were brave and upright; they, too, broke with the prince, but not in the manner of Marko Miljanov. What I want to say is that if the voivode had not possessed artistic, creative power he would inevitably have become involved in the squabbles of the Kuči and been plunged into everyday humiliation and isolation. He had to feel and to know that, as well as moral and spiritual force, he possessed also a whole world, a world of possibility such as exists within the artist, sufficiently rich and varied that he could spend all his days within it. Men always do the possible. To do the impossible, to convert the impossible into the possible, is the prerogative of genius.

It would be anomalous and, above all, unjust if this supposition led to a lessening of the greatness and significance of the voivode's action. He would have broken with the prince even if he had not been a storyteller of genius. But that gift made it possible for him to behave in an impossible manner, according to his own will, paying no heed to the most essential needs of existence.

He was not to blame that he was so gifted. He could see that by his revolt he had involved the prince and the camarilla in a dilemma of conscience. He had deprived them even in their own eyes of character; that is to say, he had revealed them as ready to renounce the very ideal by which they had risen, merely to preserve and extend the form of their existence—power and lordship. For he had stripped from them the shining armor of unselfish knights of Serbdom—at one time they were so in many ways—and thereby had brought down upon them terrible hatred and danger. In the prince's retinue there was continual talk that Marko Miljanov should be killed as a traitor, for there was no other way. Marko could guess that not only had his open and unambiguous opposition made him loved by the people, but also that they would preserve him from hired bravoes and murderers. Neither mountains nor waters would have washed the prince clean had a hair of Marko Miljanov's head been touched. He paid no heed to danger, nor could he have done so, for he could not exist, could not be as he was, other than by a clash with the new order, the new injustice. All he could live by was what he called humanity and—I would add—also by literary creation.

It is generally held that Marko Miljanov, finding himself an exile, decided to pass his time writing. The truth is quite the opposite: Marko Miljanov, though able to go into exile, would not have been able to endure exile with such astonishing equanimity had he not been of an artistic and creative nature. To the average man such a casual renunciation of power would seem incredible. In truth, there is no more powerful passion than rule over men. Really, that is so. And to exchange the sword for the pen is a feat that requires exceptional moral and creative qualities rarely found in one person. Marko Miljanov had both these qualities, and many others also. In him knightly moral attributes and irresistible creative power, if not fused, could at least not be separated. Even his self-willed raiding during his early youth was creative in another manner. The voivode himself regarded his writing as a moral duty—to save moral exploits from oblivion. If his literary work could be summed up in a phrase, it seems to me that the most accurate would be: ethics as beauty, ethics as poetry. His ethical themes stimulate emulation in the way a gifted love poet stimulates love. Furthermore, he has an infallible criterion —with him is it not an almost irrational quality?—in choosing his themes, not confusing them with the habitual and the incidental. Not only was Voivode Marko a hero and an upright man, but also his heroic and artistic morality gave him a power that death alone cut short.

He knew this well, since he remained unmoved by the prince's pressure and by the threat of death, though he was of an irascible temperament. It is too little, and also inaccurate, to say that Marko preferred to be an honest man rather than a voivode. In fact he did not choose. He suspected—and suspicion is sometimes more certain than knowledge—that his being deprived of his voivodeship would assure him a renown more lasting than a voivode's. He held that he had two inexhaustible sources upon which to draw, moral and artistic, though the second one had not yet, so to speak, begun to flow. Perhaps, after all, it was a single source; Marko Miljanov is a personality of one piece.

For that reason he is incomparable. Jole Piletić—let us take him as an example—was no less upright and heroic. But Jole had nothing creative within him, nothing outside his times and his milieu. So, too, others, the bravest and most upright.

In this connection, the case of another voivode, Maša Vrbica, is interesting. He was a member of the inner camarilla, the prince's favorite and protégé. He was one of the most insistent and perhaps the most ruthless in the intrigue against Marko Miljanov. But even he was not without his reward for having served his country or without good qualities, though very different from

Marko's. He was inventive, an imaginative administrator, to some extent educated, and above all he had a feeling for the modernization of Montenegro. He was a sort of minister of internal affairs, a man of all work in that little stockbreeding despotism. He founded a form of broad-based economic-educational organization, which later turned out corrupt, and for that reason he fell into disfavor. Rejected and banned—no one ever came to his house—and without firm moral foundations, he soon died, though still in his prime. How could he survive a break with the prince and the camarilla if he did not have moral foundations, he, a voivode who not only had belonged to the camarilla but also had been one of the creators of that ruthless system from which they now excluded him? For it is only possible to renounce the world of reality by the creation of another world, a world of unreality. For that Voivode Maša Vrbica had neither the gift nor the power. Marko Miljanov did.

It is not my intention, and, as I have said, I have not the material, to write about Marko's literary work. This is a discussion about Marko Miljanov only as a human and artistic phenomenon, marvelous, unexplained, and inexplicable because I do not believe in any human or in any divine power. Today there is no one who would deny the literary value of the voivode's work; its other qualities, ethical, linguistic, and ethnographical, were at once recognized. But it seems to me that, even as he by his heroism and unusual moral qualities attracts one and poses the problem of human conscience and resistance to oppression and evil, his work seeks an explanation as a work of art. What is it, how much of it was intended and how much of the creator's part in it was unintended?

Voivode Marko had no intention of creating a literary masterpiece, at least not as educated men, then and always, consider that term. Over and above the impulse to save from oblivion manly and humane exploits, it was his intention, which perhaps he was ashamed to recognize, to distinguish himself in the literary field and thereby show that he was able to create something more lasting than a voivodeship. His aspirations as a writer are evident from the first glance. He tries in his storytelling to avoid the peasant ten-syllable ballad rhythm and to assume a more formal and even educated viewpoint. It must be said that, like every self-taught man, he has not completely avoided false learning, and such parts of his work are the weakest and least literate; but into that unoriginal and old-fashioned mold he has poured new content. As well as his moral and personal stimulus there is also, and in far greater measure, that unerring and irresistible creative intensity which drove him to take up the pen and which, so it seems to me, was the fundamental, and to the voivode himself the irresistible, impulse for his break with the prince and the conditions of his time.

What emerged was something different from what he had begun—neither folk tales nor moral tracts, but gifted storytelling, sometimes rising to genius, artistically formed by moral circumstances. Devotion to duty and the ideal were the basic features of the voivode's character and the theme of his storytelling. Taking examples from actual events, from his own memories and the accounts of others, Marko Miljanov in fact speaks of himself and of his own personality, which is just what every true artist does, and in fact must do. The examples are as varied and unusual as life itself is apt to be, but ethics is the common factor in all of them, ethics in the distinct, concrete, Montenegrin view, the ethics of heroes and heroism. Almost impersonal in basic theme and material, the voivode's work is personal not only in expression but in subject as well. The world he portrays, however real it may be, is always his, his above all.

There are three important works by Marko Miljanov: *Examples of Manliness and Heroism,* a collection of anecdotes; *The Kuči Tribe in National Song and Story,* the history of his own tribe on the basis of traditions; and *The Life and Customs of the Albanians,* an ethnographical-anecdotal treatise. Only the *Examples* corresponds to the title and intention; as for the other two works, my words "history" and "treatise" express only the voivode's intention and their approximate content and character. Not only are these mainly anecdotal, but also their theme is humanity, manliness—*humanitas heroica,* as Gezemann has translated the expression—and the manner of telling is predominantly artistic. The voivode's history of the Kuči is not a history but a collection of national ballads and poetically expressed traditions. Into his exposition of his Albanian neighbors he inserts his usual anecdotes, ballads of heroism and manliness, and also one smaller prose epic about the heroism of Ilija Kuč, for which it is hard to find anything the equal in content or conciseness of expression. The anecdote with a moral theme is the voivode's most frequent and most adequate method of exposition.

But what anecdotes they are! It is agreed that no one among us had until then been able to recount an anecdote so simply and flexibly. That is mainly due to Marko's fantastic wealth of language, the charm of his use of the right word in the right place, and his gift for harmony and the elimination of the inessential. But that is not all. The voivode's examples are so chosen and so contrived as to represent the purest poetry—naturally, heroic poetry. This is ethics transfigured as poetry, teaching that has risen to the height of the most passionate lyrical ecstasy. It seems to me that here lies not only all the value but also the originality of the voivode's work. His anecdotes are one and all terrible dramas of conscience. Their content is universal, and it is in no way by chance that the voivode found humanity not only among the Montenegrins but also among the Albanians and even among the Turks, displaying it with the force and impartiality of which a poet of great gifts and a man of undeviating and inexhaustible morality alone is capable. He undoubtedly wished to do something noble and of benefit, to note down ethical models and examples, and his work turned out, thanks to his creative poetic power, as poetry. Was this not also so with his revolt against Prince Nikola? The voivode was morally repelled and disgusted at self-will and cupidity, and the shock convulsed the moral foundations of the whole social system. Deeds and personality are one, I do not know if everywhere and always, but in this case inevitably.

Such was also the case with Njegoš, though in another way. It might even be concluded that Marko Miljanov is the Njegoš of our anecdotes. This idea would not be difficult to sustain, despite notable personal and thematic differences. But I would like to say more about the man and his message.

The voivode has an instinctive and undemonstrable beauty that merges with the feeling of his work, with the surroundings of Medun, where he spent long years, and with his own life history. The voivode's heroes are as if incorporeal, observable and real only in their moral purity. They and their actions and their viewpoints clash with the established and the everyday; all are in conflict with reality, with life. Nonetheless, their behavior differs in accordance with some higher human law, which is unwritten and unspoken but which is made clear and explicable by their actions. The voivode does not lay down any moral rules, does not even reveal them, but draws from our harsh historical and living reality examples of exceptional self-denial.

In the voivode's anecdotes the moral precept, the moral example, is shown by man's behavior, by the manner in which he reacts. Man with his undisciplined conscience is faced by life, unbridled and unbounded in evil and misfortune. The voivode shows how a man behaves in a situation based upon reality, whether political, traditional, or something else. Always there is resistance to established and accepted reality, always a clash and a renunciation of the bodily and profitable conditions of existence. In the world of the voivode's heroes, sensual pleasures and passionate joys are unknown. It is a world of boundless, unsensual rewards, of unattainable spiritual serenity.

From this it can be seen that the voivode had within himself some precept by which he made his choice—and that was the precept of his morality. This precept could be to some extent identified, even codified, but then it would lose its force, which lies in the fact that it is not something divorced from actual events. Such molding would make it lose its poetic beauty; from a picture, from a sculpture, it would become transformed into a dull and dead regulation. Man and his morality, man's manliness, do not exist outside reality. The manner in which man reacts to the unforeseen, to the always differing conditions of life, reveals to what measure he is subordinate to impersonal, universal, aims and circumstances. Only the ant or the bee can react instinctively to the cases the voivode chose so infallibly; manliness, humanity and man's continuance despite death, is created and measured by man's resistance to direct reality, by his renunciation of pleasure and advantage.

Gloomy and icy does the voivode's world appear to all who have not penetrated its essence; so, too, appears his life and the fortress of Medun. He seems to have revived the terrible world of the ascetic, the renunciation of the sweets and beauties that life offers at every moment and at every step. But this is not so. The voivode does not reject, does not deny, any sweetness or joy. Nothing human is alien to him. What he says is that on whatever a man has chosen in any concrete instance—and life is merciless and abounding in dilemmas—depends the measure of his humanity and immortality—naturally, his immortality in this world and among men, for that other world, in which the voivode, like every other Christian, believed, did not greatly interest him, merely because it was not dependent upon men. The voivode's heroes renounce the real and the everyday, the pleasant and the profitable, only when they must choose between that and their own moral human existence. Indeed, such was the behavior, the very life, of the voivode himself. His asceticism was conditional and not absolute; it was undogmatic, imposed upon him, and became the reality in which a man must exist and to which he must react in his own human, that is to say moral—he would have said "manly"—manner.

This is certainly a Serb, a Balkan, viewpoint of ethics and relations with the world, individual as is the poetry of Njegoš, and beautiful to those who possess it. What to us seems universal in it is that conditional and not absolute renunciation, even as we regard the personality of the voivode and his actions as an untamed human conscience only in our own Balkan manner and in his concrete circumstances.

What is beautiful and truly his in his work and personality is not only ours and his. Perhaps what drew me to him was something more important than personal destiny and the circumstances in which I was born and must live. Is it perhaps what he confirmed by his actions? Is it perhaps that he confirmed, and later revealed, something of the bases of human existence? Anyone can pose such a question, and can even find an answer to it in Voivode Marko. But that only confirms our subjectivity, our inclinations and our weaknesses, and changes nothing of the voivode. Men always search for a support and a justification outside themselves, as perhaps I have, too, in this case with Voivode Marko. Well, so be it! Maybe I have found in him truth and immortality that do not exist, or at least not in such measure, but I do not consider that I have overestimated them. Is this not a proof of his character, since men, and I, too, always find justification and encouragement for their actions in something they believe to be of value and permanence? So, too, Voivode Marko, insofar as a man can be a man and eternal.

He said: "The powers of darkness are not worthy of humanity." That, too, is a human and Balkan and Montenegrin truth, alongside many others that have ruled and rule the world. More simply expressed: man cannot exist without doing evil, but it is human to fight against evil. You must fight against evil, you must reject life if you wish to be a man; only thus will you endure and continue to endure as a man. Surely it was something like this that the voivode wanted to say. This is not philosophy, or advice; let everyone take from this wisdom and instruction what he can, but it is the marrow of human experience, as others, too, have expressed it in their own way. Whether there be one truth of human life or countless I do not know. It seems to me the second; but that men always express truth differently is clear from the wealth and diversity of human expression. The voivode's message is not importunate, it is simple: insofar as a man is a moral being, without regard to personal circumstances, he is a man and endures. Be a man despite everything—for man's sake, for your own sake.

When the voivode's coffin passed through Cetinje, it was said that Prince Nikola came out onto the balcony of his palace and said: "Montenegro was too strait for him!" These words were interpreted to mean that the prince at the last moment recognized that Montenegro was too small for the strength and reason of Marko Miljanov Drekalović. But no! The prince wanted to say: "Marko Miljanov had nowhere to die even in Montenegro, but went to a foreign land!" Marko died where death overtook him and, dead, returned to Montenegro and his Medun—it had always been his—whereas the ruler of Montenegro had to fly from his land, and die and be buried on foreign soil, although, to be fair, even if he deserved such a death, it is rightly asked today that his bones be restored to his native land. But the prince's words, however they be understood, have nonetheless a deeper significance: by his life and work Voivode Marko had crossed, had to cross, the frontiers of Montenegro. For insofar as a man is greater, so much less is there any frontier for him, and Voivode Marko was a man, and greater than was possible in his circumstances and despite them.

His grave is at Medun. Over it a tombstone has been erected by the Kuči, that tribe which represented Montenegrin and Albanian characteristics and forged for itself a spiritual independence. Only from such a tribe and from the centuries-old unsubdued Drekalović roots could such an exceptional spirit as Voivode Marko have bloomed. Below his grave, in green peacefulness, stretches Zeta in its wealth and fertility. Even in death the voivode is placed between two worlds—the stone and the plain, renunciation and fatness. The symbolism never occurred to him, especially a symbolism of this nature, when he pledged his Stefa to bury him there. All he wanted was for his grave to be in the fortress around which he had fought so much and in which he had been so much alone. But surely that wish confirmed the human desire to continue to exist despite death, surely it was a human yearning for ease and comfort? Surely the place the voivode chose for his grave confirms his consciousness of his own value. By his struggle and by his moral isolation, he deserved that his grave be known and his name remembered.

Beautiful is the voivode's fortress. Beautiful is Medun.

In prison, at Sremska Mitrovica
September 23–30, 1959